THE HOUSEMAN'S TALE

Colin Douglas

The Houseman's Tale

CANONGATE

Published by Canongate Publishing, Ltd.,
17 Jeffrey Street,
Edinburgh.

© Colin Douglas

ISBN 0 903937 04 2

The publisher acknowledges the financial assistance of
the Scottish Arts Council in the publication of this volume.

Printed and bound in Great Britain by T. and A. Constable, Ltd.,
Hopetoun Street, Edinburgh.

Asleep, Joan breathed softly, with little sighs in expiration less obtrusive even than the rhythmic caress of her right breast on his shoulder. Rate probably twelve a minute. Pulse seventy and regular, and a twenty-eight-day cycle like clockwork. She was a very orderly human being and lay now at peace in the post-coital sleep thoughtfully prescribed by evolution to soak up his teeming millions. Not that it would get them anywhere: every night after she cleaned her teeth she took a little golden pill and smiled. What a fine thing it was to have a regular girlfriend.

Along the corridor a phone rang and was lifted right away. Within a minute a door opened and someone strode past Campbell's room and on to the stairs. Pity the poor houseman. The outside door clicked shut and the footsteps receded across the courtyard to the medical wards, then the Residency fell still again and the world contracted into quiet antenatal comfort: warmth and darkness, pulse and breathing, more felt than heard.

But Ted Main was dead. That thought, sad and enormous, broke into Campbell's calm and rang round and round in unsettling refrain. Ted Main was dead and by all the normal standards he ought not to be. Patients died and that was part of the routine. People's grandparents died and that was all right, but doctors in their middle twenties had a right to live. Every week in the *British Medical Journal* there were obituaries of eminent medical men who had successively played rugger, won gold medals, fought in Flanders, adorned the profession and doted out their declining years on committees. Their deaths were as proper as their lives, but Ted was only twenty-seven and had been a senior student when Campbell himself had come to medical school. As a senior student in his turn Campbell had assisted him in theatre, clumsily trimming the young surgeon's stitches in the time he took to tie them, and that had been less than six months back. Campbell tried to remember when he had last seen him: probably within the last month, certainly within the incubation period of the disease.

He had gone off sick three weeks before and everyone had known right away what was wrong with him because all those involved in his care had talked: porters had told all the other porters, nurses the other nurses and doctors had kept it among the hundred and fifty or so of their colleagues at the Institute, in a sort of parody of confidentiality, so that everyone knew and somehow certain proprieties had still been observed.

These bulletins had become more frequent and alarming: he was not going to get better. In the Isolation Unit he had gone into a coma and the last despairing measure of exchange transfusion had not saved him. He had arrested, been resuscitated, arrested again and then been pronounced dead. Who had performed that office for a former colleague, now a yellow bloody corpse?

Campbell stirred against Joan, who without waking rolled luxuriously to lie prone, edging him farther from the middle of their single bed, so that there was room only for him to lie stiffly on his side. When he did so the blankets failed to reach the level of the mattress at the free edge of the bed and the slightest movement brought cold draughts into his disrupted microcosm. Ted Main's death seemed somehow worse for that, and vice versa. Campbell pictured him lying somewhere on his back sheeted and boxed, waiting for tomorrow, a corpse both pitiful and dangerous, double-wrapped in polythene and spared the indignities of post-mortem because of the awful risks of infection.

There would be about an hour before the funeral in the morning to sort things out on the ward, and it was in a hell of a mess. Campbell lay in the dark thinking of his patients, and jumbled fragments of their histories, physical findings, investigations and various treatments tangled in his mind. On the desk in his office lay a row of sample tubes and lab forms. That took care of investigations which could be anticipated. Anything else that had cropped up overnight would have to be dealt with in the morning, before the registrars came round. There were a couple of barium studies he might or might not have arranged in detail: they would need checking up. Bertram had started to chase him for results as though the responsibility were his and not that of some slothful laboratory, because on one occasion the houseman had in fact been to blame. Since then there had been a sort of campaign, mainly in connection with a troublesome old man admitted for the investigation of his weight loss – troublesome, that is, because he was putting on weight and they did not have a diagnosis. Thirty-one more or less relevant investigations – blood tests, urine tests, timed specimens, samples for various suspected deficiency states, balance studies and specialist consultations – had not come up with any answers, and every day the patient looked better. With half the results back, and no leads, the registrars were getting worried and beginning to take it out on the houseman. Campbell considered his defensive position and was suddenly aware of a point of weakness. He had no recollection of having initiated a five-day absorption study, one of the more important tests on the registrar's list. He squirmed at the thought of the inquest: the patient, one Mr McTurk, by now glowing with health, would be lying to attention and smiling gratefully as the old soldiers always did; Bertram would tap the case-notes and enquire: What about number eighteen, an elementary investigation? Well, doctor? Registrars made a point of calling a houseman 'doctor' when making such enquiries.

Outside, an ambulance purred down the hill and turned in the courtyard. Joan slept on, her face turned towards him, exhaling warm regular little puffs of breath. She was comfortable and he was not. She had to get up earlier than he. He could not move to a position of comfort without waking her, so he could not make himself comfortable without also being selfish. He perched on the edge of his bed with his dilemma: nothing seemed more desirable than that they should lie together, Joan having moved just a foot or so nearer the wall, prone and touching at shoulder and hip, perhaps with his arm over her waist; together and asleep all innocence, like Eden before the Fall. He moved tentatively and as he did so a gust of cold swept around his legs.

Through the wall something stirred. There was a light female giggle, then a writhing sound which grew in intensity, then resolved into a steady pounding rhythm, and was joined by heavy breathing deepening to great hollow sighs. The lady, and she it must be, for Mac never made such noises, being in many ways a considerate neighbour, must be shifting about twenty or thirty litres of air a minute, compared with a normal resting respiration of about five or six. Granted that the subject was unlikely to be completely resting, the net effect would still be that of gross overbreathing. Was she suffering, if that was the word, from the well-known effects of hyperventilation and respiratory alkalosis? Excuse me, miss, do your lips feel numb? Are your fingers and toes tingling? If she'd noticed, the chances were she'd attributed these symptoms to love. It occurred to Campbell that he had no idea who his neighbour's noisy girlfriend was: no one ever knew with Mac.

Social and physiological speculation both palled suddenly at the realisation that three feet through the wall there were people making love. Still balanced on the edge of his bed Campbell stirred randily and another belch of cold air enveloped him. Joan slept on beside him, soft and warm: the rays of Reichian orgone energy did not appear to affect sleeping subjects. Lying as flat as he could to preserve the micro-climate Campbell moved closer, half overlying her as she slept, with his thigh between her knees and their faces touching. Without waking she moved, not to make room for him but simply to accommodate his intruding thigh. Not for the first time he wondered how far he could go without waking her, then the phone rang and between its double beats he heard the shrill fast tone of the cardiac arrest signal coming from his bleep. He responded automatically and immediately, snatching the phone to hear the operator's infuriatingly calm announcement 'Cardiac arrest, Ward Two,' getting up and beginning to dress all at the same time. Shirt. Slacks. Sandals. White coat dragged on while running, halfway down the corridor.

3

He galloped downstairs and out into the courtyard. It was as much as he could do for the patient until he reached the ward and found out who it was and what had happened. He ran as fast as he could, from a recumbent start with ten seconds to dress, with the sound of his bleep still shrilling in his pocket. It was no use trying to guess in advance who it was or what had happened: there were too many ill patients in the ward for that. You got there as fast as you could and set to work. If they came round you might spend an hour stabilising them and getting them organised for intensive care. If they were really dead you could sometimes be back in bed within the half-hour.

The action was at the first bed on the right: the bed-light was on, the third-year student nurse in charge of the ward was standing crying and an auxiliary was tidying away the resuscitation equipment. A night sister whom Campbell had not seen before appeared to be in charge.

'False alarm, doctor. Nurse didn't know, but called an arrest to be sure. Sorry to get you up.'

'Not at all.' That was the best kind of arrest. No administration and back to bed in five minutes. 'Have you told the gas man not to bother?'

'Just on my way to ring him. Horlicks?'

'I don't think so, thanks very much.'

'Go on, have a cup. The ward maid's probably started it already.'

'No thanks.'

The patient looked sleepy and embarrassed. There was a fleck of blood on his lip, and a padded spatula in a bowl on his locker.

'Mr Simpson's fine now. Just another of his wee turns.' The night sister moved closer to Campbell and lowered her voice sufficiently to command the attention of all present. 'Nurse has just come up here from the intensive care unit. We'll really have to learn that loss of consciousness in a known epileptic isn't always a cardiac arrest.'

Nurse sniffed and tucked the covers round Mr Simpson, who muttered, 'Sorry hen,' and clearly wished everyone would go away. Campbell walked up the ward to his office: a comment in the case-notes to the effect that the patient had had another brief self-limiting convulsion would look good when the registrar came to do the summary, and all the better for having '2 a.m.' beneath the date in the margin. The night sister was still at his side. 'Sure about the Horlicks?'

'Yes . . . Almost . . . Well, thanks.'

'Good. Sugar? No? . . . I'll just ring that anaesthetist.'

As she went to the phone box the duty anaesthetist charged into the ward, slowing down when he realised that all was now quiet, dark, normal. Campbell told him what had happened. 'That bloody cow Birss,' he said, turning and walking out.

Campbell wrote his note with some satisfaction. As he finished, the

4

night sister reappeared carrying two cups. She sat down, crossed her legs and offered him a cigarette which he declined.

'We haven't actually met,' she said, holding her cigarette between her lips and inhaling to light up. It was so indistinct that he let her say it again. 'We haven't actually met. Margaret Birss. I believe you're Dr Campbell.'

'Yes.'

'David, isn't it?'

'Yes,' How did she know that: on the duty rosters he was Dr D. A. Campbell. 'Quiet duty?' he enquired.

'Until just now.' She shot out some smoke. 'But there's a man going steadily off in eight and a young girl with disseminated intravascular coagulation in eleven. Quite interesting.'

'Oh.' Whatever that was, Campbell had no intentions of discussing it at two in the morning with someone who had obviously just been reading up on it.

'Dr Soutar's quite worried about her. Been up all night a couple of times already this week.'

Poor old Soutar. Was he suffering from an overdose of Horlicks and whatever an excess of this sort of attention might do to that most placid of his colleagues?

'To tell you the truth, Dr Campbell, I think he's been overworking. Getting quite short with the staff. Some of these girls in charge are only wee third-years and you doctors can sometimes expect too much.' She smiled as if she was quite sure Campbell wasn't one of that sort.

'I suppose so.' Campbell finished his Horlicks, closed the case-notes and threw them across the office on to the bench, then stretched and leant back in his chair. Sister Birss emptied her cup too but Campbell perceived a dim obligation to wait until she had finished her cigarette as well. She wasn't hurrying. They chatted about nothing in particular and as the cigarette went down he noticed that she was looking rather pointedly at the front of his trousers. From Soutar and others he had heard a little of Sister Birss, to the effect that her approach was free and easy, but even so this was rushing things. Not that she was grotesquely ugly or old: perhaps only twenty-seven or twenty-eight, and in certain lights she might even be considered attractive. Her white uniform was loose enough at the neck to show off generous samples of a perfectly passable bosom. (A non-regulation ornament of gold chain and locket made it OK to look there.) She reached across in front of him to stub out her cigarette in the ashtray. Time to go. He got up. 'Well thanks, sister, have a quiet night.'

'I hope so. But I think that DIC is going to play up again. Poor Dr Soutar. Good night.'

'Good night.'

They went together to the door of the ward, where he turned left, she right, and Campbell walked back through the warm, quiet corridors, across the courtyard and into the Residency. Fifteen minutes for not much work, a cup of Horlicks and a first look at one of the more talked about new night sisters. And so to bed. Halfway up the Residency stairs in the cold draught at the corner he realised that in the haste of his scramble to the non-arrest he had left his flies undone, all the way down.

At four Campbell was wakened again, this time by noise from the Institute kitchen three storeys below the Residency. He lay listening as domestics bickered and utensils clanged derisively. We will wake you at four, they seemed to say, while we are ruining the food you won't eat till eight. Like so much else at the Institute, the cooking arrangements seemed to have been devised expressly to inconvenience the housemen. The couple next door had been wakened too, and were at it again, more sedately this time. A smell of kippers rose from the kitchens and permeated Campbell's room. Joan slept on.

Campbell despaired: kitchen noises and smells, however early, meant morning. Totally and reluctantly he was awake. Another mental ward round gathered in his mind like a storm: fasting blood sugars, results to be quarried from unyielding laboratories, registrars hinting snidely. By a great effort he quelled it, limiting his notes-for-action to just one fasting blood sugar, round which an ethical dilemma promptly loomed: the sample had to be taken before the patient had breakfast, which meant either the houseman lost half an hour of potential sleep or the patient had a late breakfast. Campbell had almost decided to sacrifice the general good accruing to all if the houseman, that key functionary on the ward, were to be refreshed by half an hour's extra sleep, in favour of the comfort and convenience of the individual patient who would thus get his breakfast at the usual time, when he recalled that kippers were, on the whole, an unpopular dish. It would be more generally humane to delay the patient's breakfast, which would in-cidentally permit a latish start for the houseman, and allow him from now perhaps some four hours uninterrupted sleep. He settled once more against Joan, his arm over her waist, and fell into a fitful troubled sleep until his bedside phone rang again just before six. He picked it up resentfully and automatically.

'Two one five seven. Dr Campbell.'

'Good morning, Dr Campbell. Sister Birss here.'

'Uh.'

'I'm in Ward Three. The lady on the drip at left two, the old lady with the ulcer . . . I'm afraid we're having some trouble keeping up to schedule with her three o'clock bottle of . . . um . . . saline. I wonder if you could come over and . . .'

6

'Take it down.'

'What?'

'Take it down.'

'I wonder if . . .'

'Take the intravenous set down.'

'But the bottle's due through in twenty minutes and there's still about three hundred millilitres left in it.'

'Take it down.'

'Dr Campbell?'

'Take it down, it's her last bottle. She's fine now. She's re-hydrated and her acid-base balance is practically normal. She needs her sleep more than she needs her last half-pint of salty water.'

'Aw well.' Her telephone collapsed with her will to win.

'Good night.'

'Good morning.'

Click. Cursing the pointless nuisance of the call Campbell turned to Joan, who was now waking, and pulled her towards him. He loved her twilight states, the warmth of her semi-conscious responses. They embraced and he muttered in her ear, 'Bloody Birss.'

'Stupid bitch,' Joan replied so promptly that it might have been a familiar liturgical exchange. He wriggled against her and began to lick her ear, blowing softly every now and then on the wet bits: warm, wet, cool, warm and wet. The ear thing was a good thing: convenient, undemanding and in the vast majority of cases entirely hygienic. If having one's ear syringed was a kind of cerebral douche or enema, this was spiritualised cunnilingus, moist and wickedly internal. There was even a choice of sides.

Joan moved first restlessly then with firm and obvious purpose: with only an hour or two for sleep, the ear thing was getting out of hand. Lust and Sloth warred in Campbell and Lust eventually won, though not without Sloth putting up a troublesome delaying action. As Joan, affectionately impatient under him, made the running in a coquettish rape-by-seduction, Campbell's sense of duty gave way to something more spontaneous, and they finished together in profound mutual relief, then lay inert and perspiring as morning light shaded in the grim blocks of the Institute's furniture. Dawn was relentless and, as always, the bed seemed to be contracting slowly from the moment of orgasm. Campbell meditated once more on his growing discomfort. The ward reasserted itself in the form of a sudden specific worry. He gave Joan a little squeeze. 'Has Mr McTurk been started on a five-day stool collection for faecal fat?'

'He's on day four. We were lucky. Got him the first day he came in.'

'Good. I just wondered.'

'It's practically automatic. The whole Rosamund work-up is. A basic run-through they all get. Top to bottom. False teeth to sigmoido-scopy.'

'I suppose it is,' murmured Campbell. 'Like Creech's vitamins.'

'More scientific.'

'Meaning she doesn't actually talk to the patients.'

'McTurk's problem is that he hasn't paid a gas bill for eighteen months,' said Joan. 'He lives on biscuits and lemonade. And a half-bottle the day he gets his pension.'

'Hence his weight loss.' Campbell decided that the best way to utilise this revelation would be to suggest on the ward-round that a social worker might investigate old McTurk's background, and a dietitian come up and take a full dietary history. A couple of useful points to his credit in the diagnostic league competition. Joan snuggled against him, muttering something about getting up in half an hour which reminded him how much sleep he had lost. He lay morosely beside her, with flat limpet-patches of moist contact joining them: warm at the centre, cool at the edges and subtly changing at each breath. Campbell drifted back and forward on the borders of sleep while Joan became more and more her daytime self.

Her post-coital softness faded, and after twenty minutes she got up. Through half-shut eyes he watched her dress, wondering if a true voyeur actually preferred looking to doing: never an enthusiastic student of psychiatric minutiae, he couldn't remember. As she dressed, the familiar became forbidden. Pants and bra. That trick of fastening them at the front and turning them through one-eighty degrees, where did people learn it? As a footnote in a birds-and-bees chat or seen in changing rooms, or was it an unrecorded discovery repeated inde-pendently like masturbation? Then there was the triple mystery of the waistline: low for pants, high for tights and a sensible compromise outside, in this case blue denims. What did having three waistlines feel like? Too odd to ask about, experiment unthinkable.

'What did the ward want you for? The first time.'

'An arrest that wasn't. Mr Simpson.'

'Oh, him. Another fit?'

'Yes. But the night nurse thought he'd croaked.'

'I hope you weren't rude to her.'

'The night sister got there first.'

'Which one?'

'Birss. A new one.'

'She's not new. More of a re-mould.' It was odd, even nice nurses bitched a bit. 'She's just been away for a while.'

'Trained here?'

'Institute girl through and through. Used to be quite famous when she was just Nurse Birss.'

'What for?'

'The usual thing.' Fully clothed now, she sat on his bed for a farewell kiss that was all the more fun since they would be working together at a professional distance in the ward an hour or so later.

'Joan . . .' he began. She smiled down at him. 'Joan, would you keep Mr Mutrie's breakfast back till I come on. He's for a fasting blood sugar.'

'Come on, that's rather feeble. Keeping the poor old man waiting for his kipper just so that you can have an extra half-hour in bed.'

'I didn't sleep very well.' It sounded feeble.

'I slept marvellously. It's getting enough sex.' She kissed him, then stood up. 'Don't worry, slob, I'll do it.'

'What about the silly rule?'

'It's just a silly rule. Nurses do venepunctures in every other hospital in creation except ours.'

'I suppose so. Thanks a lot.'

They kissed again and Campbell spread gratefully in bed as she left.

As he slept, the hospital awoke: in underground workshops the small army of maintenance tradesmen coughed over the first tea of the day; from pit-villages and jungle suburbs came domestics by the busload – bandy nicotine-stained women sharing a tribal odour of cheap scent and detergent, who crowded into changing rooms clucking and scrabbling like battery hens. In the wards, with growing daylight, those patients who had lain awake all night began to feel less guilty about it; a few, starved and shaven for surgery, saw the day in more thoughtfully than usual. Nurses going off duty scribbled in the record cards and tidied away the small comforts of the night as the day staff arrived, and all over the hospital the little ceremony of the report, the handing over of the nursing guard, was observed: tired juniors accounted for their steward-ship of the wards to fresh disdainful sisters who might find in a sudden death or an excessive consumption of milk some point for comment or blame. The night sisters gathered together under their superintendent, then scattered like a coven on a Sabbath morn.

2

The Royal Charitable Institute had remained true where possible to its voluntary origins. Though now administratively indistinguishable from any other National Health Service teaching hospital it had retained, along with its accumulated benefactions and a certain genteel parsimony, its own dry narrowness of spirit and the complacency embodied in its full

9

title, The Royal Charitable Institute for the Care of the Indigent Sick. Evidence of the good old days lingered everywhere, from the attic where two afternoons a week lady volunteers sorted out cast-off clothing for down-and-outs, to the main door itself, where squatted a black oak chest, grim as a dungeon and slotted like a letter box, which, though it was never known to be either filled or emptied, displayed on its forbidding sides a scriptural reminder to the sick and poor of their dependence on the well and rich.

In corridors and stairways subscription lists lettered in gold leaf recorded for an indifferent posterity lists of past donations, some bizarre, as 'From the fishers of Pitmirk after the Exhibition of a Whale – Fourteen pounds,' or 'From Alex Cairney, Coalmaster, Five Bushels a Year of Smallcoals in Perpetuity,' and some intriguing, as the brief section by the Vermin Control Officer's door where King George IV's fifteen-pound donation was flanked by one of eighty pounds from a baronet and another of a hundred guineas from a lady with a suspicious number of alternative surnames. Here and there brass plaques commemorated with undying gratitude and magniloquent obsequies the consultants of the Victorian heyday: erudite, renowned, illustrious, irreplaceable, lamented and so on; all forgotten except one who persists immortal in the footnotes of medicine, the definitive authority on the syphilitic knee-jerk. The more frequented corridors were lined with pillared memorial busts lurking in alcoves, startling night-nurses as their originals never had in life. Bombazeen rectitude and joyless philanthropy still stalked the Institute, hand in chilly hand: there were places in the hospital where charity and grateful remembrance took over so thoroughly that nurses in uniform and patients in pyjamas seemed out of place, as though they had wandered inadvertently into a church or a museum.

At the very central shrine of the spirit of the Institute, a space between the main door with its poor box and a grand stairway with busts and pot-plants alternating on its window-sills, Campbell stood in the unaccustomed discomfort of a suit, glowering democratically at the deaf-mute auxiliary mopping the floor and a lady volunteer fussing over a flower arrangement. Mac and the rest of the Residency Committee were late.

A clutch of consultant physicians with a registrar in tow ascended the corridor from the medical side of the hospital. All wore dark suits and black ties. There were four consultants: would the registrar be whistled to jump into the boot like a gundog? Perhaps in the presence of death the leveller he would crowd into the back seat with two of his permanently appointed betters. The sergeant porter at the desk stowed his *Daily Mail*, walked round to the door, stood to attention, swung the door open and was rewarded by a nod from the oldest consultant. When all four had passed through, the registrar followed, winking at Campbell, but solemnly, as befits an informal exchange between two minor functionaries on their way to the funeral of a third.

Typical Stangoe, to go to the right funeral with the right people, and still spare a gesture for junior hospital doctor solidarity: he was the perfectly adapted teaching hospital animal, whom Campbell admired or despised depending on his own current career inclinations. A contemporary of Ted's but not, by virtue of his different specialisation, a competitor, he was probably genuine enough in his concern and funeral attendance; but there must be one or two aspiring physicians of the same vintage up and down the medical corridor whose demise he might have regarded with less straightforward feelings. The physicians stood briefly in the sunlit car park debating the transport question before opting for the senior man's white Volvo. As they drove off Stangoe the registrar was sitting inexplicably in the front seat.

Mac appeared from the Residency corridor, still putting on a black tie: he was bouncy and clear-eyed as ever. Drinking and the complexities of his private life never seemed to register in his appearance. Perhaps he would slide into sudden haggard dissolution at the age of twenty-eight or so, though he was just as likely to survive miraculously and end up as one of the indestructible old topers who led this strange profession.

'Christ, Campbell, you look terrible. Been up all night?'

'No. I just didn't sleep too well . . . Whose car are we taking?'

'Mine. The other two are getting a lift up with the registrar from seventeen-eighteen. Clannish lot these surgeons.'

They left by the main door, opening it for themselves. Above them in the grey façade the Institute crest proclaimed its virtues to the world: the staff of healing, the praying hands and the horn of plenty. Underneath it the hospital motto carved in cramped Latin in the weathered stone offered a tiny, indecipherable welcome to the poor of the city across a large car park marked, in letters eight feet long, 'Consultants Only.' The housemen walked between Bentleys and Alfas and Jaguars and Lancias to the dingy lane behind the morgue where housemen were permitted to leave their old bangers, got into Mac's two seater and drove off.

At the crematorium the number of cars and people converging seemed to hasten the dispersal of an earlier and more modest funeral. Mourners of the late Edward Heriot Main, FRCS, 'friends desirous of attending', as the newspaper announcement put it, gathered on the lawns and flowers-lined paths around a clean modern block which might have been a chapel or a small art gallery, but for a half-concealed chimney appropriate to some far larger building.

About a hundred solid prosperous men of all ages and a sprinkling of women stood waiting in groups and exchanging subdued recognition. Many were in their late twenties, graduates from Ted's year in medical school, called together from practices and hospitals by the first death in their year. A grim reunion but a reunion still: the little groups on the lawns and avenues reflected the intricate freemasonry of medicine. There were the young GPs from the year, gregarious and more sharply dressed, and men of similar age still intent on hospital careers, subtly shabbier and scattered attentively among their elders, established men who stood dispensing recognition and conversation, the small change of patronage, while the real leaders, the academics and committee mandarins, gathered apart playing desultory politics with the relaxed, expansive air of men who came to funerals fairly often.

Campbell and Mac hurried from the car and looked round the crowd for the rest of the Residency Committee, who were standing awkwardly to one side, their driver having joined senior colleagues. A crematorium official appeared at the door and beckoned to the nearest of the crowd. They fell silent and filed in. Mac led the housemen and contrived to find a row of seats behind some nurses in mufti. There was always something undisguisable about nurses however they were dressed: a tendency to gymnasium cleanness and the sparing use of make-up. As they sat down Mac sniffed the air appreciatively then nudged Campbell and mouthed the name of the girl in front. He looked as if he would be quite happy to spend the rest of the service just sitting gazing at the little blonde curls behind her ears.

There was a scuffle from the door and undertaker's men, in long coats and stiff collars at odds with saloon bar profiles, bore the coffin forward. As it passed Campbell noticed the handles were plastic made to look like brass: the combustible masquerading as the incorruptible. It was too sad. The foreman grimaced orders and Ted was laid on four chrome rollers. A pall of maroon pew-cloth was laid over him and the mutes slouched out.

From a door behind the pulpit a jack-in-the-box clergyman appeared and surveyed his congregation; solid prosperous rows stretching right back to the entrance. Momentarily daunted, he announced the first hymn as though one of them might disagree with his choice and after a perfunctory organ introduction found his own cheer-leading baritone lost in their singing. At the back of the congregation the housemen sang unaffectedly and the girl in front recognised Mac's voice and turned round on impulse to look. Mac smiled; she blushed and was still blushing when they sat down at the end of the hymn.

The clergyman, who wore medal ribbons and practised a manly local style of delivery possibly attributable to the influence of STV religion, enjoined them to pray: some of those present bowed their heads, and the rest further unsettled him with a volley of unbowed freethinking gazes. Familiar anodyne phrases, rolled together like advertising copy, glazed and scented the problem of death in general.

Death in particular, Ted's death, was reserved for a little sermon. 'The inscrutable mystery of a Providence which encompasses both the miracles of creation and such paradoxes as the extinction of a promising young life. . . .' So that was it: God was a Gilbertian. Campbell ignored the rest and, following a habit which had persisted since finals a few months ago, nervously sorted out his facts on the fatal disease, as though he were about to scribble an essay under the hostile eyes of an invigilator or be interrogated by a wanton pair of academic physicians in the depths of their post-prandial capriciousness. 'If you please, sirs, serum hepatitis is a severe and commonly fatal infection of the liver, and as far as I know from a reading of the newspapers during the last epidemic (Mystery Bug Strikes Blood Boffin) and a hasty scanning of the textbooks, no causative organisms have been isolated, though there is some evidence that it may be viral. I could tell you about how it appears to be transmitted, because as a student locum and as a houseman on the wards I have had ample cause to worry about it. Transmission appears – note my scrupulous academic doubt, kind sirs, – to depend on passage of the hypothetical organism – am I overdoing it? – in blood and blood products such as serum from infected cases. It is also thought that urine and faeces – forgive me – may carry the infection. Having shown myself to be in command of the basic facts, may I try for honours with a little extra? The epidemiology of the disease is complicated by the occurrence of clinically silent cases, victims who suffer minor symptoms or none and yet carry in their blood and secretions this highly dangerous infection.'

Campbell's internal viva was interrupted by the clergyman's voice rising towards a peroration. 'In the forefront, in the very thick of the fight against disease, a young man struggled and fell . . . mortally wounded. Our departed friend was a soldier in that fight and we who . . .' That was the sort of balls you could expect from someone with twenty-year-old medals for being awfully brave during the rationing and sticking it out till the Coronation because that was what most people got them for. Ted's case might have resulted from contact with one of these silent carriers. There had been no obvious cases since the big epidemic a year ago, and people had begun to stop worrying. That in itself was dangerous: if you forgot you got careless, and junior hospital doctors were never very far from the risk. Every day there were little incidents which made you wonder if what you were handling was infectious, if the blood on your finger was from someone who had had the illness years ago and recovered, or was brewing it up, or had had some illness labelled flu and become a nasty little time-bomb leaking death from a cut finger, a bleeding nose or a venepuncture site. At first they thought you had to get it under your skin, in a cut or needle prick; now they were saying you could get it through the sort of cracks everyone had around their finger nails. And there had even been an epidemic among Australian anaesthetists suggesting you could get it by breathing droplet secretions from the lungs of infected patients.

It was as if it had been specifically lined up to threaten doctors: there were plenty of hospital epidemics in the literature, and junior hospital staff, the humble blood-letters, seemed to bear the brunt. Was that another aspect of the divine irony? A plague sent from God to scourge a profession not noted for its humility, given indeed to bouts of God-like meddling in the processes of life and death? The analogy of VD came to mind; if God's little allies lay in wait for seekers after fleshly pleasure, why should he not keep a few more up his sleeve to put down the mighty who had spoiled so many of his previous little jokes – plague, leprosy and tuberculosis to name but three?

Metaphysics apart, it was still a horrendous disease. Jaundiced cases had a mortality of about one in four, and only about one in twenty of those who went into a coma subsequently survived. There was no cure, no drug that could kill the virus without killing the patient too: all the proud profession could do was wait and see, and tinker with the symptoms. Sometimes they tried exchange transfusion to detoxicate the blood when the patient's liver failed and the risk of death was highest. That was a chancy business; gallons of blood were needed and if you weren't careful it could lead to gory chaos and half a dozen more people at risk, so that the bad joke went on and on. And no one knew for months whether they were safe or not, which was the real horror, the stroke of genius that made the existence of an all-powerful and malevolent intelligence a real possibility: an incubation period of up to four or five months. The suspense ran on and on. Well done that God.

The voice explaining it all away changed smoothly down from homily to incantation; a saccharin wash of organ music swelled up and the coffin sank, its maroon pall sagging sadly, rumpled and vacant. From the front of the congregation a girl's voice in a sharp indrawn sob broke the ranks of silence, then shrieked uncontrollably and fell to undistinguished sniffling. Moments later two girls supporting a third made their way up the aisle towards the door. More nurses. Campbell took that assumption from a glance and spared himself the embarassment of any more detailed recognition, but as they passed the girl in the middle, older than the others, dressed in stiff blue coat that made her look older still, hollow eyed and red and wet-cheeked from crying took on an unexpected familiarity – it was Birss the Horlicks Queen.

Mac had recognised her too. 'Look at old Cinders,' he muttered, 'come to poke ashes of one of her old flames.' Even for Mac that was a bit strong. Campbell grimaced and the nurse in front turned round angrily. Mac's turn to blush.

The clergyman had ignored the disturbance and was dispensing more trite municipal comfort, more distantly than ever, with the air of an inspecting general averting his gaze to step over a limp unconscious guardsman. All rapport gone, he was speaking for no one but himself in an atmosphere heavy with the unvoiced feelings of the doctors: no colleague had been asked to speak, to praise Ted's skill and put the brutal fact of his death in the professional context it needed. This cleric with his tortuous special pleading had no idea how they felt, and he sensed it, narrowing the focus of his attention to the family in the front rows.

Finally he announced another hymn and the congregation rose, freed from the burden of his voice and thoughts. 'Who would true valour see?' Bunyan's plain words and their stirring martial tune united them and gave them voice at last. The clergyman was half right: medicine was an army, solid against a foe as loathsome as Bunyan's foul fiend. A comrade had fallen but the survivors marched more steadily than ever. At the back the housemen sensed that they too belonged and they squared their shoulders and sang proudly. The last echoes died and the clergyman's benediction, like the mutes' retreat, was diffident enough to be interpreted as an apology.

At the door Ted's family were acknowledging the murmured consolation of the mourners: in the slow crowding towards them Campbell lost contact with Mac who was ahead, inching up on the girl in front. Out in the sunlight again housemen and nurses said obvious, stunted things to each other about Ted and his death and as they talked Mac cornered the blonde one: Campbell's attention wandered too, prospecting for an alternative lift back to the Institute.

When Mac and girl had gone off, an old senior lecturer from the pathology department, a retired jungle surgeon who had taught Campbell and, for that matter, practically every other graduate of the medical school over the last ten years, saw him standing alone and came over as if glad to see someone he knew. 'Ah, Cameron, isn't it? D'you like a lift back into town? The Institute, isn't it?'

'Yes. Thank you very much. It's kind of you.'

His car was an old Riley with wood and leather inside. Campbell decided he would have liked the walnut fascia better if there had been a seat-belt to keep his chin out of it in an emergency. Once they had negotiated the avenue and were set on the main road into town his driver suddenly said, 'If nothing else, this has served to remind us that medicine remains a fundamentally dangerous profession.'

'Indeed.' The remark had the unspontaneous feel of one that might have been practised in the shaving mirror: Campbell wondered if he were its first recipient, or had the old boy been rubbing up his reputation for profundity with it since breakfast time? He went on to expand the notion with a catalogue: tubercle (at least he eschewed the dramatic possibilities of calling it 'consumption'); the sundry fevers; the tale of the streptococcus and the promising young surgeon who cut his finger, in three affecting acts. Normally Campbell would have played the old man along quite happily out of a genuine interest in the bygone profession, but today his routine was as balls-aching as any of old Creech's tales of housemanship in the thirties; eighty patients, one syringe, breathless hush and the match to win etc. In the quiet, at some traffic lights, Campbell noticed that his driver was breathless at rest and a little blue round the ears. He might be in early heart failure: nothing serious, but the sort of thing that was worth treating if you happened to come across it.

The account of mortality in the old profession drew peacefully towards its close, and the agenda turned to the question of Campbell's career, not out of mere politeness but in the manner of the grand old teacher and his former student. Campbell had two sets of answers, depending on how he felt and who was asking. One went, 'I haven't a clue what I'm going to do because hospital medicine is futile and depressing and I don't know any other kind.' but there was a higher alternative for occasions such as this which went, 'I feel drawn towards medicine rather than surgery, and intend to get some general medical experience and then specialise in cardiology.' The old man asked benign, fairly informed questions, pointing out some of the pitfalls without being too crushingly realistic: nobody needed more cardiologists, now or ten years from now. It was a grossly oversubscribed teaching hospital speciality, and they both knew it, but conversation would have died under the admission.

He dropped Campbell at the Institute's main gate, still happy in his role of mentor. 'Well, Cameron, I shall follow your career with interest.'

'Thank you, sir, and thank you for the lift.'

'Not at all. Goodbye, Cameron.'

Cameron or Campbell, a lift was a lift. Campbell waved goodbye and the door swung shut with a rich old-fashioned clunk. The jungle surgeon drove off to remind his lunch table at the University club of the mortal hazards of practising medicine.

3

In the cool light of afternoon the chaos on Ward Two had receded to no more than an averagely untidy day's work. Campbell was a list man when he remembered to be and the dozen or so items in his scribbled column he had divided into those he had to do himself and those the senior student could do while he was off at the funeral, the latter being the more menial and time-consuming of the houseman's chores: the form-filling and the label-licking, the simple ward tests and the various treks round paraclinical departments in search of X-rays and laboratory results either mysteriously delayed or deemed by his superiors to be urgent. Senior students were attached singly to the wards in order to learn the practical details of the art of medicine, and Campbell took their training seriously. Sometimes, when he was busy, he placed too much faith in the educational value of straight delegation, but when he did so quieted his conscience with the thought that as a student himself that was how he had learned fastest. As a reward for a strenuous morning's work Campbell planned to take the student through a real titbit of clinical experience: a bone-marrow biopsy.

The patient upon whom the procedure had been adjudged necessary was deaf: that made his guinea-pig role in the business much easier to keep from him, but it also made his intelligent co-operation highly unlikely. He was senile too, a cheerfully demented old man who wore a tweed cap in bed at night and addressed the nurses by the names of his daughters and daughters-in-law. He was in no sense ill, and his presence in the ward represented a triumph of harassed relatives over medical common-sense and health economics. And he was not alone in this: there were dozens of similar cases in the hospital, using the medical wards as lodging houses because there was nowhere else for them to go. It had been a topic for acrimonious discussion for years: no settlement was possible without a major medical upheaval, the transfer of the bulk of local medical resources to geriatric care together with a necessary but politically impossible decimation of the physicians. So eminent a speciality would not lightly admit its irrelevance. In the heyday of the hospital physician there had been a job to do, acutely ill young people to be admitted, treated and sent home. With the antibiotic revolution it had all but evaporated as GPs wielded increasingly powerful therapies against infectious illness and hospital medicine shrank towards the care of the old and incurable.

With no radical administrative solution in sight, a good working compromise had evolved in the city: geriatric services received encouragement but not support, and the physicians looked after wardfuls of fairly well old people, maintaining an interest in them by pretending they had rare diseases.

The candidate for the bone-marrow biopsy was not ill: he had simply been noted looking pale one day, and while this might have been no more than an unfortunate colour contrast with his green pyjamas, investigations were indicated. Blood had been sent off for haemoglobin, red cell count, packed cell volume, mean corpuscular volume, white cell count, reticulocyte count, serum iron, serum folate, serum vitamin B_{12} and the customary stained blood film. To Campbell's dismay the haemoglobin was slightly subnormal. Registrars closed in like exorcists scenting a demon and the patient's case folder thickened ominously. In the absence of any obvious cause for his anaemia, indeed in the absence of any very definite anaemia, their discussions took on a strange, dreamlike quality. They clutched at diagnostic wraiths. One registrar, gazing out of the window at the Pentlands, had murmured, 'You might send off ten mils of clotted blood for alpha-amino-laevulinic acid,' and when the student asked why, replied that lead poisoning could some-times present in this way. The senior registrar rapped out a question about relevant dietary history and all present looked enquiringly at Campbell who, in a bout of unforgivable negligence, had omitted to enquire of the distracted daughter who had accompanied the patient at his admission if the old boy were in the habit of biting the heads off his grandsons' tin soldiers, etc. The houseman was instructed to remedy his error and the senior registrar in his turn gazed upon the distant hills. 'Should it turn out on biopsy to be a refractory normoblastic anaemia, which is *much* more likely, we might be up against a leukaemia at the end of the day.' The student, who was slowly acquiring the habits of mind which pass the time on medical wards, pounced on an apparent oversight. 'But his white cell count is normal.' The senior registrar smiled wearily at the success of his little trap. 'Surely everyone's heard of pre-leukaemic leukaemia. Isn't it in all the textbooks by now?' The student was chastened. The lead-theorist, stung into further contri-bution by his superior's sneering aside, went one further remarking airily, 'It might even end up as a persistently aleukaemic leukaemia.' Again the senior registrar fended him off. 'That would be highly unlikely.' The registrar bristled and said primly, 'If you don't think of it, you don't pick it up.'

That was what it was all about: diagnosis by a process of wild specu-lation on unlikely clinical entities, each to be excluded by a test or series of tests which caused no inconvenience to the theorist, but brought endless nuisance to the houseman and discomfort or even hazard to the unfortunate patient. Though it was said that the oc-casional syphilitic archbishop turned up to put heart into seekers after improbabilities, Campbell had never come across one. But he had searched for rare Scandinavian fish tapeworms in the stools of a vegetarian who had strayed no farther than North Berwick, and seen a labourer lose a hand as a result of the investigation of symptoms and signs which even a policeman of no more than average clinical acumen would have rightly attributed to drink. It was pointless to object, as the relentless pursuit of the unlikely was one of the few causes which united his immediate superiors, and any dissent on his part would have been promptly attributed to laziness if not to downright clinical irresponsibility.

Although the candidate for marrow biopsy did not need the investigation he did not object to it either: he even appeared to have enjoyed the multiple blood letting he had endured already, perhaps out of a folk memory of the healing power of leeches. When Campbell told him about the procedure he seemed almost keen, as though expecting after this more arduous and elaborate form of bleeding to feel proportionately better.

Joan had everything ready in the ward side-room after lunch: a bed for the patient and a trolley of equipment: skin-prep fluid, slides and a pack from the central sterilising department. Three first-year nurses were to witness the procedure as part of their training. The old man was led in from the ward by the senior student, whom Campbell had briefed beforehand to avoid the necessity of too frequent prompting in front of those whom he might reasonably wish to impress. The patient looked worried, so Campbell sat on the edge of the bed and shouted a word of explanation into his better ear. He had clearly forgotten.

'We've seen your blood.'

'Aye. It's grand.'

'No. It's not quite right.'

'Whit?'

'So we want to have a wee look at where the blood comes from.' He tapped the old man's breast bone, from which the sample would be taken.

'Ma heart? Is it ma heart ye're after?' The student nurses giggled, and Campbell wondered if he had seen any of the great heart-transplant drama on television.

'No, It's not your heart,' Campbell bellowed. 'Just a wee bit from under the skin. Here. At the breast bone.'

'Oh. Aye. Right ye are.'

'We'll wash you here then put a clean towel over you. You'll feel me working here but it won't be sore. We'll use anaesthetic to freeze the skin.'

The old man lay back, smacking his gums in concentration, and

Campbell turned to speak to the student nurses, who were a lively trio, full of sly humour and giggly sexuality, like something from a naughty schoolgirl story. Already they had destroyed the composure of his senior student, who was fumbling with the rubber gloves as though he had never seen such things before. Under their eyes his gloves had been transformed into obscene and unmanageable octopus contraceptives which twanged and squeaked guiltily over his impotent fingers. Joan was watching, detached and amused.

'I've marked the spot,' Campbell began in his medicine-simplified-for-nurses voice. 'In the midline opposite the third rib space. An inch or so to the right lies the upper lobe of the right lung. Not to be punctured. And an inch to the left there's the left ventricle of the heart. Well worth avoiding. And if you press too hard,' he nodded to the student, 'the ascending aorta waits an inch below. Blood flows through it at a pressure of a hundred and fifty millimetres of mercury. If you get into it with a marrow needle it makes a mess of your shirt. And maybe the ceiling.'

The girls were suitably impressed. The student chose a needle with the air of William Tell picking an arrow, then started on the preliminaries of red antiseptic wash and sterile towelling. The patient was reduced to a four-inch pink target in a sea of green linen.

Once in action the student regained his cool, that indomitable air of 'Pass the brain forceps, nurse, and all will be well,' that supports doctors in training through their first inglorious attempts at everything. But the patient spoilt it: bored and scared in the green sterile tent covering his face, he pulled it down in a flagrantly unsterile peekaboo. Joan's soothing hands and a little shouting from Campbell served to calm him, and when the student began again he found that the enthusiasm of his skin preparation had obliterated the target mark, so that Campbell had to don a pair of gloves and reorientate the student among the knobbly landmarks of the old man's chest. While the local anaesthetic was going in the patient tried to sit up. No blood-letting should take so long. There was more soothing from Joan, who sat close to him holding one of his hands in both of hers with a firmness which, though perfectly professional, sparked brief pangs in Campbell. The marrow needle entered the skin uneventfully.

More pressure was required to penetrate the outer cortex of bone. With one knee up on the bed the student bent over the patient, turning the needle like a wine-waiter broaching an exceptionally hard cork. He was using so much force that Campbell, who had checked the safety device that prevented the needle from going in more than half an inch, wondered momentarily if it was really secure. One of the student nurses looked expectantly at the student's shirt (purple, flowery) and the ceiling (grubby, and at least twelve feet above). The student

20

straightened from his labours and attached a syringe to draw marrow from the sternal cavity and Campbell leaned down and shouted in the patient's ear, 'You might feel a wee twinge any minute now.'

It was said to be a painful business, but no one was prepared for the patient's reaction: he yelled and sat up, arms flailing, knocking Joan aside and pushing the student (who had unwisely knelt on the edge of the bed) backwards to splay against the trolley, which in turn toppled, spilling glassware, liquids and instruments out on to the side-room floor.

The student lay with his head in a pool of bright red skin-prep fluid which, though he was conscious and unharmed, made him look as though he had lost a pint or two of blood from a scalp wound. One of the nurses screamed and the other two went to the aid of the student on the floor, leaving Joan to cope with the patient, who sat and gibbered helplessly. The nurse who was screaming stopped and went pale, fainted, slumped to the floor and lay there neatly with her knees together, her skirt modestly disposed and her cap still in place. You can tell an Institute-trained nurse by the way she faints, thought Campbell, before turning his mind to more important things. The patient was sitting naked to the waist and staring wildly, with the needle and syringe still sticking from his bony chest in an attitude of science-fiction martyrdom. Campbell plucked it out and handed Joan a swab to press on the puncture mark, then anxiously examined its contents. Thank God: there was about a millilitre of rich golden-red marrow, enough for all the tests demanded.

Slides for the laboratory had to be made quickly, before the granules of marrow were enmeshed in clot. With slight misgivings Campbell left the patient, the student, the nurses vertical and horizontal and the wreckage of the trolley to Joan. She would cope. She always did: that was what he liked about her. Little need come of it: according to a strict interpretation of the rules the incident need not reach official notice, as nurses fainted almost routinely, glassware could be written off, the patient was intact, at least physically, and the student, having no official status on the ward, didn't matter.

So Campbell busied himself in his office-cum-laboratory with citrate solution and fresh slides, picking up the yellow grains one by one and smearing them evenly with one glass slide upon another. He popped the remainder into a green bacteriology culture bottle on the remote but tediously discussed possibility that the old man had TB, then rang for a porter to take the whole lot off to the labs. In the circumstances it was a restful and welcome task, and by the time he had finished it order reigned in the side-room. The patient, dressed and preoccupied by the thought that it was tea-time, was ready to be led back to the ward. The student, though concerned about an ugly pink stain not conspicuously at odds with the pattern of his shirt, had despaired of dignity, seen the amusing side and appeared to have found a fellow-feeling with the lately supine nurse, who was giggling again. In all, a happy outcome. Joan was smiling quietly to herself, and greeted Campbell's return with an expression of mock reproach, though he could not see how his presence could have hastened the restoration of calm.

On the wards they were always careful to observe the proprieties of professional life by the frequent use of 'nurse' and 'doctor' in conversation and by abstaining from what passes in lighter hospital fiction as romantic behaviour: no moments of passion in the big linen cupboard, not even a lingering glance across a crowded ward-round betrayed their relationship to their colleagues. At first Campbell had taken such precautions as insurance against public reproach in the event of his deciding to give her up. As their relationship grew he became less anxious about covering his retreat, but they kept up the game of concealment as fun for its own sake and as a hitherto successful protection against gossip. They had discussed only the latter reasons, though he had an idea she was shrewdly aware of the first.

In the calm of mid-afternoon they were sitting together at the nursing station half way down the ward, as might any houseman and any staff-nurse in charge on Sister's day off. Together they turned over the pages of the nursing card index, and as a casual observer might have assumed, they discussed ward affairs. They had just moved on to a cryptic exchange about late and early duties and nights off when one of the patients, the diagnostically problematical Mr McTurk, appeared at the desk with his trousers and jacket on over his pyjamas and his sponge-bag in his hand.

'I'm sorry to have to tell ye,' he began, 'but I'm signing myself out. Not that I'm not happy with the way I've been treated here, and a' the attention I've had, and I'll never hear a word said against the Institute. . . . I've always said it, and I still say it, that if you need something doing it's the Institute. . . . Even since the stamps came and all this National Health. My mither died in here and they've really looked after me . . .' He fingered his sponge-bag anxiously then returned to his argument. 'My papers please . . . I'm sorry, nurse, doctor, and very grateful for all ye've done . . .'

'What's wrong, Mr McTurk? Has something upset you?' asked Joan, sweetly reasonable.

'Lettuce!' he spluttered. 'Lettuce! An impudent wee lassie not two years out of school coming and asking me if I ate lettuce! Called herself a dietitian. Impudence I call it. There was no lettuce on the Somme or up at Bay-thoon, I can tell you. And I was never as healthy in my life. Bar shrapnel.'

Campbell sighed; as a frequent mediator between scientific medicine and a public too human he had met the problem before. Wearily he mustered the arguments that might persuade a healthy and indignant patient to await the convenience of his superiors. It was either that or an inquest in the morning.

'I'm grateful to ye for all you've done, the pair of ye, and I've kept all the rules and done my best with the specimens. I'm grateful to you, and the sister with the porridge, and those other doctors ye bring round whiles, but I can't stand invasion of privacy.'

'No. Quite. I'll try to have a word with the young lady concerned and see what she was getting at. Perhaps she's new.' Three months qualified himself, Campbell was tolerant of the inexperience of others, at least in public. 'But it would be best if you could stay maybe a few days more until we've found out what's causing you to lose weight.'

'I'm putting on weight. Nine stone three this morning.'

'Yes. You're putting on weight now, but we still haven't found out what was causing you to lose it before.'

'With all respect to your profession, doctor, I'm past caring. I'm feeling fine and my privacy's been invaded. So I want my papers.'

Joan reached into a drawer for a blank certificate headed 'Irregular Discharge: Against Medical Advice.' Mr McTurk relaxed and Campbell muttered to Joan, 'He's only on day four of his five-day stool collection. You heard them this morning. As if nothing else mattered.'

'He can bring it up tomorrow. It's only ten minutes' walk.'

After Campbell had explained in his sternest desk-sergeant tones the full implications of the act, Mr McTurk signed the form and they both witnessed his signature. Joan went off and came back with a large wax carton. Her instructions to the patient were absolutely explicit.

'Thank you very much,' said Mr McTurk. 'I'll see you in the morning when I bring you back your carton.'

'Good,' said Joan. 'Now let's get you dressed properly for going home.'

Feeling somehow he had done a grand job, Campbell sauntered down the ward to Sister's room a little early for tea to get there before the research people had eaten all the food. When he had made himself comfortable with tea and a fair proportion of the sandwiches Joan came in.

'At last we are alone together,' he whispered hoarsely.

'Yes. . . . That was intensive care on the phone. They're giving us a wagon train of coronaries.'

'How many?'

'Four.'

'Four? At this time in the afternoon?'

At less inconvenient times of the day, Campbell enjoyed looking after coronaries: they came gratefully to the open wards after a spell in

23

intensive care festooned with monitoring equipment, boxed in single cubicles and slugged with opiates. Most of them had a shrewd idea that having stayed the course thus far – the intensive care unit had a mortality of about one in five – they would survive, and were correspondingly cheerful. They were young, in relation to the rest of the hospital's population, and simple to look after, as they suffered from a single system failure rather than the insidious and pervasive state of decay that assailed the real oldies. The various complications of their recovery were genuine physician's territory, an area where a medical clinician might swing his stethoscope to some effect: there were clinical signs, and remedies, for the different disturbances of rhythm and degrees of heart failure. True, a few of them died suddenly, and a few more relapsed and had to go back to intensive care, but the majority did their twenty-one days, getting cheerier and more active all the time, then walked out to go home. They were a welcome relief from the dements and the grandads with nowhere to go, but four all at once so late in the day was too much. Campbell abandoned his plan to leave straight after tea.

'What about this evening?' he grunted to Joan after a silence.

'Aren't you tired?'

'Not as tired as that.'

'Come round to the flat. I'll cook. Latish.'

'Thanks, but if I get through these coronaries by five we can go . . .'

He was interrupted by the entrance of two of Rosamund's research team, who ate the remaining sandwiches and talked about a third colleague who came in shortly after, to a sudden silence, and complained that there was nothing left to eat. Conversation died and Campbell went off and gathered his tool-kit of stethoscope, tendon-hammer, spatula and ophthalmoscope to go and admit the fortunate eighty per cent.

They proved to be a pleasant bunch, joking nervously among themselves as though they had been plucked from a life-raft together and put down in front of a television camera. Campbell screened off their beds one by one and interrogated them, with his customary amiable haste, about their current illness and previous health, while prodding them and tapping them, peering into ears, throats and eyes and listening for the various sounds of heart, lungs and intestines. Given an agile and quick-witted patient the whole routine need take no more than ten minutes; the four proved better than average: devoid of entangling sagas of past illness and free of time-consuming physical abnormalities.

Two had tattoos and were therefore allotted to the care of Creech, the senior consultant. One had been in the RAF, and went to Dr Kyle, and the remaining patient, with a possible ulcer to be sorted out as well, went to Dr Rosamund Fyvie, who enjoyed what she called 'tummy

24

troubles' and took coronaries only on sufferance. Indulgence of the foibles of his superiors ranked high on any houseman's list of priorities.

Campbell was finishing the last one when Joan came along, no longer clinking: she had handed the ward keys, the symbols of her responsibility, over to her relief at the end of her duty.

'Dr Campbell, I'm going off now. Mr Levison's overnight potassium will have to be written up when the lab results come back. Mr McDonald's four o'clock urine was negative. And when we cleared out Mr McTurk's locker we found three days' worth of his calcium absorption test tablets . . .' She came closer and lowered her voice. 'And I'm feeling quite randy. What were you saying before these people came in to tea?'

'I'm off duty for all that list except the last bit. I was going to say come round to the Residency now.'

'That would be very nice, thank you. I'll go and change and then come over. Ten minutes?'

'Fine. Come in by the top door.'

'Don't worry.'

After two days and the night between continuously on call, Campbell was off duty: he went into his office, took off his white coat and put it on a hook in the corner. Weighed down with his instruments it hung straight and heavy. With it he had taken off the care of thirty-two hours of duty. He sat shirt-sleeved at his desk shuffling papers, wrote himself a list for the next morning and walked quickly out of the ward before the nurse on duty could ask him about anything.

As he walked from his ward, sunlight slanted through the windows of the pavilions to the west. The three-storey blocks, softly lit from behind, made a small silent peep-show of ward life: patients neat in bed, nurses working here and there, flowers, calm, order. The same little scenes were repeated in triplicate down the vista of the four medical pavilions. It was peaceful and reassuring: a prospect for the public, for the relatives, for patients, for schoolgirls contemplating a career in nursing. From the outside his own ward would look no different. It was a comfort.

The tar underfoot was cracked and blistered, and a pair of blackbirds disported as though by appointment on the Institute's only lawn. Campbell re-entered the building and walked on towards the Residency. Harsh chattering and a musty human smell filled the corridor: he turned a corner and found himself walking past a queue of domestics waiting at the pay office window. There were dozens and dozens. He had often wondered how the hospital could have so many of them and still be so dirty. Perhaps they employed only the practically unemployable: the components of the queue, undersized and dispirited, had the defeated, knickerless air of women waiting in gynaecology out-patients. They did not smell nice. Passing the head of the queue Campbell held his breath and thought of Joan.

4

Campbell entered his room in the Residency with relief and turned on the radio. A man was talking about the drum music of the Fulani. On the assumption that anything else was liable to be worse, he stuck to Radio Three, and lay on his bed listening for a few minutes then went for a shower.

When he came back Joan's clothes were folded on the only chair in the room and she was standing naked by the window: she was a very unambiguous companion. Still in his dressing gown, Campbell walked over towards her and they stood for a minute, not talking but looking out together over the net curtain thoughtfully provided by the Institute to prevent voyeurs with telescopes in the higher southern suburbs from espying the solitary dressings and undressings of the housemen. Their second floor window overlooked a drive and a stone wall, with a little flower bed between bordered by a four-foot welded steel fence there for no other evident reason than to keep half a dozen spindly marigolds out of the traffic. It was too familiar and depressing even in the sunlight. The Fulani drums beat a fractured rhythm.

He loosened the cord of his dressing gown and it fell open, then she put her hands on his shoulders and they looked into each other's eyes. He tried to pull her close but she resisted, still holding him at arm's length, then flicked the dressing gown from his shoulders so that it fell around his feet. They closed in a long embrace and her hair brushed around his neck: it smelt of the ward, but her shoulders were fresh and fragrant. She moved to accommodate his arousal then held him loosely between her thighs.

When he was ready, she always was too. At first when they had slept together he had conscientiously gone through the routine of starting from cold, the whole pedestrian procedure of endearments of decreasing articulacy phased with graded physical stimuli. He had been aware of the progression – talk, neck, back, breasts, thighs, abdomen, grunt – even before she had pointed it out. Then it had embarrassed him. One morning he had wakened erect and eager from a dirty dream, and they had joined with a promptitude, facility and gratification not anticipated in the standard manuals. Since then their preliminaries had been minimal or simply jocular. He smiled to think of it, and so, a moment later, did she.

Laughing, they walked over to the bed: Joan lay down in the middle.

26

'Move over.'

'No.'

'Move over. Come on. It's my bed.'

'No.'

He lay beside her on the familiar outside eighteen inches of his own bed. She turned face down and Campbell half overlaid her, sliding a hand underneath to infiltrate between her thighs. She laughed and turned over again, arms and thighs welcoming. He flopped on to her and entered her roughly, then lay savouring the contact. 'Mmmmmm,' she said. 'It's one of your big days.'

Or was it one of her small days? He wriggled closer into her and she began to move. A delicate pink flush spread from the base of her neck across her shoulders and breasts, she moved more insistently and then lay still. Campbell, erect and inert, sensing only, felt the diminuendo of receding ripples as she lay still and soft under him, seeking his lips with hers and roving over his back with her hands.

As usual, having claimed a lazy orgasm, Joan became more lively and soon Campbell was lying back as she reared over him, her hair swinging round her breasts and her thighs tense over his own. He felt himself losing control and reached blindly up to her, then deep inside tensed for the end. She fell on him, grinding and writhing against him. Telepathy? At the last moment of perception, he felt her come again, then abandoned himself, supine and helpless, to overwhelming orgasm.

They lay as they had finished until he slid from under her weight and she whispered, 'I want to be cuddled.' He obliged and they lay side by side in a loose embrace.

'How do you always know when I'm coming?'

'You. The end goes very very hard.'

He smiled and lay against her, tired and relaxed. The room faded and he fell asleep.

Mr Alester Ravelston Orr was making a fuss: an official explained the procedure again and a queue of medical men built up behind him. There was music and the officials, in shiny white suits, were working like customs men at a barrier beyond which there was a tall gate flanked by chimneys. The clergyman, now haggard and deeply jaundiced, walked around ranting a sermon and pointing accusingly at each doctor as he approached the barrier. Ravelston Orr's voice boomed out over the organ music. 'As a senior consultant in administrative charge of a highly regarded surgical unit I absolutely refuse to be washed in the blood of the Lamb on the grounds that crucifixion constitutes an inadmissible risk of the transmission of serum hepatitis.' Campbell, in some menial accompanying capacity to the great man, was embarrassed but stayed with him. The official seemed jaundiced too and Campbell became more anxious to get away, but Ravelston Orr was determined. A lorry approached: it was a square, olive-drab one-ton army truck. Campbell lifted the surgeon's bag and waved to the driver.

He awoke to Joan's nearness, his face a few inches from her breasts, and fell against her in sudden amazed realisation of her, kissing her and holding her. She looked down at him and ran her fingers through his hair. The waking world reasserted itself as Joan, bed, Residency.

'I had a funny dream . . . with Alester Ravelston Orr. He was trying to get into heaven.'

'Ooooh. Was he rude to St Peter?'

'We didn't get that far.'

'An ambulance woke you.'

'That what it was? . . . He *is* a rude old bugger.'

'You'll still have to work for him.'

'I know. I only applied because I didn't think I'd get it.'

'Hard luck. Still, they say he's mellowed.'

'He must have been bloody awful before.'

'He's still bad enough for Matron's office to use him as a punishment posting.'

'See you there in December then.'

'No thanks. I like it where I am.'

'Really?'

'Yes . . . Even today.'

'The marrow?'

'Poor old man.'

'Mmm.'

At the recollection of the incident Campbell gave a little snort. An inch from his nose Joan's right nipple, fuzzily in focus, shed its creases and lifted itself a millimetre or two like a drill squad recovering from 'Stand easy' on the precautionary order. He snorted again. It liked that. By the time he had put out his tongue to lick it, it was standing to attention.

On the left the response was similar but quicker and the tubercles of Montgomery, the little knobbles ringing each areola, joined in the excitement, stiffening in a brisk 'Attention' that the field-marshal (no relation) would have admired. Joan squinted down at his observations.

'What about me?'

'I'm coming to that.'

She shifted under him and reached downwards to guide him in: she was awash with lust, past present and to come, and lay passively as he worked on her at first calmly with the leisured expansiveness of, say, the last theme from Brahms' No. 1, then with urgent climactic force in the manner of the opening bars of Strauss's 'Also Sprach Zarathustra'.

She stiffened and writhed, thrusting back at him and clawing his shoulders, then sighing and finally shouting wordlessly so that Campbell, himself at breaking point, had to shut her mouth with hard, biting kisses. When she was silent he raised himself up on his elbows and looked down at her: there was a little pool of sweat (hers? his? theirs?) between her breasts. She smiled, then opened her eyes. 'They don't do too badly, these lady missionaries.'

Not long afterwards Campbell and Joan left the Residency, got into his car and drove from the Institute. At the gate Campbell paused, wound down his window, drew a deep breath of non-institutional air and took in the street corner scene with the heightened awareness of one set free from bondage.

Sometimes when he left the hospital cars seemed large and fast, and drab townspeople, by contrast with the inmates of the wards, glowed with preternatural health. Once after a particularly hard set of four days and nights on call he had walked to the main gate and out into the street not to go anywhere special but simply to get out of the hospital: an ordinary sky had seemed glorious, and the traffic noises sang choruses of liberation; even a black-and-green-stained monument to a Victorian provost had acquired the sort of aura the Statue of Liberty might have for an oppressed exile. It was good to get out. They went for a drink in a seaside pub.

Joan was a good cook. In her flat Campbell dozed contentedly over a paper as she worked in the kitchen, then sprawled asleep. He awoke, for the second time in twenty-four hours, to the smell of food. This time it was good food, to be eaten right away, the food of freedom and comfort prepared not for the suffering hundreds by domestics in noisome kitchens, but by Joan in her flat for only two. The little luxury of a sherry – South African, cheap, dry – seemed excessive. She had cooked veal in a creamy sauce with rice. Campbell ate more than he had intended to. Joan did not eat much.

When they went to bed she seemed subdued: Campbell was beginning to wonder if she was brooding about their future when she told him she was feeling ill.

'I noticed you didn't eat much.'
'I didn't feel like it. Funny. Vaguely sick.'
'Any pain?'
'A bit. Mid-abdominal.'
'Since when?'
'In the pub.'
'Is it getting worse?'
'It's coming and going.'
'Any other symptoms?'

'You're playing doctors. It's nothing. Let's go to sleep. It'll go away.
Lie still. You're comfortable that way.'
'All right. Good night.'
'Mmmmmm. Good night.'

At one o'clock Campbell awoke to find himself alone: the bedroom
door was open and the hall light on. He lay half awake waiting for Joan
to come back from the loo. She was taking her time, and when she came
back to bed she said she had been sick.
'Odd. Has the pain gone away?'
'No. It's still there. Worse if anything.'
'Same place?'
'Lower.'
'Gynae type pain?'
'Doesn't feel like that. More over to one side.'
'Which?'
'The right.'
'Bleeding?'
'No. And I'm not pregnant. I'm on the Pill and I remember to take
it. No irregularities and no nasty complaints.'
'Sorry. I didn't mean it like that. I'd just like to know what's making
you ill.'
'Honest, I'm not ill. I've got a sore belly and I've been sick once.
Most people who have that never get near a doctor. Lucky them. Let's
go to sleep.' She lay on her side behind him, her arms round his waist,
warming slowly against him.
'Your breath smells funny. Like ketones.'
'Oh, no. I'm not going to have diabetes just to give you the pleasure
of diagnosing it in the first few hours. Lots of people smell of ketones
when they've been sick.'
'True. D'you feel any better now?'
'It's not so bad when I lie still.' They lay silent, Joan ignoring her
pain and Campbell drawing up an impressive list of possible causes
for it. Despite her protests he felt it might be gynaecological in origin,
and panicked briefly at the thought of an ectopic pregnancy. Acute
inflammation of the Fallopian tubes was another possibility, again with
social overtones: as a rule people who got that were dyed blondes with hap-
hazard sex lives. Joan should have been exempt on both counts. There
were one or two other possibilities: he reviewed their activities of the
previous twenty-four hours and toyed with the idea of something harmless and vaguely flattering, like a strained uterine ligament, then went
to sleep, and dreamed that she had serum hepatitis and was going to die.
At half past three Joan woke him and told him that she had acute
appendicitis. He switched on the bedside light and sat up. She looked

30

ill now, pale and hollow-eyed. Her tongue was coated and her breath quite unpleasant.

'The pain's there all the time now. Down on the right. And it hurts like hell when I press it.'

'D'you still feel sick?'

'No. That's gone away, but I feel quite hot now.'

He laid a hand on her brow. Fevered. 'Can I have a look?'

She flopped the duvet down towards her feet and Campbell knelt beside her. There was nothing special to see, just Joan's comely and approachable abdomen, but he found himself viewing it in a strikingly different light. The clinical signs were unmistakeable: marked tenderness centred on a point at the junction of the middle and outer thirds of a line joining the umbilicus to the right iliac crest, where lies, as every Boy Scout knows, McBurney's point. And the history, in retrospect, seemed to confirm the diagnosis: pain, becoming more severe and moving towards that point, with one episode of vomiting and a low fever. So it was appendicitis.

That meant he had to get Joan into hospital. The problem was how best to do it. He could ring her general practitioner, who might or might not come out at this time of the morning, and if he did might conceivably miss the diagnosis. That was not on. Or he could take her into Casualty himself, right away in his own car, which would mean being met by a small but interested gathering of his and her colleagues. That wasn't on either. Or he could phone for an ambulance and go in with her – same hazards – or simply phone an ambulance and once she was safely taken care of stay at the flat the rest of the night by himself.

Campbell phoned, then helped Joan get together the sort of things one needed in hospital: paperbacks, soap, tissues, lots of nighties. That last surprised Campbell. He didn't know she had any.

The ambulance took only ten minutes to come. When the door bell rang, Campbell kissed her good night and went to the loo and there overheard a conversation which made it clear that Joan was among acquaintances. 'Nurse Masson! Would you credit that? I never expected to meet you in this capacity. Abdomen, is it? Well, I hope you'll not be long off, for we'll miss your cheery face around the ward. No, don't trouble yourself. We'll carry you down. Never take a chance with an abdomen. Got everything? There we are. Comfortable? Nothing to worry about, I'm sure. Happens to everybody, and it's nice to see a kent face. And if we see that young fellow of yours before he hears about this, we'll tell him where you are.'

From the loo Campbell heard her surprised reply. 'My young fellow?'

'That's right. The houseman laddie. We saw the pair of you down at Cramond about six o'clock. Lovely. Fair warmed the cockles of our hearts. There we are. Hold tight.'

31

5

When Campbell went into his office next morning there was a folder of patient's case-notes lying on his desk instead of in its usual place in the trolley. It was a convention among housemen covering each other's wards, signifying death. The name on the folder did not immediately convey anything to him. He opened it and read his own admission notes on one of the coronaries. A further note in his colleague's neat familiar hand read, 'Became distressed with chest pain and breathlessness late p.m. Arrested 2318 hrs. Resuscitation attempted without success. Pronounced dead after flat ECG trace at 2331.'

Fortunately it was one of the two Campbell had allotted to Creech, so the consultants still had one each. No consultant could complain that he hadn't had one when in fact he had but it had died. Strict numerical fairness had prevailed and the deceased need hardly be mentioned.

The sad thing was that the coronary who had died had been the one with the best set of tattoos, a collection covering the inter-war history of the British Army. A full-dress pipe major with strangely oriental features, one that old Creech would have really enjoyed, was wasted on a chest now still for ever. It was a pity. It could have made his morning. He was always rattling on about them: his favourite after dinner story concerned an old sailor with a lighthouse on his promontory. 'It's not what it was, sir, but you should have seen it in its prime.' It made a bad start to the day.

Sister rushed into his office. That was one of the forty or so habits she had that irritated Campbell. Every morning she would come into his room to tell him something or ask him something or just to make sure that he was there at a reasonable time and had not grown a beard or dyed his hair red to confuse her. She was a simple soul, permanently stretched to her intellectual limits by the chores of ward administration, and always in search of little reassurances from everyone from Creech to the ward maid. What form would the morning ritual take today?

He should have guessed. She was brimming with the news that her staff nurse had been admitted to a surgical unit and taken to theatre at six that morning for an appendicectomy. 'Near to perforating according to the night-theatre sister, but otherwise uncomplicated and now she's comfortable. Ward Sixteen. You should take flowers.'

Campbell's response showed a judicious combination of surprise and concern: 'Was she taken ill suddenly?'

'Yes. At her flat. Last night. Poor girl. You should go and see her this afternoon. Take some flowers. Dahlias are nice just now.' She drew

breath for further revelations: 'And one of your coronaries is dead.'
When patients died they became his; otherwise they were hers. 'Mr
Auld. No. Mr Irvine. The rest are all right. Mr Auld's bowels moved
twice. To tell you the truth, Dr Campbell, I don't think they've heard
of bowels down in that intensive care place. Blocked solid, the half of
them are by the time they come up here.'

'I expect you're sorting that out.'

'Right, dear, I am.'

Laxatives she felt to be within the scope of her comprehension. That
aspect of her approach to the care of coronary patients was not as absurd
as some of her ideas: until a few years ago laxatives had been part of the
medical orthodoxy for the condition, when bowels generally were more
highly thought of and the patient striving at stool in dread of the daily
inquisition might overstrain his weakened heart and expire a victim of
the doctrine of regularity before all. Nowadays no one seemed to care
except the occasional ward sister.

Campbell settled down to consider his list before venturing into the
ward. The student could cope with the routine blood samples, except
for the old man from whom the marrow biopsy had been taken. He
might require firm handling. Admission specimens of urine from the
coronaries could be tested in a minute. The late Mr Irvine's contribution
was exempted and respectfully disposed of down the sink first. The rest
were normal, and the fact duly recorded in their respective case-notes.
There was a motley sheaf of lab results from the previous evening.
Campbell glanced through them circling the various abnormal or significant values in red, then spread them along the edge of his desk in
alphabetical order of the patient's names. In a few minutes the scattered
forms were all buried neatly in the folders. At least once a day, in his
capacity of clinical teacher, he reminded his student, 'Look after the
paperwork and the patients will look after themselves.'

Something in the list reminded Campbell of Joan and he began to
worry about her again. In the ward phone booth he tried via a more than
normally slothful operator to get through to Ward Sixteen. The nurse
who answered was too well trained to be helpful: her replies were
straight from the textbook. 'Good morning. Ward Sixteen. Nurse
McKay speaking.'

'Good morning. I'd like to know how Nurse Masson is this morning.'

'Who's enquiring please?'

'The houseman from Ward Two. Where she staffs.'

'Wait one moment please.' There was a pause of many moments.
'She's comfortable.'

'Oh. Could you tell me any more? Has she recovered from . . .'

'Would you like to speak to Sister?'

There was no point: she too would simply say that Joan was comfortable, perhaps in a louder voice. And there was no point in prolonging a discussion with the Institute's nurses' phrase-book.

'Thank you, no, nurse. Goodbye.'

'Comfortable,' was one of a spectrum of generalities used to abbreviate or deter telephone enquiries about patients' well-being. It was worse than 'very comfortable' but not as bad as 'as well as can be expected', which meant just that, or worse, or even dead already, as it was not done at the Institute to announce deaths to relatives over the phone. 'Comfortable' meant she was alive, probably conscious, and unlikely to be on either a mechanical respirator or a cardiac monitor. She might even be sitting up.

Thus fortified Campbell took a heap of the case folders on Creech's patients and went into the ward. In the four-bedded cubicle the three surviving coronaries eyed each other with renewed interest. The fourth bed, its mattress disinfected and its crisp new bedding turned down in anticipation of the next occupant, looked as cold and uninviting as a fishmonger's slab. The student moved among the patients with a tray of blood-letting gear, putting up with the usual badinage. 'No me the day, son, ye got me yesterday.' 'Whit's wrang wi' Tam? Is he ower auld?' 'Whiles I think ye're making black puddings wi' a' that ye take.' It never seemed to change.

Campbell lifted a syringe and specimen tube from the tray and went up the ward to the deaf old man in the corner. 'Good morning. I want a drop more of your blood,' he shouted. The old man lay back, bared his chest and began to cry.

'No. Not that this morning,' yelled Campbell. 'Just your arm.' He sat up, grinning through his tears.

'Thanks, son. Thanks very much. Here you are.' He bared his skinny arm and the houseman drew ten millilitres of blood and handed him a swab to press on the spot. He seemed grateful.

Creech began his ward rounds on time because he had nothing else to do in the mornings, and because, if he could be said to have a personality, it was probably an obsessional one. His retinue of senior registrar, registrars and research fellows gathered in Campbell's office, sitting on his chair and his desk and smoking their pretentious pipe tobaccos in his air space: they too appeared to have little else to do in the mornings.

Campbell was about to join the registrars waiting in his office when one of Rosamund's research fellows buttonholed him. He was carrying a tube of serum and a sheaf of computer print-out paper, which might or might not be significant, as it was a common mannerism of research workers in medicine to be seen carrying such things in the simulation

34

of pressing business. Evidently it was significant. 'That weight loss chap, McSomething. How are you getting on with his five-day stool collection? Finished?'

'Yes,' said Campbell, unsure whether the promised specimen had arrived or not. Completed or abandoned, the collection was finished.

'Good. We want another fortnight's worth. Have you seen these results.' He waved the print-out in Campbell's direction. 'He's got partial deletion of his phytamenadione fraction.'

'Um. Vitamins.'

'Yes. Vitamins. We want him for the faecal vitamin pilot study. There's a whole sewage farm of normals in the freezer. This chap's the first really interesting one we've come across. Rosie's quite excited.'

'Oh.'

'Let's go now and talk to the old boy. He might need a bit of persuading to stay.'

'Actually . . .' Campbell's explanation was cut short by the appearance of Creech at the end of the ward . . . 'He's gone home now. Signed himself out yesterday. It was all we could do to persuade him to come up with the last specimen today.'

'He's what? Does Rosamund know?'

'I shouldn't think so. Look. I'm sorry about this. I've got to go . . . Here's old Creech.'

'You just let him go?'

'I tried to persuade him not to. He was very determined. And very upset.'

'The most interesting specimen since the study started . . .' he hissed indignantly. 'And you just let him go.'

'Sorry,' said Campbell, 'I did my best. Excuse me.'

Creech was tall, stooped and woefully thin, the very model of an expert on nutritional science. As he approached his retinue it chorused 'Good morning sir.' He handed his bowler and briefcase to the houseman. 'Morning, Campbell. Morning, morning.' 'Morning sir, morning sir,' said the chorus, its ensemble faltering at the multiple stimulus.

'The flowers are lovely this morning, sister,' said Creech. 'Lovely flowers, beautifully arranged.' Sister smiled, blushed, curtseyed and said, 'Thank you, sir.' Creech turned again to his houseman. 'D'you garden, Campbell?'

'No, sir.' In this job? A pot plant would be taxing enough. Chief was having a Marie Antoinette day.

'Wait till you get out into practice. Big garden. Flowers for their souls. But vegetables for their vitamins. Ideal.'

'Yes sir.' One or two of the more enthusiastic present endorsed Campbell's agreement. Creech looked round. His sad encircled eyes

35

and the way his neck emerged horizontally from his collar made him look like an old and probably vegetarian vulture.

'But where are the students?' he said. 'Our colleagues of the junior clinic?'

A nondescript bunch of colleagues straggled up the corridor led by a tall blonde girl in a miniskirt. The sad eyes focussed. 'Look at that. Does she wear that to every session on the wards?' Still looking at what a longer skirt would have concealed Creech intoned, 'My personal ideas and opinions as to what is permissible in the cause of fashion have nothing to do with it, but how would that poor girl feel if one of my more frail coronary patients were to arrest at her feet?'

It occurred to Campbell that too few dying men enjoyed such a view, but that he would be ill thought of by all present for saying so. Bertram, keenest of the acolytes, explained, 'She has been instructed to wear a white coat of the usual length over it, sir, fully buttoned in accordance with the Dean's ruling.'

'The Dean's ruling?' Creech's voice piped and whistled in pained incredulity. 'The question's certainly never come up at Council. You know, he just decides these things himself without going through the proper channels. What do we have a Council for if I find out about these things from my registrars?' Bertram looked worried, as though somehow implicated as an instrument of the Dean's presumption. 'If anything were to happen as a result of that young lady's dress,' Creech droned on, 'I would feel compelled to raise it in a full session.'

Amazing scenes. Food Boffin, 64, Raises Girl Student's Dress in 'Full Session'. 'I felt compelled,' says father of four.

'But we must be getting on.' The junior clinic, by now all decent, gathered round and the entourage regrouped from audience to processional formation.

Progress round the ward was slow and uneventful: they discussed the cost of geriatric care in acute medical wards in relation to the cost of sending such patients on Caribbean cruises at the tourist rate and it was agreed that the latter solution was an economical and universally pleasing alternative; it was also agreed that the manner of vegetable preparation and cuisine in the Institute's kitchen amounted to scandalous negligence. A set of tattoos was examined and a Hong Kong dragon pronounced inferior to a 1938 Quetta Union Jack with Britannia inset. The possible role of dried blood on a careless tattoo artist's needle in the transmission of serum hepatitis was also briefly touched upon: Campbell remembered that Ted Main, whom he had often seen in theatre changing rooms, had had no tattoos.

No clinical decisions of any importance were taken but a series of sparring matches in diagnostic speculation between registrars provided Campbell with a list of investigations, the results of which would in due course give rise both to recriminations and further bouts of speculation. Meanwhile among the patients nature would continue to take its course: those with strokes would continue to get better or worse or die; those with tickets in the coronary lottery would continue to bow individually to the immutable overall statistics and those frail abandoned creatures who simply lived in the ward would continue to do so, paying the modest rental of submission to sporadic clinical investigation.

Eventually the ward round broke up in sticky deference and the junior clinic drifted off. With Creech gone and no one else to impress their presence upon, the registrars disappeared too. Campbell went to his office, glad to be alone, and had just started to write out the laboratory forms for the investigations on his list when the senior student wandered in and sat on the bench testing his own knee jerks. 'Why do they think Mr Lindsay's got de Guglielmo's disease?'

'They don't. They only want Creech to know they know about it.'

'Bertram didn't. Know about it, I mean.'

'He'll look it up. Then we'll spend a fortnight excluding de Guglielmo's in everybody, then we'll go back to vitamins full-time.' The student returned to his knee jerks for a little while then asked, 'What is it?'

'A funny blood thing. Very rare. I think they die.'

'That's a pity. I like Mr Lindsay.'

'Don't worry.'

6

As Campbell left the ward for lunch, Sister shrilled after him, 'Dr Campbell, Ward Sixteen, remember. And give her my regards.' She made a strange circular gesture with her right fist, perhaps a reminder about the flowers. It was hard to tell.

At the door of Ward Sixteen he met the houseman. 'Come over to see your staff nurse? She's in the left-hand single cubicle.'

'Thanks. How is she?'

'Fine. Consultant job. Old trade-union rule for nurses apparently.'

'Difficult?'

'Didn't see it. But I'm told it was an average sort of appendix. Retro-caecal. Neat incision if you're interested.'

'Not particularly. Thanks.'

Joan was sitting up in bed: no monitor, no respirator, no infusion, no naso-gastric suction, no wound drainage bottles. Apart from her nightdress and slight pallor she looked normal.

'You look funny in a nightie.'

'Ssssssh.'

He took a chair and sat down with his back to the door. There was a card on her locker: he picked it up and read in a fluting Joyce Grenfell voice, ' "The Matron and Nursing Office Staff of the Royal Charitable Institute wish you a speedy recovery." Have you got friends in high places?'

'No. Nurses all get that. Except the abortions.'

'Really? How do they know.'

'I don't know.'

'How are you anyway?'

'All right. It hurts when I move. And when the physios come to make me cough.'

'What's it feel like to be a patient?'

'Too early to say.'

'What's the food like?'

'I haven't had any.'

'Are you hungry?'

'Not really. How's the ward?'

'Oh, Creech was terrible.'

'Of course. It's Friday. Big round day.'

'Not more terrible than usual. But terrible.'

' Come on. He's really quite nice.'

'I suppose so. He told me to take up gardening when I got out into practice.'

'For the vitamins?' They both laughed and Joan winced. Then she looked thoughtful. 'They shaved me.' It was odd how girls used the first person singular as a synonym for the external genitalia. 'I'm like a wee girl.'

'Grrr.'

She reached out a hand and touched his face. 'I suppose I'll go all bristly now.' Campbell moved forward on his chair, then settled for holding her hand.

'Is there anything you want? I can come up again latish.'

'Some flowers would be nice.'

'Dahlias?'

'Not dahlias.'

'I'll do my best. But we're receiving and I might be busy.'

'Of course.'

Each Friday night Creech's unit took its turn of receiving. All acute medical admissions to the hospital came into its wards. Campbell could reasonably expect to have ten or more emergencies to admit and care for, and would be lucky to get an hour's sleep.

'I'll come over. Maybe very late.' He squeezed her hand, glanced quickly round to the door and kissed her.

'Bye.'

'Bye.'

7

It was one of the traditions of the Institute that the duty medical registrar ate dinner in the Residency as a guest of his housemen on receiving nights. On the whole it was a useful custom: they could relax together and most of the registrars, having been housemen at the Institute themselves, enjoyed the visit at least as much for the dip into the past as for the free meal it afforded. The duty registrar was Bertram. Away from his competitors and Creech's distorting influence he was normally good company, with a line of sceptical mocking patter piquantly contrasting with his official, get-ahead, yes-Dr Creech persona. Tonight he was off form, distant and distractable. He accepted a beer and began to scan the rows of old group photographs round the dining room to find his own year. He succeeded and called the housemen over to look: of that drab gathering, proper in dark suits and as uniformly close-cropped as a squad of national servicemen, he was the drabbest, sitting on the left of the front row with his arms folded and his knees pressed together as though wearing a kilt. He began to rattle off a list of names with brief lives attached: 'Hedge. The first consultant in the year. Psychiatry of course. Scott drives a Rover 3500. General practice with own dispensary. Miller emigrated. And Bert there, I went down to his place one weekend – he's in practice near Berwick – he had one of those digital clocks in the spare room. The *spare* room. That really got me. Beaton's cracking chests but he won't make it. Thinks he will but he won't. Not smooth enough. He emigrated. She's having babies and has forgotten everything else about medicine.' And so on to the top right-hand man of three rows.

To any local medical graduate with a good memory for faces it was a diversion of endless possibility: the photographs lined the dining room and overflowed three deep along both sides of the corridor all the way to the television room, where the prints were sepia and the sitters long since gone. Most of the Institute's present-day consultant staff was drawn from these ranks, so that occasionally a houseman, passing to the toilets or the TV room, would find his eye caught by the half familiar features of his chief thirty years younger. Bertram seemed to know his way around them and called the housemen out into the corridor to pay their respects to a portrait of the senior consultant as a young man. Creech also sat on the left of the front row, with his knees primly together, just a few inches further than need be from the next man, with the same downtrodden expression as the young Bertram. Campbell was glad to note that the registrar was spared the discomfort of recognising any similarity. They glanced over the moustaches, centre partings and double-breasted suits of the forties and fifties before returning to the present day and dinner.

Coffee was interrupted by Campbell's bleep: a steady medium pitch buzz meaning that the exchange had a call for him. He took it in the phone booth under the stairs and reported back to Bertram, 'An eighty-five-year-old man in Casualty with a left bronchopneumonia. And weak down the right side.'

'Is there a doctor's letter?'

'Evidently so.'

'Sounds like the beginning of a great night's medicine . . . After the coffee.'

The general practitioner's letter turned out to be a note scribbled on a page from a memo pad, courtesy of a drug firm selling Penaurin. Bertram read it out. ' "Dear Doctor, *Re* Mr George Outram, 85 etc . . . This pleasant old boy noticed his right side rather weak this a.m. On examination right sided paralysis. Chest query left consolidation. Abdo seems OK. His wife is not coping and I am grateful to you for admitting him." I can't read his signature and Penaurin is expensive bloody rubbish. A real GP drug. Eight thousand a year some of them get for writing letters like that. I'm in the wrong job. At least he examined him. Say that for him. More than some do. Let's see if he got the sides right.'

Sometimes it seemed that Bertram regretted his decision to stay in hospital medicine: he had risen to his present position easily enough, but there were many other equally promising junior hospital doctors in similar posts all jostling towards a small number of permanent consultant appointments. He was halfway through a two-year job and looking round already for another with the appropriate combination of clinical experience and research opportunity. He hated research, but a steady stream of original publications was as much a prerequisite for advancement in his chosen path as pushing a pea with the nose is to a man sworn to approaching Mecca in that particular fashion. His early papers had been no worse than anyone else's: a few trials comparing drugs not previously considered worth comparing; an account of a device he had thought of to help arthritis sufferers wipe their bottoms; and a lengthy publication which proved conclusively that occupational therapy did not speed the healing of duodenal ulcers. (The original intentions had been far more sanguine; it had been decided to publish the results of the experiment anyway, if only to prevent someone else inflicting hours of raffia work on innocent dyspeptics.) Of late his clinical inventiveness and the persistence required to do long series of ten or so cases had failed and he had submitted little papers optimistically headed 'An interesting case of . . .' with uniformly disappointing outcome. Apart from the faecal vitamin pilot study in which he was a minor shareholder and which in any case had not yet proved fertile, there was nothing in the pipeline.

Even clinical work was beginning to pall: receiving nights formerly a challenge to his skills became with the passing months just another burden to be borne. They kept him away from his bungalow and his marquetry, and provided recurrent reminders of forms of medical life less demanding and more lucrative than his own; careers which, in retrospect, seemed to have attracted all the really sensible people from his year. While they dozed at home, or practised the sort of off-hand medicine demonstrated in the patient's letter, he of the gold medal in clinical medicine scraped by on half their salary, labouring among the detritus of a hundred practices and sorting out social problems as often as medical ones. Mr Outram looked like one of the former. By morning he would be immovable. Creech would mutter about a blocked bed. Sister might cry.

Despite his reaction to the letter, Bertram's conduct towards the patient was a model of tact, sympathy and expertise, probably for the house-man's benefit. He chatted up the old man in a disarming local accent reserved for the purpose and elicited a story of intermittent but progressively more severe episodes of one-sided weakness, then went over the nervous system for signs. By extending the patient's neck and rotating his head slightly he demonstrated a tremor in the eye-balancing muscles, during which the patient complained of dizziness. The reflexes on the right were brisk and there was some loss of power compared with the left. He finished by examining the chest with a rapidity and skill that reminded Campbell of how slack he had become in the few months since finals; then replaced the old man's smelly blankets as though they were a dowager's silk sheets. 'We'll take you into hospital a wee while to sort all this out. Dr Campbell here will be looking after you and we'll make you very comfortable. It'll be Ward Two. They're expecting you. We'll see you again up there soon.'

Campbell was suitably impressed. They went outside the screens and Bertram lapsed from bedside saintliness. 'Vertebro-basilar insufficiency, but the pneumonia's disappeared. He must have coughed on the way in in the ambulance. Still, we have to take him. I'll speak to his wife. How many beds does that leave us?'

'Four.'

'Not much for a Friday receiving.'

Campbell looked at his watch. Eight o'clock. Twelve hours to go. If, as was likely, they had to take in another six or eight patients, extra beds would be set up in the ward, which was awkward for patients, hard on the nurses but one of the great traditions of the Institute. We never closed. Doctors might despair, nurses might drop with fatigue and patients lie in conditions of Crimean congestion, but the Institute could take it.

For peculiar Scottish reasons, the Institute was quiet on Fridays until the late evening. No self-respecting Scot could admit to illness before the pubs closed on pay night, then from ten o'clock onwards those with strokes, coronaries and perforated ulcers realised something was amiss, and the rest set about each other with razor blades and broken bottles. By half past eleven Casualty was its usual Friday night mixture of Hogmanay and the Battle of Solferino. Lacerated drunks wandered convivially through waiting rooms busy with bruised youths from dance halls. A man from a wedding was trying to lead community singing in the walking patient's area, a traffic victim lay dying in one of the re-suscitation rooms and two ambulancemen were drinking tea with a policeman in the porters' box. The casualty officer who had summoned Campbell to his department took it all in his stride: he knew that by three in the morning they would all have been admitted to the wards or gone home or died or gone to sleep, and he himself worked a genuine night shift with all day in bed, to the envy of every houseman. 'It's another man from that bloody wedding,' he explained. 'A great party I hear. This one's got chest pain and a long history of angina. There might be something on the ECG. Mr Barclay. End trolley. Nice old boy.'

If they wanted you to take a patient it was always a nice old boy: where did all the cross-grained mean-minded old warlocks in the wards come from? It was like brides and wives, thought Campbell, stepping over a pool of vomitus (probable Chinese meal) to get to his patient.

His carnation was drooping and Moss Bros would not welcome his returning suit. But he was in fine fettle. 'Is that you Jimmy? When are we going back?'

'No. You're in hospital. The Institute. You've had another of your attacks.' That was usually a safe approach.

'Whit attacks?'

'Pains in the chest.'

'Listen here, where's Jimmy? We're going back to the wedding. They'll still be dancing.'

'Were you dancing when the pain came on?'

'Oh, that pain. It wasna bad.'

'Where was it?'

'Here.' Behind and below the carnation. 'And down here.'

'Into your left arm?'

'Aye.'

'How far down?'

'Jist tae the elbow.'

'To the elbow?'

'Oh, that's not bad. If I'm enjoying myself I let it go down to my wrist and then stop for a wee breather.' That was not in the textbooks. 'Listen, son. It's my pain. I'm going back to the wedding and where I go, my pain goes. Right? Jimmy!'

'Mr Barclay, it's time we sorted out this pain for you. So we'll take you into hospital. Just for a few days.'

'Is it all right if I smoke?'

'Not in Casualty. You can smoke in the ward once we get up there though.'

'Here, here, son. I'm not coming into no hospital just for a smoke. Can I not smoke in here?'

'No. There's oxygen and you'll blow us all up.'

Bertram had gone off at eleven to the garret bedroom reserved for the duty medical registrar. He believed in clinical responsibility for doctors under training and regular sleep for registrars. There was the usual let-out, 'If you're at all worried about anything, just ring me up,' followed by a slightly menacing 'See you in the morning.'

Campbell decided he would have to admit Mr Barclay: the worst case of angina he had yet encountered, who might even prove sufficiently interesting to get old Creech on to something vaguely medical on tomorrow's round. The only problem was how to ease him into the ward without upsetting him too much. Perhaps left to himself he would become drowsy on his drink and a bit more tractable.

Mr Barclay coughed loudly. 'D'you hear that, son? That's what not smoking does to my chest. One fag and it all comes up a treat. Just one fag.' He was wheedling like an alcoholic. 'Come on, son. Give us a break.'

He coughed again, spluttered and turned very red. These smoker's coughs could look quite alarming. He inhaled deeply and groaned, and as Campbell was about to reproach him for overplaying the symptoms of tobacco withdrawal he fell back staring and inert. A purple shade crept into his ears. He had arrested.

Campbell leapt forward and felt for the pulse behind the angle of the jaw. There wasn't one: he was dead, and unless Campbell did something dramatic, he was going to stay dead. He struck the patient's chest very hard with the edge of his hand. No response. He gave him six sharp jabs of external cardiac massage, compressing the heart between the sternum and the spine. Still no response. He needed mouth to mouth respiration. His teeth were dirty yellow and his last breath lingered with stale drink round his purplish lips, but that was where he needed air. Campbell whipped out a handkerchief and laid it over the patient's lips, applied his own, pinched the nostrils and blew hard. The chest

43

rose and fell and stayed down. He blew again then returned to the chest and gave him another six, pressing the sternum two inches or more. Ribs creaked. Campbell yelled, 'Arrest. End trolley.'

His voice was lost in the noise of the drunks so he wheeled the patient, still on his trolley and bluer every second, feet first across the corridor into a vacant resuscitation room. The casualty officer, who was standing talking to two policemen, noticed and loped in after them. 'Gone off, has he? That was sudden. Nurse!'

A staff nurse appeared, one of the cool seen-it-all Casualty breed, and began to pump the chest as though she were mixing dough. The casualty officer worked at the patient's head trying to get an airway into the trachea. A bluish congested forearm swung out towards Campbell and he realised it would be useful to put up a drip. When he turned round another staff nurse was standing with everything ready: intravenous bicarbonate solution, giving set, cannula. All this calm efficiency was infectious and he slid the needle into a vein without hesitation or effort.

The casualty officer, his airway in at the first attempt, squeezed a black rubber bag like a football bladder: the patient's chest moved up and down most gratifyingly. The nurse who had helped with the drip was still one jump ahead: she trundled out an electrocardiograph on a trolley and threw Campbell a handful of leads colour-coded for the different limbs. She saw him hesitate. 'Like traffic lights from the right arm. That's yellow, left arm, and green, left leg, you've got there.' Of course. They wired him up, started the machine and a strip of paper rolled out with the news. It was a chaotic scribble.

'Fibrillation! I'll fry him!' The casualty officer unwound cables from the red shock-box. 'Disconnect the ECG. Hands off the trolley. Stand by! Now!' Two hundred watts of direct current went in and Mr Barclay jerked and grunted like someone starting an epileptic fit, then lay still again.

'ECG?'

'Sinus bradycardia!'

'Atropine!' The drug went into Campbell's drip, which was still running beautifully. The room began to fill up: a couple of students who prowled endlessly in Casualty, a porter, a student nurse and last of all the duty anaesthetist, who was employed to get to arrests quickly and take charge. He shuffled up in carpet slippers. 'Managing OK? Tube all right?' He pulled out a stethoscope and listened to the patient's chest to ensure the tube was inflating both lungs, then asked the casualty officer what he was injecting. Satisfied, he stood over the ECG tracing as it emerged. The machine whirred away, churning out five feet a minute of paper strip which fell in loops on the floor. Disorder of rhythm followed disorder of rhythm: and drug followed drug into

44

the drip line. The cycle of overactivity, shock and underactivity in the diseased heart was repeated twice and began to look as though it might go on for ever, while one nurse squeezed the oxygen bag and the other pumped the chest, then slowly the trace became more feeble and flickered down like a guttering flame. It was time for desperate measures, the last rites of the resuscitation process: the anaesthetist plunged a needle into the heart itself and injected adrenaline. No response. He looked at the casualty officer and they shook their heads. Campbell glanced at the clock and saw that they had been in the room for twenty-five minutes. It had seemed less.

With sleeves and trouser legs rolled up and chest bared, the corpse was still dressed for a wedding: the carnation lay trodden on the floor among the garlands of agonal ECG trace. The students, bored by failure, left and the anaesthetist jotted notes on a record card for someone else's research series of cardiac arrests. The casualty officer had gone and Campbell had a feeling that he was going to be the one who would have to tell the relatives. He was unaccustomed to the task: he had an idea that most people said either, 'At least his suffering is over,' if the patient had had a hard time, or, 'At least he didn't suffer,' if he hadn't. Probably one for the latter, and perhaps the little group waiting in the casualty sister's room would have had some warning from the sudden appearance of cups of tea, which the Institute did not lightly dispense to relatives.

It went badly. They were drunk, half-sobered by the news and very weepy. The wife kept saying, 'If only he had taken heed of the doctor at home,' and a brother patted her arm and thanked Campbell for doing his best. The little party, sniffing and beerily bedraggled, balanced their teacups with a fierce gentility that defied both booze and bereavement. Reluctantly, Campbell was involved: it was all so sudden and pathetic. And dying in clothes you didn't own. He sat with them mainly listening and uncertain how to get away.

When he left the department it was almost one o'clock. The whole business from the condemned man's last request for a cigarette weighed him down and he suddenly found himself longing to tell Joan about it. At one o'clock she would be asleep. There had been nothing to prevent him going up to see her earlier, between the only two cases of a long evening. Now that he needed her he felt guilty.

The stairs and corridors were as quiet as ever they were, with only the sounds of ventilation and distant lifts clanking and straining. He met no one until he was in the top surgical corridor where a night nurse with a cardigan over her shoulders and a little-red-riding-hood basket passed on her way to some meal break or rest period. They seemed very organised for night duty. Not like the medical staff who did it in addi-

45

tion to and regardless of their daytime work. No days asleep and meals at night for the twenty or so housemen who covered the whole hospital between five at night and nine the next morning. You just went at it as though there was a war on, without thought of complaint. It lasted a year and afterwards you were different: you collected your own horror-stories of fatigue and endurance, and you joined a profession of fellow-survivors and became as contemptuous of the hardships of your successors as your predecessors were of your own.

Campbell walked quietly into Ward Sixteen and glanced into Joan's cubicle. She was asleep and someone had brought her flowers. Dahlias, probably from Sister: a reproach for the morning raid if she could find no other. The nurse in charge, in the white collar and cuffs of a third-year student, emerged from the pool of light at the nursing station.

'Can I help you, Dr Campbell?'

Campbell, who didn't know her name, wondered how she knew his.

'I'm receiving and just dropped in on the off-chance the staff-nurse from my ward might be awake. I see she isn't. I didn't realise it was so late.' It didn't sound at all casual, and the student nurse savoured his embarrassment with polite leisure. By three a.m. a lot of third-year nurses would know that a houseman had just happened to drop in at one in the morning to see a staff-nurse/patient from the same unit, officially in with appendicitis, though the balance of diagnostic opinion would probably swing in favour of a discreetly handled ectopic pregnancy. Campbell retreated ingloriously, glancing again at Joan, pale and lovely in the night-light, and remembering her emergent bristles.

At four a.m. he was called down to admit an acute heart failure. Casualty was quiet, the nurses efficient and helpful. The patient, a Mr Thomson, was on oxygen already, but in a bad way, gasping to get breath into sodden, congested lungs. His pulse was feeble and too fast to count and there were ominous flecks of pink foam on his lips. By the old textbooks he'd be dying. Ten years ago no drug could have dried out his lungs quickly enough. With no particular sense of wonder Campbell administered a therapeutic miracle that had become common-place: intravenous frusemide with the old stand-bys, morphine and digitalis. These and the oxygen snatched him from the jaws of a fine old-fashioned death and in ten minutes he was better. His pulse slowed down and he passed vast quantities of urine. His breathlessness disappeared and he became positively garrulous, reeling off a story including a dozen similar episodes. It was not only the houseman who took therapeutic miracles for granted. Under questioning Mr Thomson admitted that this miracle would have been unnecessary if he had remembered to take the tablets prescribed after the last one. He would certainly be back and one day, just as certainly, he would leave it too late. Campbell wrote down the story and clinical signs automatically, saw the patient to the ward and went back to his bed praying for a few undisturbed hours, the remains of a night's sleep.

He had been in bed for half an hour and had just fallen asleep when he was called again by Casualty to see an eighty-two-year-old with a slipped disc. He lay with the receiver in his hand, knowing that if he didn't get up right away he never would, then jumped out of bed cursing casualty officers, discs and eighty-two-year-olds and dressed angrily.

The general practitioner's letter was on the smallest notepaper Campbell had ever seen. He had a theory that the mental deterioration of a practitioner could be charted by the diminishing size of his letters but had not yet observed single cases for long enough to be sure. The writer, to judge him thus, must be mad, but professional etiquette dictated an attempt at decipherment. 'This grand old gentleman . . . who has had for many years' "back trouble" (were inverted commas a substitute for accurate diagnosis in the GP world?), fell while attempting to get up early this morning. He complains of pain. Query lumbar disc. Yours etc.'

Remembering Bertram's example he spent a moment composing himself before going to see the patient, who was indeed a grand old gentleman, all profile and silver locks like an old actor, and very pale. He gave a precise and patrician account of events. 'I called my physician this morning, regretfully, because of pain. The site is a familiar one, in the lower back, but the character of the pain is quite new. And severe. I collapsed when I rose intending to stretch my legs.'

'The pain was there before you fell?'

'Quite definitely, though between ourselves my physician seemed to think the fall caused the pain. One didn't argue.' A dark heavy rug of regimental tartan covered him from his chin to his feet. A third of the way down it was throbbing quite clearly at the rate of a fast pulse.

'May I examine your abdomen?'

'Certainly, dear boy.' Campbell unwrapped rug, dressing gown and pyjamas and laid a hand on the pale skin of the old man's abdomen. What he had suspected became chillingly certain: a firm pulsing mass rose centrally from under his ribs and extended downwards as far as his umbilicus.

'How bad is the pain?'

'Quite the worst one had experienced.'

'We'll give you an injection. Very soon.'

'Thank you.'

He might live an hour. Certainly not much more. And no surgeon would want to touch him. The pulsing mass could only be the distorted remnant of the great blood vessel lying in front of the spine, with pints

47

of blood and clot round it. The patient was paler than he had been only a few minutes before. Campbell remembered a gem of surgical teaching, 'Nothing goes so pale so fast as a leaking aortic aneurysm.'

'Am I very ill?'

'I'm afraid so.'

'Am I going to die?'

Campbell said nothing and the old man spoke again. 'Sorry, perhaps one shouldn't ask.' He looked at Campbell with calm alert eyes, then said, 'I don't mind.'

'I'm going to fix up that injection.'

Sometimes if the patient were relatively young and the aneurysm discovered early, a surgeon might be tempted to try an arterial procedure to replace the damaged vessel with a dacron graft, but the operation even in fit subjects had an appalling mortality. In this case there was no point in asking a surgeon to come in and look at him, and if no active treatment were contemplated it would be meddlesome even to put up a drip. What he needed was the poppy and plenty of it, as Ravelston Orr said when he slugged his terminal cancers with opiates. To be sure, Campbell rang his registrar's bedroom.

'Dr Bertram? Campbell here.'

'What?'

'Dr Campbell.'

'Oh, what?'

'I've got an eighty-two-year-old leaking aortic aneurysm. His pressure's right down and his pulse is one twenty. I've given him twenty of morphine.'

'Fine.'

'Is that all right?'

'Yes.'

'Drip?'

'No.'

'Surgeons?'

'You're kidding. What time is it?'

'Twenty to six.'

'Thanks. See you on the ward at nine.'

'OK. Thanks.'

Campbell went back to the patient hoping fervently and disloyally that he would be dead before the ward round. He could think of nothing more awful than old Creech muttering about experimental arterial aneurysms in vitamin-depleted rats while half a dozen students queued to feel the pulsing mass. A comfortable bed, for not too long, was what was required.

The nurse had repeated the readings. She emerged from behind the screens writing on his chart. 'Funny name he's got. Quothquan. Oh, and there's a relative in Sister's room. A granddaughter. D'you want to see her?'

She was tallish, blonde, in her mid-twenties and well turned out for six in the morning, in a slightly dated way, like the *Scottish Field* fashion pictures of about three years ago. She was standing looking at Sister's duck prints, and turned and smiled when he came in.

'How is he?'

'Not well, I'm afraid.'

'It's just his back, isn't it?'

'I'm afraid it's rather . . . more than that.' It wasn't that or anything remotely like that, but GPs, even micrographic demented ones, deserved some professional consideration. He's bleeding internally. From a sort of disease of the arteries he's had for a long time. It must have started to actually bleed last night. But it could have happened at any time.'

'Is he awfully ill?'

'I'm afraid so.'

'Is he going to die?'

'We'll make him as comfortable as possible.'

'Is he going to die?'

'I'm afraid so.'

'Isn't there anything you can do?'

'Not really. No, I'm sorry. When it's like this . . . you can't do anything.'

'But if he's bleeding can't you give him some blood?'

She would have to be a teacher or something like that: most people just took your word.

'The main artery in the body is giving way. Transfusion just couldn't keep up. At best it would just slow things up and only prolong the . . . whole business.'

'I see.'

There was something odd about her reaction: things in it other than anxiety and grief, almost as if she wanted to be sure about the outcome. He glanced at her ring finger and hazarded a guess: unmarried, looking after an ageing, demanding relative. She noticed his glance and relaxed a little as though she could now assume Campbell knew a lot more about things.

'I look after him,' she announced. 'Sometimes he's difficult. Sweet most of the time. But sometimes definitely difficult.' She paused perhaps uncertain whether or not to make some other revelation, then said, 'He will be comfortable?'

So that was it. No hardships: he didn't mind and neither did she.

'How long will it be?'

By the time they started out for the ward the cosy world of the hospital at night had been dispersed. Cleaners, to judge from the noise, were throwing buckets at each other and playing dodgems with the floor-polishers. A night superintendent of some six years' training and God knows how much experience was proceeding slowly along the corridor switching off lights in an exercise of the sort of self-defeating parsimony for which the Institute was famed. Quothquan lay on his trolley as pale as a marble effigy of himself and Campbell and the grand-daughter kept pace on opposite sides level with the site of the pathology. She walked nicely, fit and feminine, and the hand resting on the trolley rail was tanned. Campbell wondered idly where she had been on holiday, and with whom.

While she gave details to the junior nurse, the houseman, the porter and the nurse in charge lifted the patient on to his bed in a single cubicle. He was white and weak but still the grand old gentleman. 'Thank you again, dear boy. My pain is much relieved. Will you send the girl in when it's convenient?' His voice was fainter.

Campbell spoke to the nurse in charge and arranged half-hourly readings to keep track on his decline. When she asked if he was going to put up a drip he snapped, 'No,' then told her why not. Even doing nothing had to be explained. As he left the ward for what seemed like the twentieth time in twenty-four hours the granddaughter was leaning over a desk still talking to the nurse. She had nice legs but he couldn't think of anything else he needed to talk to her about. She saw him passing and turned round.

'Dr . . .?'

'Campbell.'

'Thank you very much for all you've done, Dr Campbell. You've been most kind.'

'Not at all. No trouble.' He remembered the old man's summons. 'Your grandfather asked if you could go in when you can.' Her eyes smiled and the corners of her mouth turned down in a comical resigned grin as though she had been summoned very often. There was an odd death-bed scene coming. Campbell left the ward. The nurses would summon him for his next and last duty to Mr Quothquan.

There was no point whatsoever in going back to bed. That realisation always marked the lowest moment of a night on duty, but there were things you could do that made it easier to pretend that you'd had a night's sleep: the routine of showering and shaving, and breakfast even if you weren't hungry normalised the morning just a little. Campbell went back to his room to shave and turned the radio on. It thumped out

50

something considered by the BBC to be the equivalent for the few of the mindlessly cheerful breakfast programmes for the many: a Donizetti overture. He turned it off and shaved then lay on his bed and realised he was waiting for Mr Quothquan to die. It was a funny name. Perhaps it was familiar, or seemed so because it was so singular, or because having met the granddaughter he wished it was. He reconstructed her features in his mind: blonde, with quick frank eyes, a wide mouth and good teeth – traditional good looks of the kind that could make you a model for twin-set knitting patterns.

From the pocket of his white coat the bleep sounded slow and steady. He rang the exchange and they put him through to the ward. 'Mr Quothquan died a few minutes ago, Dr Campbell. Could you come over and certify him. Oh, and his granddaughter's quite upset now. We didn't think she would be but she is.'

He lay as he had died. No pulses. No respiratory effort. Cardiac apex silent to one minute's auscultation. Pupils fixed and dilated and retinae very pale. The abdominal mass was less well defined. Had it ruptured as the terminal event? For the record, death by exsanguination from a leaking aortic aneurysm secondary to generalised atherosclerosis. A good solid certifiable death.

Campbell noted down his findings with some satisfaction: the old boy had died quickly and with reasonable dignity. A few months ago such a death would have been upsetting: now Campbell saw it with a sort of compassionate detachment. Hospitals existed to provide facilities for tidy dying, though fifty per cent of those eligible preferred or happened to die at home. The old man had not been anxious or afraid and the girl would find someone else to look after.

She was sitting in the visitor's room sobbing. In front of her was the ritual cup of tea which Campbell could have cheerfully kicked through the window. He sat down beside her and she looked round. 'I'm sorry, Dr Campbell . . . crying and so on . . . but it's so confusing. And it all happened so suddenly. I was told at five this morning that his back had gone again and then you told me it was bleeding and now it's eight o'clock and he's dead.'

'In the early stages the symptoms are very similar . . . You can't really blame Dr . . .' Professional solidarity, even with cretins.

'No, I didn't mean that. He adored Dr Mansie. He was more like one of the family than just the doctor. No. I wasn't complaining. It's just about him dying. I'm so confused.'

'You say you looked after him.'

'Yes, and sometimes it was awful. Especially if his back was bad. He wanted me there always, either for his pills – he was on hundreds – or just to have someone to talk to.'

'Old people, especially if they've been left on their own, can be . . . sort of . . .'

'I know.' Suddenly she lifted her head and looked directly at Campbell through her tears. 'When he was alive I was angry at myself for wishing he was dead, and now he's died I'm angry at him for . . . doing it.' She wept again and put her hands up to her face. 'It sounds so silly and so selfish.'

Campbell looked at her hands and her hair and said nothing. After a moment she straightened up and shook her hair back: a strand was wet with tears and hung sadly, darker than the rest. 'You must think me very silly.'

'No. Not at all.'

Her eyes were green and filled with tears and there was a little mole under her lower lip. The wet bit of hair had fallen forward again. Campbell sat looking at her helplessly: he was so tired he had forgotten what he was going to say. She gazed back at him as though trying to help him remember. He did. 'I think that's quite common. When someone dies, I mean. Grief isn't usually simply grief. Most people don't realise that. You do.' A blue paperback. He was glad he'd read it.

She dabbed her eyes and sniffed. 'What makes it worse is that everyone here is so kind and marvellous and efficient. And I just sit here crying and talking about my feelings.'

'You've done your bit,' said Campbell. It sounded pompous and he realised he was probably no older than she was. Medicine put old heads on young shoulders, with inconstant results.

They sat together in silence. Campbell was dog-tired and momentarily comfortable and slightly puzzled by the reactions of the girl beside him, who had seemed so much tougher three hours before. She sniffed back more tears and turned towards him. 'Is there a phone I can use?'

'Yes. This way.'

He should have directed her to the public phone-booth downstairs. That was the Institute rule but he was in no mood for it. The nurse in charge raised an eyebrow as he showed her into the ward kiosk. She thanked him again and he made his way across the courtyard to the Residency. On the way he reviewed the receiving night and its patients: one social admission, one professional case of heart failure, two corpses and no extra beds. It didn't seem much.

8

When Campbell went back to the ward at nine o'clock Bertram was sitting on his desk smoking a pipe.

'Morning, Campbell. I see you haven't been very busy.'

'Not very.'

'There's a nice big blonde lassie out there looking a bit down in the mouth. Who's she?'

'The aneurysm's granddaughter.'

'Is he not dead yet?'

'Yes. She's waiting for his things or for someone to come up or something.'

'Oh. I see you've got my old friend Jimmy Thomson in again. Had him in with heart failure when I was houseman here. Cured him. Thought I was marvellous. He doesn't take his pills.'

'He still doesn't.'

'Miller's got eight female admissions upstairs. Some of them real crumbles. Crumblitis crumblosa crumblans. Diffusa. The slow kind. Look as if they'll be here for years. You got off lightly.'

'That's the way it goes.'

'Never mind. There'll be other receiving nights.'

Campbell took his blood sampling tray and sought refuge in the wards. It was muddled and busy and he found it all but impossible to get near the patients he wanted. Nurses swarmed around making beds, shifting chairs and linen baskets, toting bedpans and doing obscure nursing things to patients behind screens. He picked his way through the chaos savouring the symptoms of his fatigue, the irritability and incoordination, the gritty eyelids and the headache. As he was finishing the blood round his senior student arrived and offered to help with it and then Sister whose dawn raid he had thus far avoided walked the whole length of the ward to tell him Joan was 'comfortable'. Such pinpricks on top of the frustrations and deprivations of the night reduced him to a state for which no expression of his feelings short of arson or aerial bombardment would have sufficed.

The junior clinic and yet more registrars straggled in at the top of the ward. Creech, to whom the fates of the consultants receiving rota had allotted the patients of the night, liked to make much of these ward rounds. They were his fancied contact with the real untidy world of medicine, though by the time he saw the patients they had been admitted, scrubbed, investigated, treated and sometimes cured. There were only two new cases and both of them were dull, but he would indulge his whimsy to the full: custom dictated that he spend the whole

53

morning between the two wards to give substance to his claim that his duties encroached far into the weekend. He arrived promptly at nine thirty.

'Morning, Campbell. Busy night?'

'Not really, sir. Two patients on the ward. There was one who arrested in Casualty. No luck with resuscitation. And there was an eighty-two-year-old who died shortly after admission.'

Creech turned to the students. 'Let us proceed to review the problems of acute clinical medicine which have kept Dr Campbell from his bed, and on the way round we shall cast an eye over some more familiar faces.'

Creech's first patient was a gaunt and speechless ninety-year-old who had been in the wards for eight months. 'Good morning,' said the chief.

'Aghaagh.'

'I think he's looking better.'

Bertram coughed and spoke up. 'We thought he looked a bit pale yesterday, sir, and wondered . . .'

Creech was eager to see his new patients. 'He's looking better.' The ward round moved on. Bertram looked crestfallen. Another silly game of anaemia had been averted.

Becalmed once more in the geriatric doldrums beyond the nursing station the ward round heard out Creech's views on the nutritional value of pine needles. Campbell found his attention wandering. At the door of the ward an outlandish figure – male, sixtyish, in green poacher's tweeds with a large watch chain – had appeared. Campbell categorised him as a GP on a hospital prowl and Bertram, who shared the house-man's indifference to the subject of their chief's discourse, whispered to him, 'Mansie. Nice practice in the New Town. Rotten doctor. Well, daft but not dangerous. Have we got any of his?'

Campbell, befuddled by fatigue, couldn't remember. The green tweeds advanced up the ward, closing on Creech with an idiot smile. 'Henry, old chap!'

'Tug! How are you?'

'Awfully well,' said the GP. 'Busy of course. And you?'

'Keeping busy. Not only you chaps who have to work at weekends you know.'

'I don't doubt it. But then you always were a worker.'

'Habit, Tug, habit, Work hard . . .'

'And play hard,' said the general practitioner, who was evidently familiar with the aphorism. The old comrades laughed delightedly together.

'To what do we owe the pleasure this fine Saturday morning?' said Creech.

'You have a patient of mine, I believe. Admitted last night. To tell you the truth, Henry, I'm glad he's in your care, because he's one of my favourites. Grand old boy. Hamish Quothquan the poet actually. Quite famous in his way.'

'Always a pleasure to look after your patients,' said Creech, 'and I'm sure Dr Campbell, my resident house physician here, has made him comfortable. What's wrong with him, Tug?'

'Oh, nothing very exotic, I'm afraid. A disc. He's had trouble with his back for years, as I told your resident in my letter, and he had a fall last night. I just popped in to see that everything was all right. And to see that my old friends and colleagues aren't overwhelming him with an excess of scientific medicine.' He chortled roguishly.

'I'm surprised my resident didn't ring me up at home.' said Creech. 'I'm always available and glad to come in. Consultants are on call full time as you know. But I expect Dr Campbell here has got it all sorted out by now.'

Campbell glanced round for Bertram, who had been at his elbow moments before: he was ushering the students down the ward to some patient of interest, at a safe distance.

'Well, Dr Campbell? How is the poet's lumbar spine?'

In the circumstances indecent exposure was preferable to striptease. 'He's dead, sir.'

'He's what?' The GP goggled at Campbell, and Creech gasped, 'Dead? Of a lumbar disc?'

'It wasn't quite a straightforward disc, sir.'

'Can't have been if he's dead,' snapped Creech. 'Why didn't you call me in, Campbell?'

Dr Mansie wallowed between amazement, indignation and loss of face at this extinction of a prize patient he had worked on a Saturday morning to come in and see. Creech hesitated, sensing the risks of further revelation, then said, 'If you'll excuse us, Dr Mansie, Dr Campbell and I will discuss this unfortunate case. Perhaps a few minutes?'

Chief and houseman walked towards Campbell's office. 'Well, Campbell, I hope you're covered. "Slipped disc" on a death certificate would hardly get the support of my signature.'

'I don't think it was a disc, sir . . .' Creech got the whole story, from the beginning and including the phone call to Bertram.

'Well, I believe you,' said Creech when Campbell had finished 'Diagnosis was never old Tug's strong point. Even as a student. He preferred shooting. If what you say is true there shouldn't be any difficulty, but we'd better get a post-mortem if the relatives are agreeable.'

'Yes sir. There's a granddaughter.'

'Good. Well, see what you can do.'

'Yessir.'

'Oh, and . . . Campbell . . . It would have been a pleasure for me to have come in last night or this morning or whatever it was. There are times when a . . . perhaps a physician of . . . more experience . . . and discretion than yourself . . . would have realised that . . . there are certain situations . . . when consultants should be called, um . . . regardless of the hour.'

Campbell, still fighting off tiredness, listened with sarcasm simmering inside him like heartburn: call Creech for all moribund eighty-two-year-olds? Or only for moribund eighty-two-year-olds with undiagnosed aortic aneurysms? Or would it be less trouble to call you, sir, only for those moribund eighty-two-year-olds with leaking aneurysms who happen also to have achieved minor fame as poets?

'I don't think I fully understand, sir.'

'Well, Campbell, how can I put it? It seems you were rightly concerned with the questions of diagnosis and management, and perhaps too concerned with them to envisage the care of the patient as a whole. A man in the position of the late Mr Quothquan is used to . . . certain . . . Let me say it again, Campbell, it would have been no trouble to come in last night regardless of the hour.'

'I didn't realise he was famous.'

Creech went on as though Campbell had not spoken. 'Ideally, of course, some surgical colleague such as Mr Ravelston Orr should have been called in. However unfit you considered the patient to be for surgery he should not have been denied the benefit of a full and expert surgical assessment. And I know that Mr Ravelston Orr too would have gladly come in.'

Sure thing. Social finds from the ruck of NHS patients were not for hoarding, but to be fingered and passed round like the sheep's eye at a Berber feast. Campbell could picture all too well the solemn futility of a Creech-Ravelston Orr consultation in the grey hours of dawn, the nuisance and sheer boredom of waiting for the great men to make up their minds to do nothing. He had no regrets.

'I'm sorry, sir . . . I . . .'

'I understand, Campbell, I was a houseman myself once . . . It's when you're most tired you have to be most careful. That's when the mistakes happen.'

'Yessir.'

'Now I'd better go and have a word with Dr Mansie. It might be better if we were to confer alone.'

They went out into the corridor, where Mansie and the granddaughter were standing talking. Mansie introduced Creech to the girl.

'Let me offer my condolences,' said Creech in his finest graveside manner. 'It is all so sudden and so tragic. I myself was a great admirer of your grandfather's work. His death will leave a distinct gap in the literary life of the nation. It's a consolation that a great reputation will survive with his poetry.'

Campbell, who suspected that Creech's exposure to verse was limited to television commercials and the twenty-third psalm at funerals, sought distraction in an oblique view of the girl's legs and listened to her voice, low woodwind, with an accent just within the reach of mockery – Edinburgh delightful.

'Thank you, Dr Creech,' she said, 'and may I thank you also for the way the staff of your unit took care of my grandfather. They were all so kind. Particularly Dr Campbell, who was most understanding and efficient.'

Campbell kept looking at her legs, thus avoiding a glance from the chief possibly accusing him of violating her on the coffin of her ancestor.

'Glad to hear it,' said Creech gruffly. 'One can't always be in attendance oneself. Regrettably. Now if you'll excuse me, Dr Mansie and I must have a word.'

After their conversation Dr Mansie left abruptly and Creech returned, not smiling, but with an expression suggesting to those who knew him that he might have been a moment before. 'I shall continue the round with Dr Bertram and the young colleagues, Campbell.'

'Yessir.' It sounded like a reminder about the post-mortem permission form. He went to his office and started to head up a blank: the poet's name assumed an Aztec complexity of qs and us to his fatigued mind, but a second attempt was passable.

In the corridor he was alone with the girl again. He ushered her into the visitors' room and they sat down. She was now composed, alert and sympathetic, as though Campbell were the one with problems. Sitting down made him feel tired again and she leaned forward and said, 'You look exhausted.'

He smiled and then remembered why they were there, but the sense of intimacy made him pause. A lot had happened to them since six a.m., and soon afterwards they would be strangers again, but before that he had to persuade her to sign a form permitting the hospital to eviscerate the corpse of her grandfather. He started gently, 'Miss . . .?'

'Quothquan.'

'Miss Quothquan, in view of the fact that your grandfather's death was . . . rather sudden . . .'

'Yes?'

'Dr Creech would like a sort of examination carried out on the body.'

'A post-mortem?'

'Yes. That's it. It's quite routine.' She hesitated and Campbell went on, 'Nowadays it's quite normal. Very few people have any objections . . .'

57

She coloured slightly. 'He would have done . . . He did in fact.'
She bit her lip then said, 'He said he wanted . . . just cremated.'
'Oh.'
'So I really couldn't sign. I'm sure you'll understand.'
'Certainly.' Campbell tore up his form: Creech was not to have his
PM, the wishes of those most concerned would be respected, and in due
course he himself would get a few guineas for signing another form
required before cremation. He stood up.
She stood up too and said, 'I'm sorry about that. But thanks very
much for all you've done. And please say thank you to the nurses for
me. Goodbye, Dr Campbell.'
They looked at each other for just a moment longer than necessary
then she left and he watched her walking away. She had nice legs.

Much later that morning, after the interminable ritual of coffee
with Creech and his eventual departure to the female ward upstairs,
Campbell went round the ward with Sister to translate anecdote,
digression and hypothesis into practical clinical management, then
prepared to leave. At the door of his office a shabbily dressed old man
was waiting. He carried a carton wrapped in polythene. 'I'm sorry I'm
late, but I didn't like to take this on the bus and I don't walk as well as
I used to.'
Campbell experienced a familiar momentary blank. Not only did
patients remember doctors better than doctors remembered patients,
but the horizontal, pyjama-clad population of the wards bore no
relation to the people who stopped you out in town after their discharge.
These beneficiaries of modern medicine, who might be snatched from
the jaws of death one week and be passed in the street the next by the
same doctor, must find it confusing too. By concentrating on the man's
face and imagining the rest of him in green Institutional stripes Campbell joggled the recall process quite successfully. Carton. Collection.
McTurk.
'Oh, Mr McTurk. Weren't you supposed to come up with that
yesterday?'
'To tell you the truth, doctor, I was that glad to get back to my own
wee house that I forgot all about the collection until . . . it was too late
for yesterday. I only remembered when I came across the carton in the
lobby last night.'
'Thanks for coming up anyway. I believe one of Dr Fyvie's assistants
wants to talk to you. It might be about more samples.'
'Oh well, after all you've done for me I can hardly refuse to make a
wee occasional contribution.'
'Good. I'll take your sample and get Dr Elder to come down and see
you.'

Campbell rang Elder, who was overjoyed, then went off to the lab deepfreeze, which was full of similar cartons all neatly labelled and dated. As he deposited this latest and most valued addition to the collection it occurred to him that the massed samples were surprisingly inoffensive. Frozen shit does not stink.

Campbell took a beer from the Residency bar and went up to the billiards room. Mac and Soutar were there already, drinking beer and watching another two playing a game. The green light and the dark walls and the click and mutter of the game were restful. The beer helped too. The billiards room was a place at peace with its past, another of the Institute's little shrines. Round its walls hung the carved tops of the mess tables of long ago, to which successive vintages of residents had added their names until there was no more space and the table top was removed and hung here and replaced by another blank one which would be filled and removed in its time. Here, as in the corridor of photographs was a place at peace with its past. There were hundreds of names. Of these only a few score enjoyed the minor celebrity of a local consultancy, and a handful more some wider esteem – a few college presidents, a talented young suicide, a royal physician and a poisoner – a handful from the hundreds named and forgotten. The signatory woodcarvers had played billiards and had once been also in Arcady and now their successors drank beer and played billiards as the genial shades of the place would have wished.

'You're still looking hellish,' said Mac. 'What's up?'

'Nothing. Except I'm too buggered to enjoy what is laughingly referred to as my weekend off.'

'Hard receiving night?'

'Fairly. And a bollocking from old Creech for letting a dying poet die.'

'Like Keats? Man, that's beautiful.'

'No, older.'

'Seriously, a real poet?'

'Could have been Shakespeare, the fuss Creech made.'

'Oho. You didn't call him in.'

'That's right.'

'Don't worry. Happens to the best of us. Missed a retired dean's wife first day in the job. Got hell . . . Seriously? A real poet?'

'Quothquan.'

' "Speak to me soft-flying ghosts of the twilight . . ." '

'That's him. I knew I'd heard of him.'

'Owls somewhere.'

'Glenfiddich?'

'No. Glenlivet.'

59

'Yes. Him.'

'I thought he'd been dead for years.'

'So did I.'

'Strange how you think they're dead.'

'He is now. Certified him myself.'

'Never mind. Look on the bright side. Any ash-cash?'

'Only just. Creech wanted a PM, but his granddaughter refused. He's for burning.'

'There you are. The silver lining.'

'Nice granddaughter too.'

They stood watching the billiards game. A long shot trickled steadily towards a pot with every appearance of getting there, then slowed and curved round suddenly just three inches short. The players converged on the corner and examined the baize. The man who had played the shot picked something up and held it against the light.

'A hair! Crinkly.'

'Pubic?'

'Or negro?'

'Here?'

'It's pubic. Some dirty beast has been bagging off on the billiard table. Bloody vandalism. It could just as well have been stained or torn. Mess property too. What's your committee going to do about that, Campbell?'

'Well, we could have a silly meeting and put a notice up: "Mess members are reminded . . ." '

The other player was intrigued more by the incident itself than by its possible consequences. 'Who's been getting a bit in here then? I never heard anything last night.'

'Match the sample,' said Mac. 'Basic forensic science. All you need is an identification parade.'

'But there's no way of telling whether a hair is male or female.'

'Think of the identification parade we could have,' said Mac.

'You've all got dirty minds. Couldn't you just play the shot again?'

'Have you thought of sniffing it?' said Mac.

The aggrieved player screwed up his face. 'You seem very interested in billiards all of a sudden.'

Mac smiled. 'I suppose you could say I am.'

'You're a dirty beast, Mac.'

'No, Campbell, I think this is truly love.'

'On a billiard table.'

'We fell in love rather suddenly.'

'With the lights on?' said a player, aghast.

'The lady was a little shy, I must confess. But if at some future date we choose to use your lights, don't worry, we'll switch them off afterwards. Come on, Campbell, let's leave them to their game. We could go across to the pub. The great God Ashcash has recently smiled on my fortunes too.'

They walked down the main staircase past sunlit flowers and busts.

'What's this love business? Not like you, Mac.'

'That's maybe putting it a bit strongly. But this one's different.'

'First on a billiard table.'

'Yes. But more than that. She is . . . different.'

'Aren't they all different?'

'In the strictest anthropometric sense, yes. Perhaps I mean gynaecometric. But this kid's got spirit.'

'Kid? Not a first-year nurse. Surely not on . . .'

'Relax. This girl. This girl's got spirit.'

'Do I know her?'

'I don't know if you do. But you'll meet her tonight.'

'Really?'

'There'll be a party somewhere, I suppose.'

9

On Saturday night there was always a party somewhere, a predictable and reliable party, a party that might resemble last week's so closely that it could have been reconvened after a seven-day adjournment, a party perhaps so congenial that it was difficult to imagine that a revival had not already been planned for next week. Only the venues changed, flitting mysteriously from Bruntsfield to Stockbridge, to the higher tributaries of Leith Walk or the fastnesses of Lauriston, but returning always to the emergent ghettoes of the young, the solid tenements of Marchmont and Bruntsfield where spinsters, widows and cats shrank before the new waves of the young and the noisy: nurses and students whose very nameplates on the doors – temporary, crowded, amended and even mixed – spelt imminent social collapse.

Without benefit of a social register, the parties ran and ran and ran. Hostesses planned two or three weeks in advance, told their friends, issued clever little hand-done invitations and sometimes suborned a houseman into putting up a note in the Residency. They purchased small eats and a ballast of cheap drink and then on the night stowed their valuables, cleared a couple of rooms for action, and waited. When the pubs closed boyfriends were posted at the door and at a quarter past ten the faithful first-comers arrived to a routine of suspicion, recognition, admission, coats over there, drinks over there. Guests with money brought more than they intended to drink, those without, or without conscience, less or none. Wise hostesses skimmed off a couple of bottles of Riesling for Sunday lunch and ploughed the rest of the customary surplus back into the occasion. Success, measured in din and overcrowding, could be judged by eleven, and when the booze ran out everyone went home.

The people were Institute people: nurses, doctors, medical students, physiotherapists, ward secretaries, radiographers, occupational therapists, electrocardiographers and a smattering of the pushier lab technicians, one of whom, Billy, an adenoidal Peter Pan from some den of haematology, discharged a central function for the party circuit: girls throwing parties took it he could be relied upon to produce the men, and men who wanted to go to parties knew that Billy was the man to ask. In his grubby diary were all the fixtures. People told him things. He remembered things. And things they chose not to tell him he found out anyway.

At parties he was always there, shifty and watchful, thinking ahead and sniffing out yet more parties, trading promises for information and hints for company: a go-between so perfectly adapted that his sexual orientation was desultorily discussed by both sides of his clientele, without conclusion or experiment. But he always knew. Something different, classy? Physiotherapists in Royal Circus a fortnight tonight. A midweek thing? The dietitians' flat in Minto Street next Wednesday. Oddment, reduced. His pasty features and adenoidal sniff irked but hung around. He was monumentally unsnubbable. His social contribution was entirely specialist and mercantile, that of the snivelling broker, and to his small enduring joy he was tolerated for it. It occurred to no one, least of all himself, that he might enjoy parties.

When Mac and Campbell went into the pub, Billy was sitting with a glass in front of him containing just the three-eighths of an inch of beer that would prevent a roving barmaid from removing it. Without discussing whether or not to join him the housemen did so. Saturday night was only once a week and time or even beer spent in reconnaissance was never wasted. Mac offered him a drink, noting his half-pint glass and silently daring him to up it to a pint.

'Just a half-pint, thanks.' Strange. Sometimes he could take a hint.

Mac brought a pint for Campbell and had a whisky and half-pint himself.

'Whisky, eh? Been burning somebody then, Mac?' This was part of Billy's stock in trade, a quite unreciprocated familiarity with housemen and their ways which sometimes even went as far as emulation: he had been known to appear in the pub with a borrowed bleep on the pretext that he was on call for urgent haematology. Mac grunted.

'Cheers anyway.'

'Cheers.' They chatted generally, the conversation orbiting around but well clear of the subject of parties for this evening, the housemen holding back out of a fastidiousness which at least delayed the asking of favours from such a person, and Billy from an excess of commercial prudence which impelled him to drink at least half the inducement before parting with anything of value. It was hard going. Eventually they let him prattle through a technician's eye view of some catastrophe committed in the name of thoracic surgery in which the patient had oozed blood from every orifice, natural and surgical. The housemen listened quietly to his account, a mass of technical detail relieved by the occasional clinical malapropism. 'And do you know what her residual one-stage plasma re-calcification clotting time was when the Prof. wanted to resect her other rib-cage?'

'No.'

'Fifty-eight seconds.'

'Oh.' That was evidently the point of the saga.

'Ridiculous!' said Billy, sniffing to supplement the lack of any other response. In his confusion he took an injudiciously large gulp of beer. Mac and Campbell watched. He remembered himself. 'What's the action for tonight then, lads?'

'Quiet evening, I should think,' said Mac. 'I might look in here again later.'

'See you here,' said Billy eagerly.

'Or I might go out somewhere for dinner.'

'And get away from Residency food?'

Mac ignored that too, and after a pause Billy said, 'There are one or two parties on, around and about.'

'Really?'

'Nothing very great.' Campbell began to wonder how the hunched pudgy little man opposite would look staked out and lightly done with napalm; Mac had the patience of a born negotiator. 'Oh. That's a pity,' he said from a great distance. Billy glanced at the last inch of beer in his glass. There was another silence.

'There's one in Abbeyhill. Some X-ray secretaries. Twenty-nine Abbey Place, top flat.'

'Yes?' said Mac, leaning forward. Billy began to talk more quickly.

'And the theatre-staff nurses from thirteen and fourteen are having one. One-eighty Thirlestane Avenue.'

'Yes?' Mac put both hands flat on the table, fingers pointing towards Billy. Billy sniffed and his eyes swept round the bar.

'And there's another one.'

'Oh?'

'Some first-year nurses. Marchmont.'

'Yes?'

'Seventy-two Marchmont Terrace. Top right.' Billy gabbled the words out and stopped for a sniff. 'And for God's sake don't go telling everyone. They want a nice quiet grown-up do.'

'Quite.' Mac sat back and finished his whisky. Billy gulped the last inch of his beer.

'Have another,' said Mac.

'No thanks. Thanks very much. No. I've got to be going for my dinner. I mean lunch. Honest. Bye. See you at the party, maybe.' He got up and scuttled out sniffing.

'Fucking little pimp.'

'Seventy-two Marchmont Terrace.'

'Top right.'

'Right.'

Campbell got up for another round and came back. 'First-year nurses seem to be getting younger since I was a student.'

'That's a poorly defined clinical impression. You can be sure they're all still seventeen at the very least.'

'I suppose so. Anyway, I thought you were supposed to be in love or something.'

'Yes. But that doesn't preclude the pleasures of mixing in society.'

'You mean sniffing round first-year nurses.'

'That's one of the pleasures of society. And some of them are quite grown up. I've got three really lively kids on the ward just now. All they wear under their uniform is black tights.'

'Really? How d'you find that out?'

Mac smiled into the froth of his beer. 'That hairy blue uniform stuff. It must keep the little dears all of a tingle the whole live-long duty through. It's awfully good for morale. I'm thinking of writing to Matron about it.'

10

'Hullo.'

'Hi there.'

'How d'you feel?'

'Better now, thank you, doctor.'

'Seriously.'

'Not too bad.'

'I came to see you last night.'

'So I heard. You should have wakened me.'

'I couldn't get near you for the night nurse.'
'She's a funny girl.'
'I suppose it was rather late,'
'Busy?'
'Rather. I didn't get much sleep.'
'Ward full?'
'Not quite. Some died.'
'Anything interesting?'
'One sad one. A coronary from a wedding. Croaked in Casualty.'
'How awful.'
'I wanted to tell you about it last night.'
'You should have wakened me.'
'How are you anyway?'
'Comfortable.'
'Really?'
'Yes. Comfortable.'
'How's the wound?'
'Not bad.'
'And the bristles?'
'Funny . . . Feel.'
'Mmmmmm.'
'Mmmmmmmm. Gently. Mmmmmmmmmm.'
'Mmmmmmm.'

II

Campbell slept for most of the afternoon and evening and went down
at about half past nine and had a beer with the duty houseman. Soutar
was there, off duty too, so Campbell told him about the party. He had
heard already from Billy. They took some beer from the Residency bar
and reached Marchmont at about a quarter to eleven. A lanky youth,
perhaps a medical student, admitted them with a careful show of
offhandedness. The second person they met was Billy, who welcomed
them warmly. 'Hello lads. Find it without any trouble then? It's going
well. Just the right amount of people.' Campbell wondered how the
lesser gatherings, unfavoured by Billy's personal attendance, were
faring. 'Mac's here already. You'll never guess who with.' As a sideline
to his main business Billy dealt in gossip too. They would never guess.

'Sister Birss.' Campbell affected the nonchalance appropriate to such
a revelation from an irksome inferior.

'Christ!' said Soutar. 'Shaggy Maggie!'

'She's called herself Margaret ever since they made her a sister,' said
Billy.

'Shaggy bloody Maggie,' sighed Soutar. 'Did you know about this, Campbell?'

'So it must have been her on the . . . table.'

'Must have been.'

'Oh, bloody hell. Birss. Getting too much sex must have softened his brain.'

'They're dancing very close together,' said Billy.

'Perhaps you should warn her.'

'Ho ho,' smiled Mr Billy McDivot of the Haematology Service, sharing a joke with some doctor friends at a party in Marchmont. 'Everybody knows about Mac. Dirty Mac. And they don't call him that for nothing. Ho ho.'

'Jee-zus. Her!,' said Campbell.

'He might just be doing it for a bet. No point in worrying about him. He can look after himself. He'll probably find someone else tonight.'

'Isn't she sort of . . . desperate?' Campbell made a mental note to get more of her track record from Joan next time he went up.

'I've had to tell her to piss off, if that's any indication,' said Soutar modestly. 'I don't think she'd had a man in months.'

'She's dancing pretty close as well,' said Billy. Campbell exploded. 'For Chrissake where's the drink?' Billy smiled. 'Over there, lads. Nice seeing you. Enjoy the party.'

There were no glasses and no cups, not even paper ones, but there was plenty to drink and an impressive variety of cheeses. Campbell took a can and tore it open, drinking the top half far quicker than he intended to: he was driving and the dose was two cans taken slowly over two hours. Across the hallway in a dark noisy room people were dancing, and among the couples shuffling in and out of a pool of light by the door was Mac, who winked at him over the dark and elaborate coiffure of Margaret Birss, fresh from her recent triumph as the madonna of the billiards table. They turned and Maggie came into profile: she was tensing forward into Mac, with a silly eager smile on her face, as though determined to make it as obvious as possible that she was enjoying herself. In doing so she became almost pretty, Campbell noted with some surprise. The gentle lighting in the doorway softened and flattered her features, and she had dressed well considering she was thin and her tits were one size too large. High waistline and low neckline made of her bosom an eager offering like her smile. Mac liked breasts: his falling in love was a little more explicable after this fresh look at Maggie, but the thought of her spread on green baize still caused Campbell to shudder.

At the food table beside him three girls were slicing cheese as though it was bread. A fat one was talking. 'With five ill patients, there was I supposed to know, just to know without so much as being told, that all the professor's hernias had to get up to sit for three-quarters of an hour on the morning of the third post-op day. So I told her . . .' Her friends believed, or appeared to believe, her account of this stand. Campbell squeezed past them and made for the door just as Billy appeared from nowhere and joined the girls. 'Been bullying Sister again then, pet?'

He found himself in a lighted room agreeably full of people talking.
'Food's dirt cheap and the way we worked it anyone who didn't have diarrhoea cooked.'
'Very sensible.'
'MOT'd until the 20th November.'
'Absolutely arseholed.'
'Bit of piston slap, but OK for seventy-five quid.'
'And the funniest thing was I felt fine the next morning.'
'Louise went bright red all over. Literally lobster. Especially her boobs. Serve her right.'
'Charlie?'
'I've done several actually. But this was my first retrocaecal – that's the hardest kind of appendix – so I had to be quite firm with the gasman. Bloody cheeky, he was.'
'Seventy-five is too much. Take my word for it.'
'On a billiard table! Really? No, I won't tell a soul. Who saw them?'
'No thanks. I just put one out.'
'Of course the patient's delighted with the incision. So bugger all gasmen.'
'Well we *were* looking for a fourth, but I'm afraid . . .'
'Then the patient let out a bloody great fart and said, "Is that what you're asking about, professor?" '
'But how do people *know*, if nobody saw them?'

There was a girl, a pale slim girl standing by herself and not drinking but eating a stick of celery. Straight dark hair fell forward on either side of her face and met under her chin. She was barefoot and wore a tawny caftan in plain rough material and a noose of chunky beads which gave her an air of ascetic modernity like a nun from an avant-garde order. Campbell asked her if he could get her a drink.
'D'you think they'll have gin and tonic?'
'No. But I'll see.' He swiped an unattended whisky and tipped it down the sink, rinsed the glass, filled it from the table of bottles and returned to the girl. 'That's vodka and tonic. Nearest thing. Not bad. I tried it.'
'Mmmm. Thanks.'
'V & T. It sounds like a real shopgirl's drink.'

67

'Like brandy and Babycham.'

'Or dark rum and pernod.'

'Bacardi and raspberryade?'

'Drambuie and green ginger?'

'What's that you're drinking?'

'Export and angostura bitters.'

'What? Oh.'

Who was she and where had he seen her before? Given the party, probably a nurse. She wriggled her neck in a pleasant equine gesture which cleared a lot of hair from her field of vision. Each could now see more of the other. She watched him wondering then said, 'Done any good marrow biopsies lately?'

'Oh.'

She put her hands up to her face and pulled her hair back in bunches behind her ears and made a little mock curtsey. 'Student Nurse Wallace, if you please, Dr Campbell.'

'Oh gosh. Sorry. Yes. That. Are you all right now?'

'Why shouldn't I be?'

'Aren't you the one . . .'

'No I'm not the one that fainted. That one was Student Nurse MacKintosh. And she's all right now.'

'Good.'

'That was the first marrow biopsy I've seen.'

'It wasn't typical.'

'Pity. I enjoyed it.'

'The bloke didn't.'

'Neither did the student.'

'You lot put him off.'

'Yes.'

'Why?'

'Well . . . Medical students . . . Oh, they're all right when the big daddy doctor's around. But when he's not they take it out on us. Because they're the lowest form of medical life, I suppose.'

'Take it out on you?'

'Over here nurse. Nurse this and that. Are you making some tea nurse?'

'I didn't realise. I'll have a quiet word.'

'I'm sure you were just as bad. Probably worse.'

'You seem to have it all worked out. How long have you been nursing?'

'Weeks and weeks, doctor.'

'You can call me Doctor Campbell.'

'Eight weeks actually.'

'And before that?'

68

'Travelled a bit. My parents live in India.'

'Hence the sackcloth and rosary?'

'Afghanistan.'

'I'm impressed. Intrepid Edinburgh nurse braves Pathan hordes in search of beads.'

'There were six of us in a Land-Rover. And I wasn't a nurse then.'

'Do you have any other names apart from Student Nurse Wallace?'

'Lee.'

'Lee?'

'That's it.'

'Is that short for some dreadful mouthful like Letitia?'

'Never mind.'

That was something: a toehold in the glassy slopes of her self-possession. Perhaps it actually was Letitia.

'D'you know the girls in this flat?'

'Sort of. They're in the class above mine. Hearties.'

'What?'

'All on the big side. Hiking boots under the bed and that sort of thing. That's them over there.' The mighty sister-crushing cheese-eaters.

'I see.'

'Who's that with them? A houseman?'

'No. But he'd love to hear you say that. That's Billy.'

'What's he?'

'A ubiquitous androgyne.'

'A what?'

'A creature of both sexes that gets everywhere.'

'Oh. I thought it was something else about the hospital that I ought to know. There's such a lot.'

'I suppose so . . . D'you like it?'

'Nursing?'

'Yes.'

'I suppose so. But they post us around such a lot and it depends so much on where you're working.'

'What about Ward Two?'

'It's not bad. You're rude. And Sister's daft.'

'Is she? Even so's you'd notice?'

'Yes. You should hear her reports!' She put on a prim mouth and mimicked Sister's report voice. ' "Left four. Mr Ochiltree. Quiet night. Ate his porridge. Moved his bowels. Oh no. He died last night and the doctors couldn't start him up." '

Campbell laughed out loud. 'What about the rest?'

'Fingers Bertram?'

'Fingers?'

'That's him. The last of the old-time bottom-pinchers and bra-strap snappers. But we've stopped wearing them.'

'Because of him?'

'Not really.' Campbell spared a thought for Mac and his exciting discovery. New light cast.

'What about your bottom?'

'There's not much you can do except keep a sharp lookout and never go into the big linen cupboard alone.'

'I see.'

'Creech is sweet though. Quite the courtly old physician.'

'Not the way I think of him.'

'Of course not. You're in the doghouse.'

'What am I supposed to be in the doghouse for?'

'You are. The poet.'

'Oh that.'

'Tough luck. Creech must be the last consultant left alive to expect his houseman to have heard of poets.'

'I had heard of him. It was just I was too tired to remember.'

'Poor tired houseman.'

'Careful.'

'Too tired to dance?'

'Not quite.'

Campbell, who danced badly when forced to dance at all, worried about her bare feet. She didn't seem to. In the corner Mac and Birss were still dancing, in the sense that they were standing in a clinch swaying to the music. Maggie was hanging on as though her life depended on it, as though the lean white arms round Mac's waist were lined with double rows of suckers.

The mood changed with darker, even slower music and Campbell relaxed; under its sackcloth his partner's long torso came close and her arms lay across his shoulders. She closed her eyes as though inducing some state of altered consciousness in which Campbell was a non-participating accessory, a mere hookah. She turned her face inward and muttered something which it would have been pedantic to ask her to repeat even though he did not know even what language it had been in. She snaked against him, cheek to cheek and thigh to thigh, more than ever the wayward nun, her soft breasts pressing him on either side of her unyielding rosary. He thought first of St Anthony in the desert, and then counted the days since Joan had taken ill.

They went for drinks and took two cans of beer from a forlorn half-dozen. There was no cheese left. They found a dark corner and sat close and innocent on the floor, leaning against a wall. She seemed to fold herself up under the caftan thing which, with her hair falling over

70

her shoulders made a soft untidy wigwam. The legs of disembodied quadruped couples shuffled past. They talked.

Later in his room in the Residency she sat on his bed, again barefoot, sipping sherry from an indestructible Institute tumbler. She looked tired and he recalled a fragment of military wisdom from a cadet corps handbook to the effect that all forward troop movements should be conducted so as to ensure combat readiness on arrival. That happened a lot: people incurred pointless delays that not only deferred sex but blurred and tainted it with fatigue. He put a record on quietly, an innocuous and familiar classic, took his own glass and sat down beside her. She looked nervously around and said, 'Your rooms are better than ours. Bigger.' She looked round again as though measuring. 'This is the first time I've been in the Residency.'

'It's not Bluebeard's Castle,' said Campbell reflectively into his sherry. She sat up, curling her legs under caftan.

'I suppose not.'

There was the merest stirring from next door, then a grunt and a giggle. She appeared not to have noticed. Suddenly she finished her sherry and Campbell hastened to follow suit. She handed him her glass then sat with her hands folded in her lap. There was providential silence next door.

'You look like a minor saint.' She blushed and he warmed to the topic. 'A really minor saint. The kind they're abolishing. Saint Sesquipedalia, virgin and martyr. One of those.'

'I'm not,' she said, blushing yet more. 'A saint I mean. Oh . . . You're just sitting there laughing at me.'

'No, I'm not,' said Campbell, taking her hands. 'You're sweet. And sometimes funny. But I'm not laughing at you.'

'You're nicest when you're not talking.'

'That's a bit harsh.'

'It's true. On the ward too.'

Campbell braced himself for the sort of verbal harpoon she had demonstrated on Sister and Bertram but it did not come.

'Since we're not on the ward . . . David . . .'

'Lee . . . What's that short for anyway?'

'Come closer.' She whispered, very close, 'I'm not telling you,' and kissed his ear. They smiled and kissed again, lips this time.

'You smell nice,' Campbell heard himself say for perhaps the hundredth time.

'They scrub us down with saddle soap every morning. Then sprinkle us with lavender water.'

'That sounds fun.'

'It promotes the Institute complexion.'

71

She lay back and straightened her legs. The caftan lingered agreeably high on her thighs. Campbell shifted to lie prone propped on his elbows in the classic ready-to-lunge position. She put her arms around his neck and he lay over her. The string of beads between them was hard and intrusive: Campbell lifted himself up and hoisted them out so that they lay round her neck then fell gently on her again.

'Take them off,' she muttered.

'Mmmm?'

'The beads.'

'Oh. Yes.' They rattled to the floor and he kissed her neck where they had been. She made little eager whimpering noises and he moved a thigh between hers unopposed. As a raiment of chastity the caftan had its drawbacks: sliding his hands up her arms to her shoulders he found its sleeves so wide as to be positively welcoming.

Confirm no bra. Breasts light, tending to conical even when supine. Nipples unusually large, responsive, stiffening. The little noises became more enthusiastic and she lay with her eyes closed seeking his mouth with hers and rotating her hips gently against his thigh.

Campbell decided to consolidate the position prior to further advance. He lay closely on her to indicate his own state of readiness before proceeding to phase two. The disposition of the caftan was propitious: at least he had been spared the Victorian handicap of starting from the ankles. An interim tactical appreciation now envisaged an unopposed phase two. After delaying just long enough to create a state of receptive uncertainty he made a move.

She moaned and once more pulled his head down to whisper in his ear as though they were in a roomful of people. 'David, please not. Please not everything.'

Mais certainement, madame . . . If *madame* wishes any programme from holding hands to nut-bursting ninety-nine percenters our highly trained staff will be only too pleased . . .

'Mmmm?'

'Please not everything, David.'

'Mmmmm.' Action not words. Don't debate, masturbate.

A swift conventional right-handed ascending thigh glide then hand flat on abdomen, a brief reassurance like patting a horse before dumping a saddle on its back. Her thighs opened slightly. He advanced down the lightly defended reverse slope of the female lower abdomen and she moaned an equivocal welcome. In her pubic hair he paused and contemplated its texture. The rough with the smooth. He advanced again as she inhaled sharply then clung to him still moaning, her eyes closed in another of her instant trances. Virgin and martyr on reflection seemed unjust. She was more of a sexual mystic.

She emerged abruptly and sat up, muttering, 'Wait.' Fifteen seconds

72

would be about right. She wriggled out of her caftan and it joined her
rosary on the floor. Campbell tore off his shirt, ripping a fragment of
material with the last button, and fumbled with the waistbelt of his
slacks.

'No please no. Not everything.'

At a point such as this, corresponding to the penultimate stanza of
the ballad of Bollocky Bill the Sailor and the Fair Young Maid, and with
the end clearly in sight, Campbell saw no harm in marking time for
the duration of the second last chorus, as it were, before pressing the
point home. He lay down beside her and regained the objectives of
phase two, this time without the preliminaries.

'Thank you, David,' she whispered.

'What for?'

'For not.'

'Not what?'

'You know . . . But that's lovely.'

'Glad you like it,' said Campbell with a note of self-pity lost on
virgin martyr sexual mystics. He wriggled to relieve the discomfort of his
acutely congested groin then applied himself to his allotted task with
intelligence, sympathy and an understanding born of sound knowledge
of the associated anatomy and physiology.

'Oh thank you . . . Oh oh thank you . . . Oh oh oh thank you. OOh oh
ooh thank you. Oooooh oooooh . . . . Oooooooooh OOOH Thank you
Very MUCH.'

'Don't mention it,' said Campbell absently. His groin ached with a
deep tense agony. She popped out of her trance. 'Most men simply
don't understand.' Campbell groaned. She went on, 'But you're very
kind. That was marvellous.' She sighed and reached to the floor for her
caftan and began to put it on. Campbell lay back and groaned again.

'Are you all right?' she asked through the sackcloth. Her head appeared and she watched him move a hand to his bulging groin. 'Oh,
that. Will you be all right?'

'I'll live. But it's actually quite sore.'

'Really?'

'Yes. I think it's acute congestion of the seminal vesicles.'

'Oh, that.'

'The machinery's not built to take it.'

'What?'

'Getting worked up and then not.'

'Oh.'

She wiggled her caftan down to her feet and put on her beads and
sat on his bed beside him, stretching out a comforting hand.

'Don't touch,' he moaned, 'Unless . . . .'

'Then I won't . . . Sorry.' She lay down beside him, kissed his ear and whispered, again below the threshold of hearing of the imaginary roomful of listeners, 'You're sweet.'

'Sometimes I surprise myself . . . Perhaps I should have raped you.' She recoiled. 'Gently of course. It's so bizarre. Unnatural. And it hurts like hell.'

'That's lust appealing to pity,' she remarked, as though explaining an allegorical painting. 'You're trying to make me sorry I didn't let you. And why should I anyway?'

To underline her argument, a familiar plunging heaving sound struck up next door. Campbell wondered what had delayed them after the initial warming up noises of half an hour ago. Perhaps Mac had felt compelled to listen to the life and hard times of Sister Margaret Birss, RGN, SCM. Perhaps it *was* love. Lee cocked an ear.

'Have you got a keep-fit enthusiast next door?'

'I hadn't thought of that.'

A horror-struck expression swept across her face and she put her hand up to her mouth. Campbell sat silent.

'That's it,' she said. 'You just expect it. Not you . . . Men . . . Doctors. Me Tarzan. You Jane. Bed. But not this one, brother.'

'What's all this?'

'Doctors. They act as though they had a right to . . . unlimited access to nurses to make up for not being able to sleep with their patients.'

'But I never . . .'

'No . . . Because you're a . . . gentleman coward.' He sat up and reached for his shirt. She took his hands and said, 'A nice gentleman coward . . . I'm sorry.'

'I'll walk over to the home with you.'

'Thank you.'

'Limp maybe . . .'

She giggled. 'Are you? Already . . .?' She giggled again. 'Sorry.'

They walked out of the hospital into the dark summer streets, holding hands. The nurses' home was a block away down a hill past the end of the Institute's grounds. For the first time in many years Campbell prepared for a pavement good night, a social art-form whose existence he had forgotten. They arrived outside the front door and stood face to face. She took his left wrist and twisted it round so that she could see his watch in the light from the doorway.

'It's twenty past one. You'll be just in time for your visit to Staff-nurse Masson. Please give her my regards and best wishes for a speedy recovery.'

But for a thoughtless gibe from a first-year student nurse, Campbell would at that point have gone up to Ward Sixteen to visit Joan. He did not, but resolved to go and see her the following day.

Instead he went back to the Residency lounge, where Soutar was slumped in one of the big fireside chairs, throwing fragments of something at a corner of the fireplace.

'Cheese,' he explained. 'A mouse. He was right out before you came in.'

'Sorry.'

'No, I was thinking of having a beer. A mouse is company. Better than drinking alone anyway. Will you have one?'

'Thanks, an export.' Campbell flopped into the other fireside chair and sat with his feet on the fender savouring the quiet of the place and the ticking of the clock. Soutar came back with two cool red cans of beer.

'How long did you stay?'

'Not much longer than you,' Soutar replied.

'Who did you end up with?'

'Nobody. I got sick of it.'

'Of what?'

'The system. The circuit. Rentagrope.'

'How long have you felt this trouble of yours coming on?' asked Campbell, pressing the points of his fingers together and leaning back in his chair.

'Tonight. When I saw Rab Kyle feeling up a wee girl in the corner.'

'That's not unusual.'

'But a year and a half ago at a similar party he was in a similar corner with a similar wee girl who's now at home looking after their baby.'

'Well, it's different for the married men. All right for us though.'

'Sure. It's all right for us. Never a dull moment or an empty bed unless you want it. To recover.'

'That's a bit of an exaggeration.'

'Not much. Look around the Mess.'

Campbell had looked around the Mess for some time before following the example of his contemporaries; then he had been surprised at how simple it all was, and even a little irritated at his own diffidence in having refrained for so long. Housemen had it easy. As though he had been reading Campbell's thoughts, Soutar went on, 'How many birds d'you think you'd trap if it wasn't for your MBChB?' Campbell looked down at his shoes, noticed they were dirty, and sucked morosely at his beer. 'Did I ever tell you how I got started in medicine?' Soutar asked. 'When I first came up to University I did a year in Social Anthropology. I thought it sounded great until I found out that everyone thinks it's to do with apes or chimpanzee's tea parties or something. And every time I told a girl at a party or something what I did she said, Oh, and seven times out of ten she'd end up with some birk sporting the blood, liver and pus-coloured famous medic tie. I didn't tell them that

75

at the interview but they let me in to confirm the observation from the other side. And I did. Often. And now I'm sick of it. It's bad for people.'

Campbell, who had never heard Soutar say so much all at once before, wondered what other than the Kyle thing, which sounded too altruistic, had prompted these insights. Or was he just drunk?

'People?'

'Nurses mainly. From bloody old Birss clutching at Mac as though he were the last leading man before the menopause rings down the curtain, to that dewy, dawn-picked fresh green student nurse you sneaked off with tonight.' He stopped suddenly. 'What happened? Why are you down here?'

Campbell found virtue, chivalry even, in his defeat: one did not admit to making a heavy pass at a first-year student nurse from one's own ward and failing. 'I left her on the doorstep of the Argyll Robertson Home and am now en route to a chaste and solitary couch.'

'Complaints, complaints.'

'We are just good friends.'

'And another thing,' said Soutar with his back turned on the way for more beer. 'Has it occurred to you what would happen if one of us, or one of the charming and obliging young ladies that we keep meeting at parties, were to get a dose of the gram-negative intracellular diplococci or clap?'

'No.' VD was for patients.

'Can you imagine what the nice lady from the venereology department would say when she turned over this particular stone.'

' "Put her down. You don't know where she's been." '

'But you *do* know where she's been. And where he's been. They've all been in and around the jolly old scene for months.'

'Who?'

'He. She. Everybody. It's bloody musical beds in this place.'

The problem facing the contact tracer gripped Campbell's imagination. 'She could make a sort of flow diagram like one of those maps of the kings and queens of England. Gonorrhoea starts hoea.' He jabbed a strategist's finger at the empty chairs around the room. 'And ends up hoea and hoea.'

'It bloody would.'

'Maybe it has already.'

'People would talk.'

'Or at least groan in the loo.'

'Disgusting.'

'Disgusting.'

'Beer?'

'Beer. But it makes the pain worse.'

'What?'

'Alcohol does. The pain of the gleet or clap.'

'Does it?'

'So I've read. Part of the ancient punitive wisdom of the order of things. Calvinism immanent in Nature. If you drink when you've got the clap the pain gets worse. Thus ye shall receive of the Lord's hand double for all your sins. Anyway, I haven't got it. But beer would make it worse if I had. Yes thanks. Another beer.'

'And another thing,' said Soutar. 'It's bad for you, screwing around.' This was a more familiar Soutar. Short and to the point.

'Rots the brain? Lowers the vital spirits? Enfeebles the spinal cord?'

'No. Fucks up your emotional sensibilities.'

'I suppose it does.'

'It has mine. Right up.'

'Maybe mine are beginning to be. Just beginning. "I waive the quantum . . ." '

'What?'

'Something something feeling. A poem.'

'You've had a bad day with poets.'

'Burns. Not that dead bugger this morning. "I waive the quantum of the sin, the hazard of concealing; but oh it hardens all within . . ." '

' "Wee sleekit cooerin timorous beastie . . ." '

'What?'

'It's back.' Soutar was picking little pieces of cheese from his lump and rolling them towards a mouse which was sitting, alert and delicate at the corner of the fireplace and skirting board.

' "And petrifies the feeling".'

'Fucking right.'

The mouse inched towards a golden ball of cheese then sat clasping it, eyes rolling furtively like Charlie Chaplin with a stolen watermelon.

'I like mice,' said Soutar. 'Better than cockroaches.'

'At least we've got a choice here.'

'They're more our sort of vermin. You know. Mammals. Not like great bloody black clanking war-of-the-worlds cockroaches.'

'We really ought to have a go at them about it. Via the Mess Committee.'

'Only the cockroaches. Your committee kills our mice over my dead body.'

'OK. We'll keep the mice.'

'And massacre the cockroaches.'

'Carried unanimously.'

'Now. Well, after another beer.'

'All right.'

They had another beer and fed the mouse to satiety. When Campbell rose to his feet he experienced an unsteadiness that he attributed to tiredness and overwork. Soutar was steadfast. They went through to the servery, crept in and switched the lights on. A dozen cockroaches scuttled aimlessly in the sudden brightness. Soutar ground one under his heel murmuring, 'Snap, crackle and pop,' and Campbell swung a broom end-on at the fleeing targets.

'The lift. The top of the lift.'

A small hand-operated lift brought food to the servery from the kitchen below. Soutar raised the shutter and a warm stale gust of air swept up the shaft. He pulled on the rope and brought the lift up so that its top was level with the ledge of the hatch. It was swarming with fat black cockroaches. Soutar held a bucket under the sill while Campbell swept them into it with his broom. More than twenty seethed and crackled in the bottom of the bucket, scrambling vainly against its walls. Drunkenly the housemen pondered the question of their further disposal, then Soutar disappeared into the dining room and came back with a large envelope which had contained drug advertising. Between them they manoeuvred the insects from the bucket into the envelope: some escaped and scuttled to safety under the warm-cupboard.

'Under Matron's door?'

'The Secretary and Treasurer's letter-box?'

'Staff Suggestion Box?'

They decided on the last. Nothing personal, but a silent and eloquent gesture that would make its point without provoking hysteria. And in the box a premature dispersal of the collection would be least likely. They went out of the Residency and along the corridor to the Staff Suggestion Box near the main stairway. Soutar tore one corner off the envelope and held it over the slot: the cockroaches baled out one by one like paratroopers and plopped in. The housemen listened for a moment to the tiny frantic shufflings within then turned and walked back to the Residency.

'When d'you think they open it?'

'Maybe never.'

They had another beer and then went off to bed. From Campbell's neighbours there was silence. He fell asleep and dreamt that he had slept with his ward sister who halfway through had turned into a giant Kafkaesque black beetle, and given him the clap.

78

12

At nine the following Monday morning Campbell was at his desk trying to write a list to get himself started.

'Another of your patients died, Dr Campbell.' Sister began talking even before she got into the room. She had resumed human shape but even so he resented her intrusion and felt it all the more keenly because it was Monday morning. 'Another of those coronaries. That Dr Miller from upstairs came down but he didn't come round. While I was just going off duty too. So I had to stay behind and do the body because it was only a wee third-year in charge on the late. That's two. D'you think there's something wrong with this lot?'

For his psychological war against Sister, Campbell had a secret weapon in reserve. He had concocted a tenuous but plausible hypothesis connecting excessive purging with sudden death in cardiac patients. The purging might, at the utmost stretching of physiological credulity, cause sufficient internal shift of fluid and disturbance of the equilibrium of fluid components, particularly the potassium concentrations, which were known to affect the stability of the heart's rhythm, to put a recent coronary patient at risk. It was an idle and malicious conjecture, but a damaging one for Sister, whose enthusiasm for laxatives was well known. Now might be the time to use it.

'Perhaps,' said Campbell solemnly.

'D'you think so?' Her face became suddenly serious and he recalled she cried easily. 'Oh, I hope not. The other two are quite nice. Well, Mr Gavin is. I heard that other one talking dirt to an auxiliary. And him maybe at death's door.'

She was very much herself. Silly but not threatening. She was not a large black beetle and she had not given him the clap. He decided not to upset her. And there was always a chance that a more damaging opportunity to air his hypothesis might present itself later.

The demise of Creech's second coronary was the only event of the weekend. At the far end of the ward the geriatrics continued their small scenes of drab lodging-house changelessness, by Pinter out of Chekhov, and among the surviving ill patients only the predictable slow improvements and deteriorations had taken place. Working among them asking routine questions about symptoms and listening to their chests Campbell wondered at the healing power of unassisted nature. Patients survived the neglect of the weekend every bit as well as they did the excesses of attention lavished on them through the week.

From half past nine until coffee time a steady trickle of registrars came into the ward, chaffed Sister, took fresh white coats from the cupboard and descended on the patients propounding their meddle-some notions with the singleminded enthusiasm of the underemployed. Campbell, the survivor of many such Mondays, jotted down the minimum acceptable action on each diagnostic or therapeutic flight in the knowledge that a certain surliness on his part was the patient's main defence against the zeal of the registrars.

With Joan off sick and Lee and her two contemporaries for some reason absent, nurses seemed to be thin on the ground. Only Sister and a married part-time staff-nurse with a bristly chin were on duty, and in the course of the morning it appeared to Campbell that they were not coping very well. He found patients' readings skimped, and deficiencies in ward stocks. He concluded that Joan had been carrying more than her share of the nursing load and that Sister was in the process of being revealed as a fussing, feather-brained incompetent. With an air of panic barely contained she flitted between patients and cupboards, from phone-booth to sluice and back again, while the part-timer tramped stolidly round, doing routine things routinely and addressing curt gruff sentences to the patients. She was services-trained, old and bold: campaign ribbons would have gone well with the chin and manly bosom. Campbell speculated as to which of the three services had shaped her attitudes, or did the Royal Marines have a nursing corps of their own too?

At coffee-time two registrars swapped accounts of the weekend's golf, punctiliously exchanging three- or four-hole gobbets with a passable show of mutual interest. When Sister came in, flushed and flustered, Campbell asked her if more haematology sample tubes had been ordered. She stared at him moist-eyed and sniffed. The golfers fell silent and Sister sniffed again. 'I think so . . . I hope so . . . I'll go and do it now . . .' she muttered and rushed out.

The golfers turned on Campbell. 'Look at that. No wonder she gets upset.'

'But I only . . .'

'It's hard enough to keep nursing staff without unnecessary friction and unpleasantness. Housemen like you don't make it any easier.'

Campbell sank chastened into his *Guardian* and bland waves of golf washed over him once more.

13

'How are you?'

'Not too bad . . . Long time no see.'

'Yes. Sorry. I meant to come up on Saturday but left it a bit late . . . and I was away all day Sunday.'

'Oh. Good weekend?'

'Not bad. And you?'

'Quiet. They tell me I'll be in for a bit longer than I'd hoped. I'm supposed to have a temp. I feel all right though.'

'A temp? What's going on?'

'Nothing. I think. But they keep bothering me.'

'Wound?'

'Don't think so.'

'UTI?'

'No. You're as bad as they are.'

'Sorry.'

'But the flowers are nice. Thank you.' His freesias joined the dahlias, presumed gift of Sister, on her locker. 'How's the ward?'

'OK. Quiet. Nothing much happened over the weekend. Another of Creech's coronaries died.'

'Poor old Creech.'

'The sooner he retires the better.'

At the end of an awkward pause Campbell said, 'I missed you.'

'I missed you too.'

'I went to an awful party on Saturday. That's when I really missed you. Especially afterwards. I got drunk with Soutar.' Campbell talked a lot because he felt guilty. He told her about his latest brush with the registrar caste and about Sister's performance at coffee.

'I heard about that. She's been up to see me again. You just missed her.'

'Good.'

'She was rather awful. Told me all about those blood tubes. Said you were brusque and demanding and she'd had a hard morning.'

'Me? Demanding? She just wasn't coping. It made me wonder who ran the ward when you were both there.'

'Mmm, well. Sister mentioned she'd be glad to have me back.'

'D'you order things, usually?'

'Often. Yes. Usually.'

'Who makes up the off-duty?'

'Me usually, I suppose.'

'So what does she do when you're both on there together?'

'Well, she teaches the juniors.'

'But you teach the juniors.'

'Sometimes.'

'They're a bright lot, the ones who are there just now.'

'Yes, That's what Sister said about ten minutes ago. She was full of them. Especially the skinny one with dark hair. Wallace.'

'Really?'

'They were on together yesterday.'

81

'Oh, Were they?'

'Yes. Precocious child, by the sound of things.'

'Really?'

There was another silence, which Joan ended by talking about his flowers. Then they talked about the ward again and eventually the lunch trolley rattled outside her room. Campbell made it an excuse and left.

He walked downstairs feeling vaguely outwitted and ruminating on the problem of counterintelligence that he faced: who knew what and from whom? In the gathering of gossip Sister was known to make best possible use of her stunted intellect and he now knew that she had been on duty with Lee between the party and her visit to Joan. From Lee's remark on Saturday night about visiting Joan it was evident that she had known at that time of what he had presumed was a thoroughly discreet liaison. Had she passed the information on to Sister on Sunday? Or had Sister known for some time and told her in the first place? And had Lee been drawn into an all-girls-together, who-were-you-with-last-night inquest all too easily imagined in the calm before the Sunday afternoon visiting time? ('A bonny girl like you must have lots of boy-friends . . .') And if so, had Sister, who might conceivably have no idea what her staff-nurse did in the time off she so capably organised, passed on some snippet to Joan, either as time-passing remark or as a gleeful briefing of the sort classically preceded by 'As a friend I feel I ought to tell you that . . .' Whatever the details, one thing seemed certain: Sister had talked.

Creech began his Monday afternoon ward round right on time and by three minutes past the hour it was established in grooves worn by the habits of decades: anecdotes and musings of an old consultant interspersed with wild sallies into the small print of medicine by his registrars. The round reached the acute beds at the nursing station via the fall of Singapore, a possible case of pseudoxanthoma elasticum, athlete's foot among the Chindits and an unproven but brilliantly suspected case of Bartter's nephropathy which if confirmed would be the third recorded in the UK literature. Campbell stuck glumly by his chief, hoping to encourage reminiscence at the expense of tiresome and potentially time-consuming diagnostic speculation.

From time to time Sister afforded unwitting light relief by doggedly reporting on the bowel function and appetites of patients at moments so consistently inappropriate that it was hard to believe they were determined by chance. Her contributions repeatedly brought breath-taking edifices of clinical-pathological inference crashing down among the porridge and bedpans. Campbell wondered idly why she hadn't been strangled years ago.

82

The bed which until recently had been occupied by Creech's surviving coronary had not yet been filled. Creech turned to Campbell for an explanation, looking so crestfallen that it was tempting to pat him on the back and tell him to cheer up because lots more people would be having coronaries soon. Instead he put on his bad news voice and said, 'I'm afraid he arrested over the weekend, sir.'

'Oh dear . . . And there was that other one of mine. One I didn't even see. The poor man who arrested on Thursday.'

'Yessir.'

'That's two.'

'Yessir.'

'Both of mine, in fact.'

'I'm afraid so, sir.'

'Oh dear,' His stoop seemed to have increased a couple of notches since the beginning of the round. 'I wonder what's doing it.'

Campbell glanced at Sister who looked as if she were trying to remember whether or not the departed had met his maker with an empty bowel: a stupid interfering woman, sitting steady in his sights. Off safety catch. He cleared his throat to speak. The chief turned round, his eyes sad and enquiring.

'It occurred to me, sir, that it might have something to do with our laxative policy.'

'Laxative policy? I wasn't aware we had one. We've never discussed it on ward rounds. That sort of thing is usually left to the nursing staff, though its true that practically everything else that goes into the patient has to be justified by a doctor's signature. It might even turn out to be an anomaly in prescribing procedure in hospitals.'

He was off: the last phrase had the flavour of one of the speculative little articles the journals accepted from him on account of his position. Sister sensed trouble and stood at a frightened alert, glancing round for support.

Slow even pressure on the trigger.

'It occurred to me, sir, that the various laxatives which act by shifting fluid into the gut might cause just sufficient potassium disturbance to put a potentially unstable cardiac rhythm into a fatal arrhythmia . . . Fibrillation or something like that.'

'Like cholera?' The chief brightened. 'I remember a Highland Light Infantry RSM in Penang . . .'

It was not a digression to be encouraged. Campbell braced himself, smiled and said firmly, 'Yessir, like cholera . . . But perhaps a less drastic shift of potassium. Insufficient to cause problems in normals but enough to trigger off a fatal arrhythmia in these coronaries.'

'Yes, I suppose it sounds possible. But I don't remember having seen it in the journals. Where did you read it?'

Campbell coughed modestly. 'I don't recall seeing it in any journal either, sir, but the cholera potassium thing is well documented.'

'Yes. Well. Maybe.' Creech was uncertain as to whether original thought should be encouraged among housemen.

In the pause Bertram jumped in. 'I think I see what he's trying to get at, sir.' Bloody cheek, thought Campbell, who had put it so simply old Creech had got it in one. 'A purgative-induced potassium shift inducing fatal hypokalaemic arrhythmia after recent myocardial infarction.' It sounded tailor-made for the *BMJ*.

He too was off. For Bertram the idea might prove a salvation. It would need working up and a few clinical trials, but it was original and related to a common fatal disease and might just make the difference between a late start in general practice and a good senior registrarship somewhere. Handled carefully, first as a letter to the *Lancet* then as a preliminary communication and a long paper to the *BMJ*, followed by contributions to all the relevant specialist journals, it could yield as many as eight or ten publications and put him ahead of the field again. It might make the *New Scientist* ('Easy does it for bunged-up heart sufferers') or even hit the jackpot in one. 'In a famous and historic hospital in Edinburgh, Scotland, a young Scottish doctor pondered on one of civilised man's most distressing killers . . .' That would be titled 'Towards Safer Heart Attacks', and 30 million people read the *Reader's Digest*.

'It wont be all that easy.' Elder was muscling in already. As one of Dr Fyvie's research fellows he attended Creech's ward rounds on sufferance only. He really was pushing his luck. 'You'll need total body potassiums, balance studies, faecal potassium estimations and a lot of co-operation from the isotope people. I know Dr Glaister would be only too pleased . . .'

That was interesting. Campbell had heard something to the effect that Elder had been trying for months to get inside the stout cotton underwear of Dr Rowena Glaister, of Medical Physics. Bertram rallied to beat off the intruder(s) on scientific rather than simply proprietorial grounds. 'But the point is that it's an internal shift. The potassium moves from the blood and the extra-cellular fluid into the gut, so these balance studies of yours will prove nothing. Short-term internal shifts are hard to pin down but I think we can do it: serial blood sampling, say half-hourly, for a start; then to prove where the potassium's going we'll need high colonic tubes to get samples and possibly even upper gut intubation via the mouth and stomach to get a picture of potassium concentrations in the gut as a whole. We'll need about twenty-five coronaries getting the usual laxatives and twenty-five getting none. That's the smallest number in which we could hope to prove both the mechanism and the mortality.'

He paused and looked round: his claim as principal potential author seemed unchallenged. 'We get about five new coronaries a week, so with one hundred per cent patient co-operation we should have the whole thing wrapped up in three months or so.'

Campbell stared at Bertram, whose sketch of the clinical trial sounded most uncomfortable, if not downright dangerous, for patients recovering from heart attacks. He had floated the idea simply to embarrass Sister and did not want men to die for the cause.

'But what more proof do you want?' said Creech. 'Two out of two is a hundred percent. I take it they both got laxatives.'

Sister had turned very red.

The rest of the ward round ignored the chief's remark. It was a pity he talked such nonsense, because he didn't have to say anything at all. As the senior consultant on the unit he was invariably the honorary principal author, inspirer, supplier of unstinted encouragement and assistance, in a phrase, 'the onlie begetter' of all publications emanating from his juniors.

Among lesser candidates there was still fierce competition: a senior house officer with a project on computerised electrocardiography put his case at length, making the team by sheer persistence, and Campbell reflected that the first paper had five authors before a word of it had been written. He ventured to speak: 'Don't you think, sir, that multiple blood sampling and intubation from both ends might be a bit risky in patients who'd just had coronaries?'

Creech looked sympathetically towards his houseman but did not speak in time.

'Surely, sir,' said Bertram, 'it's our duty to pursue as energetically as possible any lead that might result in the reduction of mortality in what is after all a very dangerous condition. If we suspect that large numbers of preventable deaths are occurring because of the casual handling of laxatives then surely the quicker we pin it down the better.'

'Maybe . . . Perhaps . . . But I'm quite in agreement with you about the casual distribution of what are essentially medical preparations. When you consider that every sleeping pill has to be authorised by a doctor's signature and yet the patients are handed any one of three dozen purgative preparations as if they were dolly mixtures . . .'

Bertram clinched his argument. 'Perhaps with fatal results.'

Sister, whose discomfort had gone unnoticed amid the onrush of medical progress, suddenly burst into tears and fled down the ward. Campbell was gratified: whatever the subsidiary benefits to registrars or mankind at large, his scheme had achieved its main objective in style.

Creech looked anxiously after the fugitive, then round his followers for an explanation. Bertram volunteered one. 'I'm afraid Sister isn't quite herself today, sir.'

'Oh?'

'Yes, sir. Unfortunately . . . the houseman upset her this morning.'

From such an inauspicious Monday the week grew steadily worse. Joan's temperature persisted for several days until she was taken back to theatre and half a pint of pus released from an abscess deep in her wound. Over this time Campbell continued to visit her, sometimes out of a sense of duty and sometimes because he was on call and had nothing else to do. The first-year student nurses reappeared on the ward without Lee and he later learned that she had taken a week's leave to go on holiday to Morocco. Relations with Sister could not have been worse and Campbell was relieved when she took two days off at short notice and left the ward in charge of the part-timer and a pale heavy third-year student nurse from the North whose powers of organisation rivalled Joan's. He found his cupboards and drawers on the ward rearranged – for the better, it had to be admitted – and received little lists from her which clarified hitherto undefined areas of responsibility between them. At first he resented such initiatives on the part of a nurse under training but soon gave in on all but a few token points and even began to like her. She was bright and hoydenish, with a faint reputation for religion, and the question of her presumed virginity was just beginning to exercise his mind when she too disappeared for four days off, leaving the ward once more to a prim and defensive Sister.

In response to Bertram's overt and covert propaganda Creech treated his houseman with more disdain than ever and seemed to be allowing the registrars much more than the usual quota of outlandish investigations. Purgative-induced potassium shift replaced the faecal vitamin pilot study, if not as the principal research interest of the unit at least as the major topic of research-oriented coffee conversation. The registrars discussed the protocol, double-blind control and statistical significance at great length and on the one occasion when Campbell opened his mouth on the subject he was firmly snubbed and given to understand that housemen had no concern with such weighty affairs.

By Thursday his morale was so lowered that he found himself looking forward to the routine but cheerful midmorning visit of Mr McTurk with his polythene wrapped carton. That morning Mr McTurk did not turn up, nor did he on Friday.

On Friday afternoon he went up to see Joan, held her hand and pitied her obvious ill-health. He told her he missed her but to himself admitted that all he felt for her now was a mixture of kindness and the dangerous itch of lust.

14

John, the Residency steward, rarely stayed sober on Saturday evenings but he had a sense of occasion about Mess functions which overcame a lifetime habit. He went to a lot of trouble to ensure that Residency parties reflected creditably on the Institute, and did great things on a slender budget by means of his various contacts in the city. At about nine thirty he was seeing to some last details in the lounge.

'I thought we wouldn't have too many pot plants, sir, seein' it's an informal occasion.'

'Quite right, John.' For formal occasions he knew someone who could transform the Residency public rooms, free of charge, into a rival for the Botanic Gardens. Perhaps one day they could have a jungle party. Campbell looked around the lounge and made a complimentary remark about the food.

'Yes, it's nice tonight, sir. I thought I was going to have difficulty with the transport but I just dialled nine nine nine and got my brother-in-law to send an ambulance. A driver he could trust, of course. I knew him too, as a matter of fact, so we picked up the glasses as well.'

'Good. It's all looking very nice.'

'You're on duty yourself, sir.'

'Afraid so.'

'A half-pint then, sir? Just to see the barrel's all right.'

'Thanks, John.'

Soutar came in and sat down. He was carrying four bleeps: some of the residents operated an unofficial collective system of on-call, so three duty house physicians must be across in the pub, or even further afield. Soutar had a pint. At ten to ten the first guests arrived: they were a New Zealand senior house officer and his wife, who had mistaken the nature of the occasion and come dressed as though for a registry office wedding. Campbell got a quick pint into the man, and his wife sat by Soutar and chirped nasally.

Not long after closing time the wandering physicians returned, collected their bleeps from Soutar and resumed drinking. With the appearance of the first unattached girls Campbell abandoned a half-formed resolution of abstemiousness, got drinks for them and had a whisky himself. They identified themselves as secretaries from Radiology, a department which appeared to recruit exclusively from the counters of Woolworth's. Conversation was difficult and he left them on the pretext of filling his glass.

One whisky later he found himself standing by the girl who had so capably reorganised his cupboards.

'Hello.'

'Hello.'

'I thought you'd gone off for four days.'

'I did. I'm back.'

'Did you go up north?'

'Yes.'

'Oh.'

It was Jean or Mary. He couldn't remember which. A simple name that meant her parents had wanted a girl, because there they called them Williamina or Georgina if they had wanted a boy. Mary.

'Is someone getting you a drink, Mary?

'Yes, thanks.'

'Oh.'

'And my name's Jean.'

'Oh.'

Campbell's senior student approached carrying two drinks. The girl took one and smiled lovingly. How long had that been going on? Campbell wondered why he had failed to notice such a development on the ward and in doing so found himself quite unexpectedly in sympathy with his ward sister. Mary/Jean drank lemonade. The student was affable and asked about one of the chief's patients: feeling somehow patronised Campbell began to explain, then the girl muttered about talking shop and took the student away.

It was a relief when the ward called him: he walked across the courtyard with the noise of the party receding behind and entered the medical block. Crickets sang in the lift shaft, and the stair-well was cool and empty. The ward was its late evening self, calm, orderly and hospitable, with the two night nurses taking round hot drinks. Campbell envied them the simplicity of their task: almost everything he did for a patient had to be explained beforehand or apologised for afterwards or both. He stopped at the nursing station and wrote up some sedations, then when the night nurse had finished her round he went through the patients' card index with her because she was new to the ward. Who might wander in the night. What to do if an IV drip stopped. Who should be resuscitated. Who shouldn't be. On the way he stopped for a word with the old man in the tweed cap, who called him Jimmy and squeezed his hand. He shouldn't be.

Campbell found it useful to thus anticipate trouble on his nights on call, and liked to walk round both wards. Among the ladies upstairs a perfumed boarding-house tranquillity prevailed in which the suggestion of illness would have been in bad taste. Was it the flowers and the talcum, or the long-suffering nature of the female of the species? He exchanged a few words with the nurse in charge, who indicated that all

88

was in order and might even have resented his intrusion, then went downstairs past his own ward recalling its very different atmosphere: slack, scruffy, chummy, like a really run-down army unit or bowling club or something, and much preferable.

When he got back the party was well off the ground: the dining room was crowded and throbbing to the beat of a discotheque, and upstairs the lounge was full of people many of whom were quite unknown to Campbell. At the barrel he met Billy.

'Hello, David.' Campbell winced: he resented the casual use of his forename, especially by hermaphrodite pimps.

'Hello.'

'Good party, eh?'

'We do our best.'

'I mentioned it to a few people. Birds mostly. Some lads too. I'm just getting them drinks. Excuse me.'

He bustled off with four pints of beer. Campbell poured himself one and drank three-quarters of it straight off from need. A small group of his fellow housemen were discussing extra duty payments. He joined them with relief and listened while they debated how best to get paid individually and generously for services they performed sparingly and collectively. The system was new and still sufficiently undefined to lend itself to abuse.

The housemen got drunker and more grasping and Campbell left them and went downstairs and danced with a staff-nurse from Casualty who was known to be currently unattached. She was large and nubile, with the placid expansiveness of a milk-yield champion Ayrshire. Campbell had always gone happily to Casualty when he knew she was on duty: she was efficient and kindly and could interpret ECG tracings, which must have been by intuition because even her best friends admitted she was stupid. Blue swimmy eyes and long blonde hair that had been blonde as long as anyone could remember plus all the rest made her somehow too good for real life. She was kind and stupid and nice to everyone: her uncritical amiability posed for Campbell a problem she could never have comprehended. That in itself was appealing.

As they danced Campbell thought his way through a scenario of going out with her, a painless exercise in speculation which went roughly: she is kind and beautiful and stupid, an earth goddess with brains of clay with whom it might be futile to converse unless you were holding her hand at the same time; but who might also be the vessel of some mystery incarnate, an earth-goddessy thing to do with dark animal truths. Perhaps going out with her would be a magnificently rewarding absurdity, reached by a leap of faith, like becoming a Catholic. His silence made her uneasy and she started a line of light chat of such terrifying banality as to put any leap of faith on Campbell's part quite out of the question. As soon as the music stopped they parted.

By half past eleven the party had achieved a steady state in which groups of the conversationally drunk disported on the lounge floor while downstairs dancers, frenetic under strobe lights, gyrated to the disco. Most of the unattached girls had gone home and only a few – the thickest-skinned and most determined, it was to be presumed – hung around on the edge of the dance floor. Trapped in the comfortless limbo reserved for those who have had too much to drink but cannot relax and be drunk, Campbell was contemplating bed when Mac appeared with an urgent request.

'Do me a favour, Campbell, there's a decent chap.'
'What?'
'Dance with Maggie.'
'Where is she?'
'In the loo.'
'Why? Dance with her, I mean. And why me?'
'Because you're a decent chap. And because Maureen's here.'
Maureen was the blonde from Casualty.
'So?'
'Why are you asking all these questions? Look, there's a decent chap, just dance with Maggie for about ten minutes.'
'So you can ditch her and go off and screw Maureen?'
'I was thinking more of talking to her at least to begin with.'
'She's a nice girl.'
'Fucks like a rattlesnake too, I've heard. So you can go and dance with Maggie and then everybody's happy.'
'Except Maggie. And possibly me.'
'Come on. For a friend.'
'You're a real bastard.'

When Maggie came back from the loo the three talked awkwardly for a moment then Campbell, as naturally as possible in the circumstances, asked her to dance.

Somehow she wasn't as bad looking as he had expected her to be. As they danced he worked it out: although she was probably only twenty-six or seven and had once been considered pretty she had become in his mind the archetype of the desperate spinster carnivore. It was hardly fair. In the dim, flashing light of the dance floor he saw her anew and had to admit that she was pleasing enough to look at and that she moved well. She was laughing a bit in a bright not-too-sexy way, as though conscious of being under scrutiny by a friend of her new boyfriend. That made it sad.

When Campbell glanced at his watch and saw that Mac had had most of his ten minutes Maggie began to appear uneasy, and might even have been looking round for Mac under cover of dancing movements. Campbell ignored this, passing time between records in febrile chatter and enthusing over the music. The ploy was perhaps becoming obvious.

If the first dance had been for her a small social display the second was simply submission: to a slow tune she moved closer and though her hair, fragrant in Campbell's nostrils, stirred automatic longings in him, she danced passively, almost resentfully. By now she must know.

Around them couples strove in each of the limited range of postures which maximise physical contact in the vertical; the evening had reached the stage where existing combinations whether ecstatic, resigned or merely habitual were likely to remain undisturbed. Campbell felt Maggie's head beside his own, scanning gently round still looking for Mac. The record stopped and the disc jockey made a one-minute speech in which the word 'wunnerful' occurred at least ten times, then the lights went up.

At this Sister Birss did not, like something from a horror film, revert instantly to the grotesque. Once more she was better looking than Campbell expected her to be, though she looked worried. As they walked silently upstairs Campbell kept an arm round her waist.

The groups in the lounge had thinned out and Mac was nowhere to be seen. Nor was Maureen and Campbell wondered if Maggie had noticed that too and made the appropriate deduction. Their undeclared search proceeded in silence to its conclusion: dining room, stairs, lounge and corridor and no sign of Mac.

'My coat's in Mac's room.'

'I'll get it for you.'

'No . . . I'll . . . I'll come along too.'

No harm in that. It was just possible that Mac and Maureen might be frolicking naked on Maggie's poplin raincoat, but it was unlikely as Maureen had a flat somewhere in Marchmont.

Mac's room was empty and Campbell collected her coat from the bed. She put it over her arm.

'My car's down in the East Car Park.' Her voice was flat and she sounded more tired than sad.

'I'll see you down to it.'

'He's a bastard.'

'You know what he's like . . . You must have known before.'

'I thought I was different.'

'He said you were.'

'That was nice of him. But I suppose I'm not now.' She stopped and fished in her handbag. Down the corridor the last of the stragglers from the lounge were moving on to the stairs. She began to cry. They were standing opposite the door of Campbell's room. He opened it.

'Look, don't get all miserable about it. Come in and calm down. Talk about it. Have a drink or something.'

He followed her into the room and closed the door.

'Sherry?' He made a mental note to get some decent sherry glasses.

'No thanks. I'm off alcohol. Doctor's orders.' She let a giggle through her tears as though what she had just said was funny.

'D'you mind if I do?'

'No. May I smoke.'

'Carry on.'

Campbell poured himself a good tumbler of sherry to take the edge off the impending conversation. He had asked her into his room mainly to offer sympathy as reparations for covering Mac's withdrawal, and had sufficient experience of girls with problems to guess the broad outlines of what was to come. Something like: most of my friends are married or at least engaged. What keeps going wrong for me? Yes there was a nice boy once but it went wrong. Most of the men old enough to be interested in me are married. Yes there have been married men. Etc. At the thought of it Campbell took a fortifying gulp of sherry and reclined on his bed. And as well as sympathy, if he were honest with himself, there was perhaps just a glimmer of speculative lust which could hardly at this point be admitted.

Maggie sat in his chair with her legs crossed and lit a long cigarette which was strange because nurses usually smoked evil little weeds the size of rawlplugs. She held it elegantly and inhaled with neurotic zeal, holding lungfuls of smoke and blowing twin plumes, dragon-style, from her nostrils. Her handbag leant against the chair. She looked like a neophyte television interviewee. ('Miss Birss, you I believe are the two hundred and fiftieth victim of the recently qualified houseman sex fiend. Can you tell our viewers . . .?')

Campbell collected himself to push out the boat of psychotherapy, gently at first, encouraging the patient to describe the problem as he or she sees it, with a minimum of intervention, just as he had been taught in the course of his training at a plush new unit whose sole apparent function was to take tongue-tied and inadequate neurotics, and turn them at considerable public expense into highly articulate but still inadequate neurotics.

'Were you fond of him?' The use of any tense other than the past would have been a cruel mockery.

'I think I was. And I thought he was fond of me . . . I don't understand it.'

'What?' At least they agreed on tense.

'How could he be so interested in me and just . . . go off like that.'
She began to cry again. Campbell got up and took a box of paper hand-
kerchiefs over to her.

'How long had you been going out with him?'

'A week. It doesn't sound long but we saw each other an awful lot.
He was very keen . . . Right up until tonight. He didn't even tell me
anything . . . He just disappeared.'

Crying put years on her. Campbell had been toying with the idea of
asking her how she had started going out with Mac but felt sorry for her
again and decided against it. Instead he asked, 'What are you going to
do now . . . to get over it?' This was short measure psychotherapy,
moving quickly towards the final directional nudge that was considered
permissible by some of the more authoritarian theorists.

'I don't know . . . I expect *he*'s got over it already.' She straightened
up and looked directly at Campbell. 'Any idea where he is?'

'No.'

She ground her cigarette into the ashtray.

'Did you know he was going to do this?'

'I've known Mac a long time. He does this sort of thing sometimes.'

'So I've heard. D'you think he knows what it feels like?'

'Shouldn't think so. I doubt if he's let himself get . . . involved . . .
Sorry. But that's the sort of chap he is.'

'I suppose so.'

'Look, it's not the end of the world . . . Put it down to experience.'

'Experience?' she said with a hysterical giggle. 'I've had enough of
that sort of experience thank you. Do you know what age I am?'

Campbell took another swig at his sherry glass and found it was
empty. 'No. Are you sure you wouldn't like a drink? Just a small one.'

'Just a small one then. Twenty-eight. I've been in nursing ten years
and in that time I've had most of the experience going.'

'Really?' Psychotherapy might be about to take a turn for the more
interesting.

'Yes really. The lot, I suppose. For the first time, all very wide-eyed
and what-do-I-do-now-doctor right down to a drunken old gasman
who just wanted company but had to have affairs to get it.'

Much taken aback, Campbell handed her a sherry.

'I shouldn't really. Oh yes, I've had enough of experience and I'm
not going to spend the next ten years sleeping around providing it for
other people. Relationships yes, experience no.'

'And you'd hoped that Mac would be a relationship?'

'I thought it might be. But it wasn't. It was more bloody experience.'

'But enjoyable experience?' Campbell remarked without really
thinking about it, half Panglossian therapist, half prurient confessor.

'Not too bad as experience goes. Most of the time he was a selfish oaf and I tried to ignore that. And he was mad about sex and vain enough to want me to enjoy it too. He was a good screw.'

She finished her sherry and began to light another cigarette. Her fingers trembled and the match went out. She blinked and her mouth twisted as though she were in pain and the cigarette fell still unlit into her lap. She made no attempt to pick it up but sat curled forward with an expression frozen half-way to crying. Campbell looked at her with tired disbelief: if she really got going, sympathy might prove time-consuming. He looked at his watch. It was almost half past twelve but Maggie was far beyond the reach of social hints: her shoulders shook and heaved, tears ran on her cheeks and she began to sob in long moist shuddering sighs with her hands up to her face.

Campbell sat on his bed still watching her. When she straightened up her face was wet and red, her eyes swollen and her mouth loose with grief. 'I wanted it to be beautiful,' she blubbered. '. . . I even believed it was. And it wasn't. It was just squalid and cheap and . . . just nothing . . . He's a bastard and I knew he was . . . I hated him but I tried to tell myself I didn't. I hated him even when we were . . . screwing . . . I wanted to believe it was real and true and lasting and it wasn't. I wanted it to be a romance . . . and he just wanted . . . one long drawn-out textbook fuck after another. And now the bastard's bestowing his marvellous timing and control on someone else.'

These belated insights of Maggie's were exasperating: hospital sex was hospital sex and Prince Charming, MBChB, didn't come into it. After ten years she was getting her share of the truth and hurting herself with it. 'Steady on . . .' he murmured.

'And I hated myself even more for loving it. It. Being screwed by him I mean. Hating him and loving it.' Campbell put up a hand to silence her. 'Oh, he takes time and trouble and he's good. And keen on it. He even had me on a table, would you believe? And I tried to think it was romantic.'

She was learning fast. She began to giggle through her tears and Campbell got up to fill his glass, smiling back at her. Welcome to the real world. Again he offered her a drink and she accepted: as he handed her the glass he unconsciously made a gesture that could have been in-terpreted as indicating that she should sit on his bed. To his blurred surprise she did, smiling. He topped up his glass and joined her.

They slumped parallel, diagonally across the bed. It was not com-fortable but whatever the outcome it was unlikely to be for long. Drunk-enly Campbell tried to sort out their respective motivations of lust, pity, loneliness etc, but gave up in the face of his patent inability to think in the abstract, recalling the words of a pharmacology lecturer on the effects of alcohol on the nervous system. First the higher functions,

94

the soul and conscience in the frontal lobes, packed up, followed by intelligence then fine muscular control. The sense of smell, phylogenetically old, survived the onslaught till later. How nice. Her perfume filled his shrinking awareness, evoking associations that eluded precise definition. What a splendid thing to be left with: unrecordable and darkly linked through the diencephalic pathways to the very core of consciousness. He sniffed loudly at her hair and a warm inexplicable sexual confidence surged within.

'Whassat perfume?' said a distant voice, his own.

'Kiku.'

'S'lovely.'

Who was Kiku? Its vivifying odour refused the precision of a face, a name or even an approximate time. He felt a nose, firm and slightly cool, below his right ear, then reached out and put his empty sherry tumbler on the bedside table. The other voice said something ending '. . . nice too.'

'Cyprus dry. Ten bob a bottle. And Boots'. Old Boots' for Men.'

She giggled, whiffling in his ear, 'Nice. Go well together.'

'Uh.' Campbell shook his head and his jowls flapped emptily. 'S'late.' He shook his head again and half sat up. Shaking seemed to get the alcohol out of the higher centres. Maggie sat up too. He remembered the party, Mac and the plot and almost apologised, trying to fish words from his muddled brain. They escaped his grasp. He felt Maggie take his hands, then she looked closely into his face and said, 'You're tired.'

'S'past my bedtime.'

'I'll go.'

'Have another drink. I won't though. Duty.'

'I mustn't.'

'You keep saying that.'

'I don't really want one,' she said, leaning forward and cupping his face in her hands. Campbell clambered grimly into full consciousness. He was in his own room. It was quarter to one. Mac had had more than an hour and might already be asleep with Maureen the beautiful blonde perfect in silent rest at his side. Campbell had the feeling that this drunken vigil was above and beyond the call of duty.

'You're very comfortable,' said Maggie, suddenly leaning back and pulling him down towards her.

'Thanks.' He lay back, wondering if this was the critical gesture of surrender. She moved again, bringing her legs up on the bed, then lay waiting on his next move as though they were playing Chinese checkers.

In manus tuas domine commendo spiritum meum.

He lifted himself to lie beside her kicking off his shoes as he did so

95

then turned towards her. How much further would they go if he just let her get on with it? Perhaps she now felt that she had done all she decently could. A second wave of Kiku jangled in his mid-brain.

Maggie snuggled against him and pressed a thigh between his. Unthinkingly he opened up for her and lay relaxed, closing his eyes: the resultant reduction in sensory input was most welcome. He wished now he had put the light out. Drink, fatigue and this sudden comfort drove him to the brink of sleep, from which only social conscience and a residual sense of sexual opportunism held him back.

The local stimulus of Maggie's thigh elicited its local effects as it would have done in a paraplegic or a half dead tom-cat in the physiology practical class. From the other end of his spinal cord Campbell sensed the mounting urgency of sexual arousal in the intact male, first with a drunken detachment then, as the pattern of response was reinforced, as subjectively as any doomed mayfly or spring-bedrunken newt. He retrieved a hand from the other side of Maggie and laid it on her breast.

The resulting sensation of contact, even through two layers of cotton, with the mass of fibrous tissue, fat and resting secretory apparatus furthered Campbell's arousal and drew from Maggie a reaction of violent urgency: one-handed but with great dexterity she flicked open his belt buckle, unzipped him, negotiated the complexities of shirt and pants and seized her prize like a relay sprinter snatching the baton.

Campbell made his decision. Muttering, 'Wait,' he switched on the bed light, got up and walked clumsy and half-dressed over to switch the main light off. When he returned again towards the bed, Maggie was clad only in bra and pants: the rest of her clothes were folded (folded!) on his chair. He took off his shirt and his trousers fell to the floor of their own accord. He left them there and sat on the edge of the bed to take off his socks. Maggie's hand reached round his waist and her hair brushed across his shoulders.

It was all very difficult. The whole business had started in deceit and looked like finishing in lust and confusion. Yet through it ran a golden thread of charity. He had first agreed to accommodate Mac in the matter of Maggie-minding as he himself would have expected Mac to help him in like circumstances. A neighbourly do-as-you-would-be-done-by sort of gesture. And if Maggie's fate was inevitable, which it was, was it not best over soon and in as pleasant a fashion as possible? Maggie must surely appreciate his consideration on the dance floor and afterwards when they had looked for Mac. Their little chat in his room must have helped too.

And now this. He recalled a grainy French black and white film about a prostitute, the moral of which, that even casual sex can be a blessing and a gift, had seemed forced and oblique at the time. He finished undressing and Maggie prepared to receive charity graciously by re-

96

moving her bra and pants. Campbell remembered it was now Sunday.

Afterwards, as they lay in sated comfort together, Campbell felt better than ever: he reflected on the wordless satisfactions of the encounter, all the variations of tempo and posture, the calms and exhilarating frenzies that had evolved: no need between them for the sort of grunted muddled instructions best left to furniture removers. Whatever else one thought of promiscuity, it certainly raised the general standard of performance.

Maggie lay asleep or very near it. That was a disturbing development. He moved just sufficiently to ascertain whether she was or not and she stirred slightly. How could she expect to stay the night? And in a room right next to Mac's: Campbell was surprised her pride permitted her to. And he had to admit to himself that the prospect of a night in a shared single bed with her was daunting. After all, he hardly knew her.

As long as the bedside light was on and she was awake, her options were open. She might still spare herself the ignominy of occupying adjoining rooms in the Residency on consecutive nights. If he switched the light off, she would probably feel invited to stay so he decided to leave it on for a little. That achieved nothing so to activate things a little more he got up and went to the loo hoping that a brief and socially acceptable abandonment might help her make up her mind. When he came back she was fast asleep. Charity, it appeared, was to be extended overnight.

15

Next morning Campbell went down to breakfast having snatched an hour's sleep between the latest time that Maggie felt it discreet to leave and the time they stopped serving breakfast on a Sunday. The dining-room windows were open and a healthy chill was dispersing the stale odour of the night before. Half a dozen of his colleagues were spread around the table reading newspapers and drinking coffee. A few brave souls toyed with poached eggs as small and hard and unappetising as the eyes of a grilled salmon. John came in and Campbell reflected that there were probably many patients in the wards less ill than the residents' faithful servant that morning, who soldiered on, walking fighting wounded, the magnitude of his self-inflicted injury telling of his heroic capacity both to inflict upon himself and resist the punishments of alcohol. The coffee cup rattled in the saucer as he laid it down.

'The eggs are nice, sir.'

'No thanks, John. Just toast . . . Oh, the party went very well. We're grateful for your efforts.'

'No trouble sir. It's my pleasure to see you all enjoying yourselves. I had a wee drink near the end myself of course . . . cleaning up . . . very few breakages.'

'Glad to hear it.'

A manly reek of stale whisky lingered after the steward had disappeared back into the servery. Campbell got up and went over to the side-table and the remaining newspapers. Hangovers seemed to have limited his colleagues' sense of intellectual adventure to the *Mail* and the *News of the World*. The *Observer* remained and he picked it up. At the other end of the table some surgical residents were dissecting the party.

'No, the one that staffs in seventeen. Big ears.'

'Her?'

'I think it was her but I didn't actually see them go. Looked like her.'

'Who invited Billy?'

'Did anyone ever? Or Billy's bloody friends. One of them asked me if there was any malt whisky.'

'What happened to Soutar?'

'Dunno. Probably nothing.'

'Maggie Birss ought to pay a Mess subscription. Her car was in the car park all night again. Fifth night running.'

Campbell felt incipient embarrassment pricking at his armpits. Fortunately Mac was not around.

'Mac?' said one of the surgeons.

'I suppose so,' said another. 'I don't know how he puts up with it. "Dr MacDonald, I wonder if you could just come straight up again and attend to an elderly night sister?"'

The surgeons laughed loudly. Campbell lifted his paper higher and busied himself with an article by the mother of a young offender with spina bifida.

'He seems to stand the pace quite well. He must have been potting it steadily for a week since the billiard table.'

'I like his approach. He just doesn't give a damn.'

Inadequate wheelchair exercise facilities at the remand centre.

'Where is he?'

'Sleeping it off, probably. Well-earned rest.'

Complaints of rough handling on the stairs to the visiting room. MP written to.

'I hope he can keep it up when she goes back on duty. If she's getting enough maybe the physicians'll get some sleep.'

Incontinence and toilet facilities.

'Imagine it though. A scrawny old crutch. And clinging on like grim death and saying "I love you" all the time.' The surgeons groaned and laughed.

98

Governor's reply. Special provision for the very infrequent disabled
. . . Unfair on all three counts, thought Campbell, but no gallantry he
could muster would have tempted him out from behind the fortress
Observer to say so. Blushing but still safe he returned to the plight of
the invalid delinquent and conversation at the other end of the table
devolved to the customary discussion of relative consumption of alcohol.

Campbell cooled off slowly through the business pages, reaching the
sports section at a shade of pink that could have been accounted for by
an unexpectedly hot mouthful of coffee. He picked up the colour
section and scanned the contents. Deodorants: the Hidden Risks.
African Statesmen: their Wives and Wives and Wives. That might be
good for a few pages of bouncy black bosoms. He set out through the
trackless wastes of adverts in search of the Africans, meditating gratefully
on his escape. No points for screwing Maggie and points off if the word
got round. Which it needn't. Mac would make another of his effortless
transitions and Maggie would find somewhere else to park her car at
nights, most probably in the Argyll Robertson Home sisters' car park
where it belonged. And the physicians including himself (especially
himself?) would get as little sleep as before.

The majority of the African statesmen's wives were by any standards
over-dressed, but their numbers provided passing interest. There was
even a little international league table showing the ex-British territories
well behind those formerly under the influence of the lascivious French.

From the car park beneath the open windows came the uneven roar
and bravura terminal snarl of an old sports car coming to rest.

Deodorants might (might, it stressed) be the cause of a predictable
selection of ailments including eczema, cancer and impotence: the
combination of everyday fears and incomprehensible chemical names
had unquestionable mass appeal but the authors had denied themselves
the more graphic possibilities of illustration, confining themselves to
armpits.

Heavy footsteps approached along the corridor and Mac, pink and
stubbly, strode in, poked his head into the scrvery and said loudly,
'Morning, John, sorry I'm late. Poached eggs? I'd better have two.'

Everyone looked up much as Mac had intended. He poured himself
a coffee and took a place halfway down the table, beaming around as
one who looks forward to being questioned. No one wanted to ask. A
surgeon opposite him leant back in his seat and looking over the top of
Mac's head said, 'Well?'

'Lovely morning for a drive.'

'Oh?'

'From Marchmont,' Mac added.

'Marchmont?'

'It's nice to get back to blondes,' said Mac elaborating mysteriously.

'Blondes?' said another surgeon, still looking down at his newspaper.
'Oho. Not Maureen,' said a third.
'The same. Lovely girl.'

Mac sipped his coffee with the air of a witness who has much to tell but must be asked the right questions. His audience feigned indifference. Campbell folded his newspaper and got up to go. He was just passing the end of the table and turning towards the door when Mac addressed his back loudly.

'How did you get on with Maggie, Campbell?' Campbell kept walking. 'I'll do the same for you some day.'

Derisive echoes of the surgeons' reaction rang in his ears all the way across to the ward.

The next few weeks passed slowly for Campbell. After his brief and unsatisfying whirl on the roundabout of hospital promiscuity he lost faith in its fabled riches. From time to time he found himself thinking of Joan, who none the less remained ill: recurrent wound abscesses were drained and she lingered in Sixteen a full four weeks after her appendicectomy. Occasionally he visited her. She looked pale and ill and they talked distantly about the ward or about Sister or about some item of gossip not involving either of them. Once he forgot to hold her hand. When she finally left the Institute she went home to convalesce with her parents in Perthshire, and it was only after she had done so that he realised he did not know her address there.

Lee returned from Morocco. He saw her once in a pub with someone else then she disappeared again suddenly and just as surely to a course in an outlying orthopaedic hospital.

Sister Birss's calls on his nights on duty became formal and forgiving: infinitely more irritating than before and much more frequent too. When he got up for them it seemed that half the complement of medical residents were up too, regardless of the hour. But a widespread awareness of her aims and methods resulted in a complete cessation of social life as she had known it.

In the wards Campbell despaired of greatness as a physician and began to mark time until his second housejob, in surgery, was due to begin. He passed his days resentfully, indulging the whims of his superiors with grudging contempt as the ward rounds seemed to grow longer and more devoid of purpose than ever. Even the pretence of research flagged in the unit: a theoretical objection to the methods of the potassium shift study led to its abandonment after three experiments and one mishap. And Mr McTurk, whose daily bounty had revived interest in the faecal vitamin pilot study, began to lose weight again: he was admitted to the ward, where he died of a rapidly advancing abdominal cancer.

16

The 1st of December was generally agreed to be an inopportune day to be in hospital in the region, and to be acutely ill in the morning was not far short of foolhardy. It was one of the two days in the year when resident medical staff changed over by a massive simultaneous shift which in theory occurred instantaneously at nine a.m. As no time was allowed for hand-over or familiarisation it was not uncommon for a houseman to find himself grappling with disaster at ten past nine in an entirely strange ward while his patient expired a martyr to administrative convenience.

True, it was the lesser of the two feasts, that of 1st June being distinguished by the advent of housemen who were not only strange to the wards but brand new to the profession: fledgling doctors who blinked and fluttered in their novel status and were frequently more shocked by the confidence of the public than by anything else in their new lives. Six months' experience, however irrelevant, made a difference both noted and approved by the perennial observers of the junior medical scene – the ward sisters, the porters and the ambulance drivers. December housemen were always considered to be marginally less bad than their predecessors.

For Campbell the changeover came as an escape from the longueurs of physicianly doubts and speculations and the end of the worst fortnight of his medical career. A misfortune of the duty roster gave him two consecutive weekends on call and only one night off in the week between. The days in hospital were cold and indistinguishable and the nights sleepless and shot through by repeated crises in wards crammed to the doors with elderly patients not quite dying of the complications of influenza.

The move to surgery took him to another world. His new colleagues from the senior house officer upwards practised a clipped and decisive habit of thought and speech even when there was nothing to be clipped and decisive about. Their views on everything from piles to politicians were so rigidly and briefly expressed that even their light conversation had the elliptic disjointed air of the subtitles to a silent film. Senior members of the unit wore white coats of rare and dazzling freshness which somehow conveyed the impression that to be seen at one's place of work in a lounge suit was a contemptible trait of post office clerks and consultant physicians. In clinical examination they affected a Luddite suspicion of instruments, leaving the use of stethoscope, tendon hammer and spatula to their most junior lieutenants, and themselves using little but their own well-groomed and often-scrubbed hands.

Campbell had been assigned to the female ward of his surgical unit, and on his first afternoon took the case-notes and strolled round his new estate with an air at once inquisitive and proprietorial. The patients were on average younger than those in his last ward, and most would leave the hospital having benefited from their stay. Some, it appeared, might well return, and one of them, according to a brief word from the SHO, was in to die.

The most striking difference was the absence of the inert cadre of long-stay patients which haunted every medical ward. Patients who came in to the surgical side of the hospital were briefly attended to and afterwards were either dead, better or not a surgical problem. Case-note folders too were agreeably light: no more tattered epics the size of telephone directories recording the dull horrors of chronic and fundamentally incurable medical conditions. The surgical habit of thought extended even to written communication: unnecessary words, like unnecessary organs, got cut out, and consultants' letters, copies of which were included in the folders, were concise and colloquial. His predecessor's progress notes on the current admissions were also short and at times seemed to Campbell, fresh from the medical side, to be almost negligently devoid of detail. It did not escape him that quite soon he too would probably write like that.

Most of the cases were routine: hernias, piles and varicose veins between them took up more than half the beds. If the human race had elected to walk upright it was destined to pay the penalty in three ailments quite unknown in our horizontal fellow mammals. It followed that junior surgeons – consultants seldom concerned themselves directly in such work, at least in the NHS – spent their days in a long and ultimately hopeless struggle against gravity, though it was unlikely that any of them saw their situation in such cosmic terms. If they thought about it at all, it was probably only in terms of pruning and landscaping: cobbling things up to correspond as closely as possible to *Gray's Anatomy*.

Happy with such musing, Campbell prepared to inspect the last of his new patients, who was in the right-hand single room. The case-notes were heavier than the rest, which was sinister, and even before he went in he noticed a whirring sound and a strange smell, rich, meaty and unpleasant, from within. He paused, recalling that in certain circles the single rooms were referred to as the departure lounges. Down the ward a nurse saw him hesitate, so he went in.

On the bed, naked but for modesty pants, lay a woman of about forty. She had an intravenous infusion in each arm and was wired up to an electrocardiographic monitor. An enormous gaping wound occupied most of the front of her abdomen. Suction tubes connected to an electric pump under the bed gurgled in its depths, drawing off viscous brown fluid. The smell was overpowering. Campbell moved closer. In the wound he could see her small intestine quite clearly, not pink and shiny as in the operating theatre, but dull grey and covered with the sticky brown liquid. The edges of the wound were like nothing he had ever seen before: irregular and gaping, raw in some places and clearly rotting in others. A wave of nausea rose in his gullet. He drew his eyes from the wound. The patient's face was pale and composed: she had a polythene nasogastric tube in her left nostril and wore a detached expression as though amused to see how he would cope.

'Hello,' he said.

The patient lifted a bandaged hand trailing drip line and ECG lead and pointed to her throat. Only then did Campbell notice that she was breathing through a tracheostomy tube in the front of her neck. He realised she could not speak. She smiled at him. Campbell smiled back as best he could then looked away. There was a nurse sitting in the corner knitting.

He glanced down at the name on the case-notes and tried again. 'Good afternoon, Mrs Noble. I'm Dr Campbell. I'll be helping to look after you now that Dr Tennant has moved on . . . I'm sorry to hear that . . . you've been poorly.'

The patient lifted her right forearm from the bed again and gave a little circular wave. The nurse stopped knitting and spoke.

'Relax. She's just about completely knocked off on top. She arrested for five minutes on the table. She's more or less decerebrate now, but quite pleasantly.'

'What's she in for?' said Campbell. 'What was her first operation?'

'Hernia. Right groin. It's fine now.'

Campbell looked down at the patient's lower abdomen: on the right he could see the top of an inguinal hernia scar, healing well, just above her modesty pants.

'So what happened?'

'Complications of surgery,' said the nurse briskly, going back to her knitting.

'I'm the new houseman . . .'

'I heard your wee speech.'

He ignored that. 'I'd like to take her charts and so on to my office . . . to sort things out from the beginning.'

'You do that, dear. She doesn't smell very nice.'

Campbell gathered up the charts, went outside and took a deep breath. He left all the notes and charts in his office, walked quickly to the staff toilet and vomited.

Someone as ill as Mrs Noble was going to take up a lot of his time, so he resolved to get to grips with the details in comfort and went over to his room in the Residency with her notes, washed, cleaned his teeth to get rid of the taste of vomit and started at the beginning of the folder.

She had presented as an emergency a fortnight before with a painful tender lump in the right groin, colicky abdominal pain and nausea. The registrar on duty had correctly diagnosed a hernia and taken her to theatre immediately because the loop of bowel trapped within was liable to perforate. At operation it had turned out to be a relatively uncommon and difficult type of hernia and with the patient still anaesthetised he had summoned the senior registrar to help him. Together they repaired the hernia then opened the abdomen again farther up and removed the damaged section of intestine, restoring the continuity of the bowel by an end-to-end repair. An unusual but well-documented problem had occurred and had been dealt with routinely and the patient returned to the ward. The absence of any progress notes covering the next few days seemed to indicate that all had gone well for a while.

Four days after her first operation she had become fevered and complained of abdominal pain again: the signs found on examination suggested early peritonitis, the most likely cause being the breakdown of the stitch line where the bowel had been repaired. Once more she went to theatre as an emergency. On this occasion a consultant operated, but that proved no guarantee of salvation. He and the senior registrar had reopened the abdomen, confirmed that the suture line had broken down and had begun to trim the intestine to re-suture it. An incident had occurred just then the details of which were buried in the decent obscurity of an operation note. 'During this procedure considerable haemorrhage occurred which was traced to a puncture of the splenic artery. This was controlled and the patient transfused with four pints of whole blood. In view of the damage to its blood supply the spleen was removed by the standard procedure.' Campbell checked the initials at the top of the page and found it noteworthy that a consultant operating with his senior registrar had seen fit to dictate the operation note himself. He read on and a ghastly sequence of events unfolded: while they were tying off the artery to the spleen deep in the abdomen, the pancreatic duct had been damaged, releasing the digestive secretions of the gland into the abdominal cavity. This had gone unnoticed at the time of operation.

It had come to light several days later: the patient remained ill, still complaining of abdominal pain, then the larger of her two abdominal wounds began to leak and its edges broke down, with the appearance of an unusual tacky discharge. Laboratory analysis confirmed an uneasy suspicion that it was coming from the pancreas. That, even to a surgical resident of only six hours' standing, seemed to be another turning point in the case. First the intestinal stitches had given way: misfortune. Then the spleen had had to be removed: the result of a blunder. Then the pancreatic damage: another blunder. Though he did not recognise the sequence, it illustrated a truth about surgical mishaps, that bad gets worse.

He read on with pity and horror: the juices of the pancreas once released from their lawful passages would digest anything from the pancreas itself to the edges of the wound. Deep in the left of the abdomen the fluid had formed a large abscess and a third operation was undertaken to drain this into the patient's stomach. It was a drastic but sometimes effective procedure for it diverted the corrosive secretions into an organ that could withstand their effects. By this time the patient was scarcely fit for anaesthetic and had arrested on the table. Resuscitation succeeded, but not quickly enough, and brain damage occurred because the heart had stopped for seven minutes. (Someone had given the nurse an edited and less incriminating version of events.) When the anaesthetic was over the patient had failed to breathe spontaneously and had required four days' mechanical ventilation.

The third operation had failed to control the secretions of the pancreas. The abdominal incision leaked again then gaped as its edges were eaten away: they extended steadily to become the gaping fistula he had seen half an hour before. The patient's hold on life was now very slender: she was being maintained by antibiotics and constant intravenous feeding. And she was still relentlessly digesting herself to death.

Campbell put the folder down and went over to the window. She was forty-five, young in the hospital's terms. That she should yield her life seemed to him shocking, a failure of a system of medicine which could fight gamely with anything but the old enemy cancer. Yet, as the nurse had said, she was dying of the complications of a hernia. There was no way out. Even if the pancreatic secretions could be stopped at this stage, perhaps by the removal of the whole gland, her situation would still be hopeless. The intestines and other abdominal organs were damaged and the awful wound remained. Any repair of her abdominal wall would be a prolonged and elaborate feat of plastic surgery, difficult enough in the unlikely instance of an otherwise healthy patient, but here complicated by her desperate debility. Campbell sat down on his bed. Her death, in hours or days, was certain. Only the manner of it was in doubt. Infection was most likely despite the vast quantities of antibiotics she was receiving: she would either develop a respiratory infection as a result of her tracheostomy and inability to cough or the infection now limited to her wound would spread overwhelmingly via her bloodstream. There was a third possibility, that she would die a sudden death as a result of the effect on her heart of the metabolic imbalance produced by prolonged intravenous feeding and the presence of so much dead tissue.

From the notes it was clear that no one wanted to give up: her death was to be delayed as long as possible though there were some surgical units where kind old consultants would have muttered about striving officiously and stopped all active treatment. Without IV lines she would last only hours and without antibiotics perhaps less than a day, but a policy had been decided: life was to be prolonged where it could no longer be saved. Perhaps even because her plight was the end result of a series of mishaps and blunders the most unkind mistake of all, that of keeping her alive, was now being made. Not for the resident to reason why, but what did it feel like? And could she smell herself? Her relatives could for sure. And did it hurt? There was so much that might, from the constant itch of the ECG leads and the tracheostomy to whatever it felt like to have a hole like that in your belly. And the speechlessness, so that no one knew except in a most general veterinary way if her pain was properly controlled. It was all so awful that her brain damage might be a blessing, however much it added to the relatives' distress.

In a case like this a perfect houseman would probably sit down and make a written summary of the story so far, both for his own benefit and for anyone else concerned with the complex and growing file. Even a mediocre houseman would do it without being told, at least on his first day in a new unit. There was the delicate question of how to make it sound like anything other than a charge sheet to be answered before the Great Surgeon on High, but a cool list of dates and events might suffice. As Campbell looked around his room for some paper his bleep went off. Slightly muffled by the folds of his white coat came the fast shrill beat. Cardiac arrest.

He swept the notes up from the desk, grabbed his coat and rushed out. The ward was three storeys up and even to get to the foot of the stairs he had to battle his way through swarms of visitors. Some stood clear like traffic giving way to a fire engine as he charged down the corridor, white coat flying: some tut-tutted or mumbled, 'Nae manners', and a bottle of Lucozade swept from its bearer's grasp crashed in his wake. He did not look back, but leapt on to the stairs and ran up three at a time so that his legs ached. Until someone else had decided to give up on Mrs Noble, he wouldn't.

More visitors crowded round the ward entrance waiting to be admitted by Sister on the stroke of three. He burst through them and crashed the swing doors. His heart thumped wildly and his head was pounding. The last few yards passed in a reddish blur and he sprinted into the right-hand single room.

The nurse looked up from her knitting with surprise. Mrs Noble looked just as well or ill as she had done earlier in the afternoon. She gave him another of her royal waves.

He turned and rushed out again. Two figures blocked his path. One was Sister.

'Who?' he gasped. 'Where?'

The other was Alester Ravelston Orr, whom he had not seen since the interview months before. Mr Ravelston Orr surveyed his new houseman and spoke.

'Dr Campbell? Ah, yes. I remember. You need not have run, Dr Campbell, though I find your misplaced concern for my colleague's . . . um . . . albatross most reassuring. Should ever any of my own patients have the misfortune to require your urgent attentions, it is comforting to know that it may take as little as three and a quarter minutes to obtain them. Though I should not have been surprised to find you on the ward already at three o'clock on a Wednesday afternoon.'

Flushed bright red and still puffing like a moribund case of emphysema Campbell blurted out, 'No arrest?'

'Not to my knowledge,' said Mr Ravelston Orr, 'Though we know not the hour or the day, particularly in such cases as my hapless colleague's hernia patient. No, no. I simply asked Sister what was the quickest way of obtaining the attendance of my junior staff.'

'Sorry, sir.'

'A not unreasonable request, I'm sure you'll agree. If some more pressing business takes my junior staff from my unit, then they may expect to be summoned via the impersonal and necessarily peremptory medium of the "bleep" system.' Ravelston Orr's inverted commas were impeccably inflected.

'Yessir.'

'Anyhow, Campbell, I'm pleased to welcome you to the unit and trust that you have settled in and familiarised yourself with the workings of my wards.'

'Thank you, sir.'

'I thought we might commence – at Mr Laird's convenience of course – to look over my cases, both pre- and post-operative. Ah. I see we are not to be kept waiting.'

A lean and anxious man with that air of early middle-aged harassment which Campbell had come to recognise as the hallmark of the senior registrar approached and spoke.

'I'm sorry, Mr Ravelston Orr. There was a muddle over your out-patient clinic. The senior house officer . . .'

'Gavin, I don't know if you've met my resident surgical officer, Dr um . . .'

'Campbell, sir.'

'Of course. But your first name. We may know your first name, I take it.'

'David, sir.'

'Dr David Campbell. Mr Laird is my senior registrar . . . Gavin I thought we might go round quickly. Where are the students?'

'In theatre, sir. Mr Lochhead insisted . . .'

'More hernias, presumably. Ah well, they must be exposed to surgery in all its forms. Who's first, Gavin?'

'The breast for tomorrow, sir. A Mrs Calder.'

'Sister?'

'Second bed on the right, Mr Ravelston Orr.'

Alester Ravelston Orr was a famous surgeon, though no one could recall in detail why he had become one. There was a theory that if an ancient medical teaching centre did not at some point in time happen to possess one, he might require to be invented. Generously equipped by nature with both presence and style, and sufficiently circumspect to maintain comparative respectability in his private life, he had emerged over the years first as a character, then as an institution.

A good war had a lot to do with it. He had even stolen a march on his contemporaries by going like the Luftwaffe to Spain to sharpen his claws for the coming conflict. The outbreak of general hostilities found him one of the few young but experienced military surgeons, and early in the North African campaign he had commanded his own field hospital. Mechanical failure of his transport in retreat had led to his capture and internment in Italy, an experience that had left him with a lifelong suspicion of all things mechanical and a loathing of all things Italian, but further enhanced his gift for survival.

The story of his escape and flight to Malta in a stolen aircraft was widely reported as good news at a time when most news was bad, and added to his modest eminence, though those closest to him then and later harboured suspicions that his captors, despairing of any solution to their mutual problems other than cold-blooded murder, may have ignored if not connived at his attempt to abscond.

In 1945 his war ended with the same circumspect promptitude that had marked its beginnings and he proceeded to fight the peace on the same overall plan. Style, opportunism and a talent for survival saw him through, and in the fifties he graduated from being the oldest young surgeon to being the youngest old one, cutting NHS patients competently, displaying propriety on committees and impropriety too in its rightful place after dinner. He had gained a late reputation as a scientist by encouraging and indeed on occasion appropriating the ideas of his subordinates. His private practice was immense and prestigious and he was very rich: for fifteen years he had cultivated the best men in the capital's clubs and had patronised charities conspicuously for the usual reasons. Therein lay his sole disappointment. He was still plain Mr Alester Ravelston Orr. There had, it was true, been a tense hopeful time about two years previously after Sir Hector Pittendriech had retired to his roses and salmon. The authorities were known to be considering him for the Institute's traditional ration of one surgical knighthood and he had heard his wife on several occasions talking in her sleep and addressing herself as Lady Orr. They had actually been invited to dinner at Holyrood, during which a diplomatically disastrous gastric upset had dashed the cup from his very lips and ended his hopes for ever. An accolade had gone to a surgical rival whom he still referred to as a competent laboratory technician and he had since developed a vociferous distaste for the whole honours system. The honour of being Mr Alester Ravelston Orr the famous surgeon was enough.

Mrs Calder, by contrast, was a thoroughly undistinguished NHS patient: thirty-five years of age, pretty in her careful, faded way, and mother of two teenage children. She had been referred by her GP to Mr Ravelston Orr's out-patient clinic because of a lump in her breast and had come into the ward that morning. A pleasant little woman, she seemed at least as concerned to avoid causing unnecessary trouble to the staff of the unit as she was by the prospect of cancer. Her husband and children were at her bedside as Ravelston Orr approached leading his entourage, and she shooed them away even before Sister had a chance to. The screens were whisked around her and she sat up in bed, fragrant, neat and anxious to please, in all respects ready for her encounter with Mr Ravelston Orr the famous surgeon.

'We'll just have this off to start with,' said Sister, descending on her and expertly whipping off her fresh red nightdress. Mrs Calder naked to the waist sat facing three men, one of whom was a very famous surgeon. She flushed slightly and patted a curl back into place. 'Good afternoon, Mr Ravelston Orr. And doctors.'

Ravelston Orr grunted and bared his teeth slightly then turned to his senior registrar.

'Where is it, Gavin?'

Mr Laird took out a large indelible marker and drew a two inch red circle just outside the left nipple. Mrs Calder smiled at him too.

'Feel it, Campbell.'

'Yessir . . . Good afternoon, Mrs Calder. If you'll just permit me to . . .'

'Get on with it. Well?'

'Thank you, Mrs Calder. Well, sir, there is a slight abnormality . . .'

'Slight? Slight, man? That's not what Mr Laird thought. Watch me. Examination of the breasts. Breastsss. Both at once. Advantages of speed and symmetry.' He sat down heavily on the bed and held his hands up, palms forward and level with the patient's breasts, then pushed as though demonstrating the shunting of trucks in a goods yard. 'Flat to the hand. Firm and fearless. You won't hurt them. Lump on the left.'

He seized the mass through soft tissue and pulled it. 'Not tethered to the chest wall. That's lucky.' He rolled it firmly and thoughtfully between his fingers. 'But fixed to the skin. That's bad.' The patient winced and sniffed.

'Now the axillae.' He slid his hands sharply up into her armpits, almost lifting the patient off the bed on his fingertips. Mrs Calder winced again, then smiled bravely at Ravelston Orr who was by now glaring round at his houseman.

'With spread on the left, eh? That's how to examine breasts.' He turned to Mrs Calder and addressed her for the first time. 'Bit of trouble on the left. Fix it for you tomorrow. Right?'

'Will you be taking the whole thing, Mr Ravelston Orr?'

'Just the breast. The left one.'

The patient blinked and sniffed. He patted her breasts and growled, 'At your age, my dear, they're a biological irrelevance. And the rubber things are quite good now. Sister'll tell you all about them and get you fixed up with one for afterwards. Less trouble in some ways than the real thing. Especially from our point of view.' He grinned fiercely, stood up and swept away, leaving Mrs Calder sobbing behind her screens.

There were no other pre-operative patients and the sum of Mr Ravelston Orr's post-operative patients was a lady from a psychiatric hospital who had had her piles done by the junior registrar. She was graphic in her description of the first test of the revised anatomy and eloquent on her present relief. Ravelston Orr acknowledged her thanks with grave courtesy.

As the little procession moved back up the ward through the relatives and friends of the patients, Campbell concluded that Ravelston Orr chose to go round his cases during visiting times to conceal the fact that he had very few, while maintaining the impression that he was very busy. Being a famous surgeon had a paradoxical effect on NHS out-patient referrals, the main source of bread-and-butter surgical cases, because GPs seemed to think that famous surgeons were busy men and referred their patients to lesser luminaries whose waiting lists were assumed to be much shorter.

The problem appeared to have been exercising Ravelston Orr's mind as well: over tea in Sister's room he announced his intention of reviving the weekly grand round, over which he presided as senior surgeon and consultant in administrative charge. He could thus extend his interest in the ward to the patients of the other two consultants, which would be unusual and unpopular but quite within his rights. In a monologue he pointed out many advantages but omitted that one, and concluded by saying that the changeover of junior staff provided an ideal occasion to begin.

The senior registrar agreed warmly, pointing out the great teaching opportunities that would be opened both to junior and senior students. The senior house officer, returned from the out-patient clinic, also ventured to agree enthusiastically. Sister poured tea and said little. The houseman wondered how long the grand round would take and what it would achieve for Mrs Noble, but did not voice his thoughts. The following Monday morning was unanimously adopted as the time for the first of the new series of grand rounds.

17

Just before five o'clock Campbell went across to the male ward to find his new co-resident, a quiet rather academic Englishman who had done his medical job a few wards along from Creech's unit. His career in psychiatry had been mapped out since the fifth year of the medical course and he was known to regard pre-registration surgical experience as simply to be endured. He was in his office sitting at the desk writing out laboratory forms and labelling sample tubes. He stopped when Campbell came in.

'Hello, David. How's it going?'

'Could be worse, I suppose. Got off to a flying start with the chief. What did you make of him?'

'Maybe a compensated endogenous depression. Or an early senile dementia. Interesting.'

'Oh. I meant as a chief.'

'Disastrous.'

'Busy?'

'Not so far. But three cold admissions coming in at half past five. On what they call my night off. Bloody Laird and his social conscience. Wringing a last day's work out of tomorrow's list. All for the public good and regardless of inconvenience to the likes of us.'

'Look, could you take my bleep and cover my ward for an hour? I want to get out into town. Leave one of these cases for me. I'll see him at six and you can go off.'

'OK. Thanks.'

It was beginning to get dark when Campbell left the hospital, and rush-hour crowds were bustling past brightly lit windows. After the confines of the hospital the streets were cold, noisy and alive. He stopped off at a bookshop and browsed hungrily, then bought a couple of paperbacks he might never read, mostly as a gesture against incarceration in the bookless wastes of the Institute. Apart from a general ache to get outside, the main object of the excursion was to get a ticket for Friday's concert. One ticket. He had found by experience that it was not worth taking girls who would not have gone of their own accord. Watching them suffering two hours of unaccustomed inactivity and boredom, or worse, feigning rapt attention, eroded his own enjoyment too much. He also had a long-standing but unfulfilled dread of taking along some poor innocent who might clap enthusiastically between movements. One ticket only. But the concerts finished early enough to permit getting back to the pub in time to track down the best party for later. Within the narrow limits of time off, culture and dissolution had to be strictly timetabled.

The music shop which booked the concerts was across in the Georgian north of the city. Campbell, who had lived and studied in the south side for more than six years, never crossed the High Street without a slight sense of going foreign. It was not simply that the streets were wider and the shops better: the people, even the rush hour crowds, seemed about an inch taller and somehow cleaner than their southern counterparts. Bright green and red displays in grand stores half a block long added to the alien festive aura.

In the windows of the music shop mute expensive instruments glistened in unlikely groups and, inside, the first storm-troopers of the Christmas rush huddled in booths listening to records and riffled through the motley racks of sleeves. There was a queue for concert tickets and Campbell took his place behind a blonde girl with nice legs. Customary curiosity about the unseen face was answered as the queue shortened and she turned in profile to face the counter. Pleasant unemphatic features and green eyes. Longish hands pointing on the booking plan of the concert hall, then picking up change and a ticket. One ticket. Interesting.

As she turned and passed Campbell to leave the shop he remembered her suddenly and totally: the aneurysm's granddaughter, the waiting night, the hands on the front of the trolley. He stopped in thought. The clerk selling tickets tapped the glass at him and behind in the queue a woman muttered. Angry at himself for not having recognised her more quickly, and annoyed at the secondary disturbance in the queue, Campbell chose a bad seat quickly, took his change and walked into the record section.

Your Hundred Best Christmas Melodies Sung by Father Sidney MacEwan and the Chorus of the Academy of the London Palladium. As he flicked through the sleeves Campbell remembered the hands pointing on the booking plan, and the voice saying what seat she wanted. Again he cursed himself: a cool operator would have said nothing, booked the seat next to her, and enjoyed the coincidence at leisure. He glanced back at the queue, which was now much longer, and tried to calculate the cost in sweat and upset of going back and either bludgeoning the clerk into swapping the seats or buying the other one as well.

A shop assistant was hovering watchfully nearby as though he suspected Campbell were about to do mad violence to the Christmas selection. He left the shop and bought an intellectual weekly at a bookstall. He had twenty minutes left: enough for a coffee and an amble through views on views on aspects of Carlyle or whoever it was this week. There was a first-floor coffee shop with a bookstall opposite.

Campbell climbed the stairs and went in, carrying his *Listener* like a pass. Ignoring a counterful of health-food snacks he asked the assistant for a coffee, which she poured into a rough earthenware mug. When he reached round the other side of it for the handle he discovered there wasn't one. The assistant smiled condescendingly.

Turning from the counter to look for a seat he saw, smiling at him across the nearest table, the blonde girl he had seen minutes before in the music shop. With his wallet and the magazine in one hand and the hot ungainly cup of coffee in the other he went over and asked politely if he might join her. She nodded.

'It's Dr Campbell, isn't it?'

'Yes . . . Miss . . .?'

'Quothquan.'

If on seeing her in the ticket queue Campbell had formulated an immediate tactical objective, it would have been something like this: a drink or a coffee straight away, somewhere close at hand. Thus presented with the situation he found it much harder to deal with than it would have been if he had engineered it himself. Having failed and morosely adjusted himself to failure, he was caught by this effortless success with his forces wrongly grouped; solitary retreat into the pages of a magazine was to be replaced at short notice by an advance to contact.

He sat down, depositing his coffee with relief and noting that her similar handleless mug was full of milk, cold and sensible. There was an intriguing difference about her appearance. The tan had faded and her hair was shorter and possibly less blonde than it had been, but overall her whole style had somehow altered as though her newsagent had stopped sending *Scottish Field* and substituted *Vogue*. Her former persona, not far short of twinsets, pearls and Jacqmar head-squares knotted just under the chin, had made way for someone younger, smarter and dressed in looser, lighter things. The change had been accomplished in just over two months.

A glance at her hand ('Observe the patient's hands, young man.

113

In the book of the hands is written the story of the life.') ascertained that she was still single. The rest of the updating of information might be harder work. He sipped his coffee, picking it up with the other hand to save his still throbbing fingers, and could not for the life of him think of anything to say. Their only common ground, concerning the death of her grandfather, hardly ranked as light conversation, which left Do you come here often?

She spared him by suddenly announcing, 'I like this place. Especially about this time. Earlier it's swarming with schoolkids.'

That was a lot: it contained *a.* a demonstration of that happy knack of anticipation which, he remembered with pleasure, was an outstanding feature of her conversation on the waiting night, *b.* a voluntary statement about her movements of possible predictive value and *c.* at least two potential points of departure for further conversation. Two school children, under the heading *c.* (*ii*) remained at a corner table: a pale thin boy, smoking a cigarette, probably just tobacco, and a girl from another school, also in uniform, who had reefed up her skirt by a couple of turns round its waistband to reveal thighs a more discriminating owner might have preferred to conceal.

'I like it here,' said Campbell, 'because of the kids. It makes me feel like a solid and respectable citizen.'

'Oh dear,' she said. 'They just make me feel old.'

Choice of two moves: either 'Did you go to school in Edinburgh?' a standard opening which Campbell, who had not, never used without feeling slightly fraudulent, but which was probably safe enough, or 'You look much younger than you did the last time we met,' for which it was almost certainly too early.

She put down her earthenware mug and spoke again. 'It's funny. I used to come here years ago from school, trying to look older than I really was.'

So they talked about where she had been to school and about her job, and about the art gallery where she worked, and eventually about his work too, though he could no more explain it to her than a subaltern could explain trench warfare to a showgirl, except to say that it was nice to get away from it for a while. As they talked he took in the details of her appearance – the way her mouth moved when she spoke, the pattern of her fingers on the rough mug, and always back to her eyes, quick, frank and green. They did not talk of her grandfather. It was as though they had decided to start again from something other than a death.

Campbell glanced at his watch and found it was five to six. He stopped in mid-sentence and explained in a muddled way why he had to go, because of the colleague who had obliged him, and because of the patients and being on call. She seemed surprised, as if expecting to terminate the interview herself, and said something about having come to look for something in the bookstall. She got up and began to turn away then said, 'It was nice meeting you again . . . somewhere else.'

'Yes.' Campbell floundered. Did she mean that was it: one home game and one away. 'Perhaps we'll run into each other again some time.'

'I hope so.' She smiled, adding a little to the formula, then walked on to the bookstall. Nice legs.

18

Back in his white coat by ten past six, Campbell found the third cold male admission for tomorrow's list ready to be clerked. He was an insurance agent of about forty with a neat little moustache and a high, old-fashioned parting in his hair. His story was elusive. 'No point in putting off the evil hour, the quack at home said. Have the old trouble seen to now. Be a new man afterwards.'

'The old trouble?'

'Had it for years.'

'How long?'

'Since fifty. Korea. Covering the Inchon landings from *Triumph*. Seafires, y'know. Great old crates. Lick anything they could throw at us until the Migs came along.'

'What happened then?'

'Well, it was a bit rough for a while, then we got Venoms. We got replaced by Venoms I should say. They said I wasn't worth re-training. Old trouble, y'know.'

'No. I meant what happened in nineteen-fifty to start off this trouble?'

'I was just telling you, doc. We were covering the Inchon landings. Seafires. I got winged. Take any amount of punishment but there was a fuel leak. Thought I'd better be getting back. Quite high. Looking round for the carrier. No idea how small they are and hard to find when you really need 'em. All of a sudden there was this bloody Mig. One of the first. No propellers, that's cheating, I thought. Ho ho. But bloody fast despite, eh? So down we went, me first. Then I saw *Triumph*. Big rusty *T*, bless 'er. No place like home, I thought, and if you follow me they'll shoot you.'

There was no stopping this fellow. Campbell put down his pen and switched off.

'Did I tell you I'd lost a whole tankful? Anyway this Mig just wasn't going away. So I tried a full power dive. Fuel a bit low but you only live once. Did damn near five hundred knots.'

He demonstrated the ensuing action by a series of wide sweeping gestures. Patients two and three beds away watched with interest.

115

'Hung on to the dive as long as I dared. Got jolly close to the hoggin, then had a glance at the fuel situation. Nothing on the clock but the maker's name. Jammed the stick right back and just made it out of the dive. Mig was still hanging around waiting for the splash and one of the escorts got him. Serve him right. Cheeky beggar. Sheer speed took me up to a thousand feet again and I got home on the last teaspoonful in the tank. That was how it all started.'

'Sorry,' said Campbell. 'What started?'

'Piles,' said the patient. 'Came on like that' – he snapped his fingers – 'Coming out of the dive.'

'I see,' said Campbell. 'You've got piles.'

'Yes,' said the late aviator. 'I thought we'd better kick off by getting it in black and white. How I got 'em. For the pension.'

'The pension?'

'Yes. For the little woman. Oh, I know it's not likely. But I want to know that if things go wrong she'll be properly looked after. Result of enemy action, eh?'

'It's a very simple operation,' said Campbell quietly, 'and it's most unlikely that anything will go wrong.'

The patient leaned forward. 'Every op has its risks. Admit it, doc. The old sawbones in *Triumph* always used to say so.'

'Things are a bit safer now than they were then,' said Campbell, trying not to think of Mrs Noble. He drew the screens around to inspect the combat damage. 'I think everything is going to be all right.'

Campbell was lying in his room with a surgery book open in front of him when his bleep went off. A routine slow beat call. He picked up the phone.

'Dr Campbell.'

'Dr Campbell, outside call for you. Putting you through now, caller.'

'Hello?'

'Hello.' A light, slightly posh female voice.

'Dr Campbell speaking.'

'Oh, hello. Alison Quothquan here. We met in the Chasuble today.'

'Oh, hello . . . Sorry I had to rush away like that. It must have looked awfully rude.'

'Oh don't worry. I understand. I suppose it's a bit more pressing than some jobs.'

'I suppose so.' But why had she phoned? Perhaps she regretted the abrupt muddle of their parting as much as he did, but even so it was a bit forward just ringing the hospital.

'Dr Campbell, did you know that you left your wallet on the table in the Chasuble?'

'What? Gosh no. Where is it now? Did you hand it in at the counter?'

'No. I've got it here.'

'Oh. Thanks very much. Where are you?'

'At home.'

'Look, I'm on duty. I can't come out now but if you hang on to it perhaps we can meet.'

'I could bring it up this evening.'

'Really, I hardly need it in here. We could meet somewhere. They're letting me out on Friday.'

'What?'

'The next time off I've got is Friday evening. I'm on duty till then.' There was an awkward gap in which Campbell wondered if he ought to be thinking more positively. The girl spoke again.

'Are you by any chance going to the concert on Friday?'

'Yes. Yes, I am. I got the ticket just before I met you today.'

'I'm going too.'

'Are you?' Cool, thought Campbell to himself.

'Perhaps I could give you your wallet back then.'

'Yes, thanks. I'll meet you at the interval. In the foyer. Near the statue.'

'All right. You're sure you won't need it before then?'

'My wallet?'

'Yes.'

'Gosh yes. My ticket's in it.'

'OK. Same place. Before the concert. Twenty-five past seven.'

'Fine. Thanks. Sorry to put you to all this trouble.'

'See you on Friday.'

'Yes. Thanks.'

Campbell put the phone down, did a handstand against the wall, shadow-boxed in front of the mirror, did two press-ups on the floor, threw his surgery book on top of the wardrobe then dived full length on the bed and lay giggling.

It was fully five minutes before he thought of his wallet, and when he did it occurred to him that her shot in the dark about his going to the concert might have been inspired by a quick look in his wallet. Then he remembered what else she might have found there. After all, not everyone was on the Pill.

19

Friday evening was going to have to serve as the whole weekend for Campbell. In moving from medicine to surgery he had stepped from the frying pan of a Friday receiving night into the fire of one on Saturday. Weekends formerly truncated were now obliterated. In a discussion with the senior registrar on the subject of the duty roster it was decided that the resident with the 'weekend off' could take Sunday afternoon and evening. Later and privately the housemen determined that whoever had the Sunday off would get to bed on Saturday night if at all possible, while the duty man would stay up, so that time off would not be wasted sleeping. True, the patients might be cared for on Sunday by an exhausted houseman, but in a disciplined organisation like the NHS sacrifices must be evenly spread around.

At twenty past seven Campbell waited by the statue in the foyer, reading the concert programme. It offered an opus one by a modern composer of whom he had never heard, a middle-number Haydn, perhaps familiar, and after the interval a solid romantic symphony that had been sitting like a mahogany sideboard in the living-room of Campbell's musical consciousness for as long as he could remember.

At twenty-six minutes past – how delicate, how considerate to be one minute late – she arrived, pink from the cold outside, and greeted him in a relaxed casual way as though they had been going out together for weeks. A lurking fear that she might have approached holding his wallet at arm's length and walked off having dropped it at his feet now seemed absurd. They chatted for a little about the programme then she said, 'Oh, your wallet,' as if it were entirely incidental to their meeting and took it from her coat pocket and gave it to him. He stifled a graceless urge to check its contents, put it away and thanked her.

'I hadn't even missed it when you phoned. But it was great to hear that you had it. I lost one before and it was horrible. Not the money, but the membership cards and things like that. Thanks very much.'

A bell rang and groups in the foyer began to break up and file into the hall. A familiar necessity to take an initiative pressed in on Campbell. This time she was expecting it.

'Shall we meet for a drink at the interval?'

'Let's.'

'Here?'

'Fine.'

They went upstairs by a succession of flights of diminishing grandeur to the gallery where the poor, nice people went and parted to go to their seats. The hall was not full and the audience on the whole rather bronchial. Campbell settled down for the first half. The overture was no more painful than could have been expected, and much shorter. The Haydn passed innocuously in contemplation and they met again on the stairway at the beginning of the interval, which made Campbell feel that his luck with her had turned.

By the time the nice, poor people from upstairs arrived at the bar it was always crowded, and they were apart for more than five minutes while he struggled for two warm lagers served with hasty bad grace by a barmaid whom he contrived to insult with a risible tip, the subtlety of which was missed. The sense that this was a proper date rather than a formal restitution of lost property grew over the lager and after the interval they went upstairs again and sat together in two seats that had been empty in the first half. To Campbell, tired from his previous night on duty, the second half was totally pleasant, the music familiar and un-demanding and much improved for being heard in the close proximity of Miss Quothquan, who was wearing a suede coat still new enough to contribute a fresh-leather smell to her general fragrance. Every sixty bars or so her hair fell slowly over her eyes and she swept it back, un-covering her profile once more to Campbell's sidelong view. Far below, the orchestra played the thing with warmth and intelligence, then when it ended stood through the applause with tradesmanlike equanimity, looking more concerned with quick drinks somewhere and the times of last buses home. Alison glowed with pleasure and turned to mutter, 'That was terrific,' with an innocent enthusiasm that Campbell found touching. They went downstairs and through the foyer again: this time Campbell was in no doubt as to what to suggest, or that she would agree. They stopped outside.

'Could you face some food?'

'Mmm, I think so.'

'Foreign food?'

'I think so. What sort did you have in mind?'

'Italian?'

'Fine . . . Where? I've got the car with me.'

'I walked.'

'Good. It's somewhere round here.'

The 'somewhere' was sweet. And the car was a predictable red mini. He felt he knew her quite well already. They got in. Girls' cars always smelled nicer than men's.

'Where to?'

'Rose Street. East End.'

'Giacomo's?'

'D'you know it?'

'Love it. But I haven't been there for ages.'

Perhaps because of a subconscious and erroneous musical association, Campbell chose something called lasagne verdi which turned out to be a green farinaceous exercise in the Mediterranean art of protein dilution. Alison had scampi. Between them a candle flickered on top of a bottle encrusted with wax in the manner of pirate dens and the cheaper eating places of the day. They drank chianti and she looked hopelessly and endearingly lovely.

After one and a half glasses she started to put her hand over her glass when he offered her more, so rather than invite scorn by the pursuit of such rakishly obvious tactics Campbell finished the bottle himself and concluded that he was in love. Coffee, three or four cups of it, came and went in a golden haze of candlelight flickering on her hair and face. He talked a lot and could not remember afterwards what he had said but remembered her expression, not disapproving, and smiling sometimes. As they left he helped her on with her coat, which proved to be an ordeal of physical restraint.

She offered to drive him back to the Institute and he accepted, dimly appreciating that her sobriety was sensible, not priggishly obstructive as it had previously seemed. Protecting an investment of fifteen thousand pounds by the nation in his medical education, and their lives too. He loved her for that as well.

In the Residency car park she switched off her engine. A good sign. But when he invited her up to his room for a drink she politely declined. With one hand still on the steering wheel she turned to face him. He took her other hand and kissed it, the first time other than accidentally brushing together that they had touched. She smiled and he took her other hand then leaned forward to kiss her, slowly enough for his intention to be clear so that she could register disapproval if she wanted to. She didn't but leaned towards him instead.

Jesusmary hallucinogenic tactile ecstasy and probably addictive too. He put an arm round her and pulled her over: she gathered against him pressing her lips against his. More ecstasy. Her hair smelt of heaven and Italian food. His free hand found the vee of her suede lapels of its own accord. She moved slightly back, laid her hand on his, shook her head about a centimetre each way and kissed the tip of his nose.

'Unless you were exaggerating, you'll be busy in the morning. I'm sure your patients will need you well rested.'

He sat back with his hands in his lap, somewhat chastened. Was this how the wild beasts felt after a few chords from Orpheus with his lute? Or did she mean he was drunk? She was giggling.

'Can I phone you?' said Campbell quietly, still playing up the hurt of her rebuff.

'Please do.'

'I suppose there are pages and pages of Quothquans in the book.'

'There aren't. Only two of us. My number's still under grandpa.'

'I will. Good night.'

'Good night. And thank you.'

As he walked upstairs the Chianti hit him first, then love. His last co-ordinated thought before sleep went back to the aneurysm: they had not quite got through the evening without mentioning the late commemorator of the owls of Glenlivet.

20

Campbell got up early for his first surgical receiving day and went round the ward on his own before breakfast. It was half empty. Everyone who could have been sent home had been, and the eight beds nearest the door were waiting with sheets drawn back in the ready position. Saturday had a reputation as a busy receiving day: in the morning the GPs saved their consciences and their golf fixtures by sending in all the doubtful abdomens that might not keep till Monday, and in the late evening came the victims of traffic accidents and other convivial weekend violence. All that on top of the routine and the inevitable: the honest perforated ulcers, the statistically inevitable appendices and the rag-bag of miscellaneous minor surgery.

At half past eight he was summoned to Casualty to opine on the first abdomen of the day, a girl who gave a textbook history of appendicitis. She was intelligent, clean and pretty; a pleasure to clerk and the victim of a disease that was easily dealt with but could kill if neglected. Compare and contrast the average medical admission: decrepit, demented and riddled with irreversible degenerative pathology. Surgery might be fun.

It was a good morning. The average age of his first five patients was under thirty. Before lunch he went round with the registrar, who decided that three were for cutting, two for watching. The residents tossed a coin to determine which was to go into theatre. Fate deemed that Gray, the psychiatrist of tomorrow, should have first chance to perform an appendicectomy.

Some light relief came in the afternoon while Gray was in the theatre and Campbell was seeing both male and female admissions. He was called down to Casualty to see what the duty SHO there called 'a paraphimosis with a difference'. Paraphimosis he knew about: a tight retracted foreskin that would not slip back into place, usually accompanied by swelling of the affected part. It was a fairly common minor surgical emergency, treated either by manipulation and reduction without anaesthetic or, in more severe cases, by a minor operation on the comfortably gassed patient. Whatever was done at the time, most patients were recalled for circumcision to make sure it didn't happen again. That was ordinary paraphimosis, but what was a paraphimosis with a difference? A hermaphrodite? Or a woman?

The patient waiting in the trolley room was a thin worried man in his middle twenties whose occupation as recorded on the documents was 'evangelist'.

'How did this come on?' Campbell enquired.

'Last night. In bed. After the Friday Youth Meeting. You see there was a group there – we don't usually have music – called Salvation Rock. And there was this girl singer . . .'

'I see,' said Campbell. 'Was this the first time you'd had intercourse?'

'Intercourse? Certainly not! I mean I've never had anything of the sort.'

'I see,' said Campbell again. 'What were you doing when this came on?'

The patient, whose anxiety seemed out of all proportion to the severity of his pathology, bit his knuckles and blurted out, 'I was in bed by myself. Having impure thoughts.'

'Well, that's not uncommon,' said Campbell with a professional tolerance acquired over six weeks' enforced tuition at a forward-looking loony bin kitted out like an airport hotel. The patient was not soothed.

'Doctor, doctor,' he pleaded. 'Will you operate? Oh soon. And get it all over with.'

'We'll have to see.'

'I'm quite ready, doctor.'

'Good,' said Campbell. 'But let me see.'

'Oh, soon, doctor. The sooner the better and it'll all be over. You'll know your bible, doctor. If thine eye offend thee . . .'

See an ophthalmologist, thought Campbell turning down the blankets. It was indeed a paraphimosis of moderate severity. 'Yes . . . Hmmm.' He prodded it. 'Does that hurt?'

The patient squealed like a branded piglet then closed his eyes and muttered, 'For it is better to enter into the heavenly life maimed than to be cast whole into everlasting fire.'

'Quite,' said Campbell absently, wondering whether he could tackle it himself and reduce it down here in Casualty, or whether the man should be admitted for a general anaesthetic.

The patient sat up and clutched Campbell's arm. 'I've lived by the Word and I never approved of having skiffle groups at the Friday Youth meetings in the first place.'

'I'm sure you're right.' There was quite a lot of swelling. It might even be one for an emergency operation. The patient moaned to himself.

'Whom the Lord loveth He also chastiseth.'

'Quite. What I'm going to do is get another doctor down to have a look at this.'

'But doctor!' The patient suddenly sat up straight and stared transfixed at the curtains in front. 'Deuteronomy twenty-three verse one. No man that is wounded in the stones or hath his privy member cut off shall enter into the congregation of the Lord.'

'Of course not,' said Campbell, trying to remember the name of the registrar on duty for Ravelston's unit. Hadden. 'I'm going to get Mr Hadden down to have a look at this for you. I won't be a minute. Excuse me.'

Hadden was sitting in Sister's room with his feet up, reading her *Daily Record*. Campbell described the case.

'Oh, a touch of the old wanker's doom, eh? Well, I've never yet seen one that I couldn't sort out in Casualty with a squeeze here and a flick there.'

'This might be your first. It looks quite tight to me.'

'Sixpence says my big right hand will do it.'

'OK.' Betting on the little uncertainties of receiving day added new lustre to the joys of surgery. 'Sixpence.'

'And besides,' said Hadden, 'we're not very well off for male beds and if he's gassed he'll have to come in. Who's on in Casualty?'

'Jock Lyon.'

'Ring down and ask Jock to write him up for ten milligrams of Valium intramuscularly. Daze him a bit. We'll do it in half an hour.'

'Fine. He's an odd bod, though. Religious.'

'There's nothing like Valium for religion, acute or chronic.'

Campbell went across to his own ward and pottered round for a while. The first post-operative appendix was snoring peacefully like Sleeping Beauty. From the notes, Gray had done her: he would be in every day to see how the incision was coming along.

Houseman and registrar went down together to the treatment area in Casualty where their patient was waiting. A pink ticket marked 'Receiving Surgeons' denoted his screens. From behind them came strange sounds and when Campbell drew them back the evangelist was revealed on his knees on the trolley with his hands clasped in front of him, swaying backward and forward in supplication. He was moaning softly, 'Lord, if it be Thy will, let this cup pass from my lips.'

'I see what you mean,' said Hadden. 'Should have given him fifteen.'

The patient opened his eyes and stared at Hadden as though he had been carrying a cleaver and a bucket of boiling tar, then blurted out, 'But if it be not Thy will then let Thy will be done quickly. Oh doctor, I'm terrified.'

Hadden took him by the arm. 'Just lie down. Careful now.'

The man of God, naked from the waist down, stood up on the trolley to get from his kneeling position to lying on his back. The pathology passed close before Hadden's eyes.

'Yes, the old man's got his scarf on a bit tight today.'

'Pardon, doctor?' His eyes rolled with fear and his mouth was twitching.

'Spot of bother with the unruly member, I see.'

The patient was extremely agitated: he sat up, lay down, and sat up again, clutching at the doctors and the rails of his trolley. He wailed, 'Oh, spare me, Lord, and pardon my iniquities. Surely my burden is greater than I can bear.'

'Lie down!' said Hadden. The shock of command did more than faith to steady the patient. He lay shaking but silent as the registrar drew on a rubber glove. 'I'm just going to shake hands with the bishop. A bit of a squeeze to reduce the swelling, then everything will just flip back into place.'

'B-b-b-bishop?' spluttered the evangelist. It was hard to tell whether he approved of them or not.

'It'll soon be over,' said Hadden calmly, lifting the patient's shirt away from the scene of the action.

'Jesus my saviour,' came the shriek, 'Anything but the knife.'

'Who said anything about knives?' Hadden grasped the nettle with once-and-for-all firmness.

'Ooooooooghoooogh.' The patient wailed piteously.

'Just a firm squeeze.'

'Oooooogh. Spare thy rod, Oh Merciful Creator.'

'That's the ticket. It's going down already.'

'A just chastisement for my iniquities which are manifold, but God be merciful.'

'Easy does it.'

'I was unclean. Uncleeeeeeeeeean.' Sweat was pouring from his brow.

'It's going down very nicely.'

'Purge me with hyssop, Oooooooh, I shall be cleeeean.'

'Almost there.' Hadden's brow was moist too and the veins were standing out on his wrist.

'I was a sinner . . . Lord in thy mercy hear thy servant . . .'

'That's enough of that,' said Hadden, relaxing his grip. The swelling was down and the work of Satan almost undone. With an expert flick of his thumb he finished the job. 'Shrunk with fear but otherwise not too bad,' he remarked to Campbell. 'Never failed yet.'

'Thanks be to Thee, Oh God, for Thy infinite mercy. And thanks, doctor. Both of you. My, what a relief.'

'Peace, be off,' said Hadden amiably. He turned to the houseman. 'He can go now but get him back in to have his wick trimmed the week after next. When you've arranged that tea will be served in Sister's room. Price sixpence.'

By late afternoon surgery was beginning to pall again: Gray remained in theatre and Campbell had to look after the growing number of post-operative patients in both wards. One of Mrs Noble's drips stopped running and he spent half an hour bent over her arm in the choking miasma of the side room, trying to find another vein to take the cannula. She was less active now and had lost her cheerful indifference. She lay pale and inert, with beads of sweat on her upper lip.

At the end of visiting time when a lot of relatives were waiting to be seen Campbell suddenly found that he was the only doctor around. Some presented no problems, such as the relatives of the appendix patients. 'Straightforward operation, not much more trouble than having your tonsils out. He/she will be out in a week if everything goes as well as it has done so far.' Others were less simple. Mrs Calder's husband had to be told something approximating to the truth. 'Mr Ravelston Orr did the operation himself and is quite hopeful that there won't be any more trouble. Unfortunately a certain number of people with your wife's complaint do have to come back. However, there's certainly no reason at the moment to believe . . .' The use of the word cancer caused needless anxiety so where possible Campbell avoided it. Mrs Noble's husband, a square little man in a cap and scarf, seemed imperturbably stupid. He thanked the houseman several times for his efforts and remarked, 'She's looking brighter today. We're all keeping our fingers crossed.' Campbell wondered how he would cope when he realised what was obvious to everyone else already.

The sixth female emergency admission of the day took him abruptly back to his time on the medical side. She was a seventy-five year old widow from one of the poorest parts of the old town. She gave a rambling story of indigestion proof to more proprietary indigestion powders than Campbell had ever heard of.

'Awfy bad the day, son, awfy bad the day. I was just going down tae the phone box tae get the doctor when I fell. A policeman, a young laddie like yersel, picked me up, and the pain was that bad I had tae ask him tae phone for an ambulance. An' the ambulance drivers were awfy nice laddies an' all. Everybody's nice here too. D'you know that, son? Awfy nice.'

Her abdomen was rigid under the fat, acutely tender and silent. Most people with perforated ulcers weren't half so talkative. Campbell ascribed it to the known decrease in pain sensitivity in the old, and the fact that she had been so swept off her feet by the gay social whirl of an admission after years of loneliness that its cause no longer counted for much. To save time he abandoned the usual systematic enquiry about health and previous illness and went straight on to examine her, chatting her up as he did to keep her amused. She giggled so much when he was testing her reflexes that a casualty nurse put her head round the screens and pointedly asked if he wanted a chaperone.

The afternoon theatre session had ended before she could be made ready, so she was installed in the ward to go in with the evening list. Gray emerged from the operating suite, a hardened surgeon in white theatre pyjamas and rubber boots, and made straight for the female ward to enquire after his first appendicectomy, who was sore and somewhat sleepy, but awake enough to ask him if he had done it himself, which made it all worthwhile. Mr Laird reappeared in an enormous overcoat and announced his intention of going home for some chop. He would be available if required later.

Over dinner in the Residency Campbell asked Hadden about Mrs Noble. He sounded hard-boiled. 'Every surgeon has the occasional albatross, and the form is that it hangs round his neck until it rots off. Lochhead's a good safe cutter and one case makes no difference because nobody wins 'em all. I'd still rather have him inside my abdo than Alester any day if I needed hacking about. Alester doesn't make many mistakes because he doesn't do much cutting. He's getting rusty.'

'Not enough patients?'

'That and too much of being an internationally famous surgeon. Which means not doing much surgery.'

'So we all have to turn out on a grand round to prop up his ego.'

'So I heard. Gavin told me. Three-line whip and no excuses. Ten o'clock Monday. It'll be a bore, or a farce if we're lucky.'

'Will it help anybody? The patients I mean. Mrs Noble . . .'

'I shouldn't think so. But she might not last till then.'

'Spare Lochhead's blushes if she doesn't,' said Gray.

'Patients take tact only so far,' said Hadden glumly, as though he didn't want to talk about that any more.

The evening passed in bodeful calm with both wards full and only one patient waiting to go to theatre. The three doctors sat in Sister's room round a bottle of sherry gifted by relatives on behalf of the grateful dead, eating biscuits paid for by the odd shillings from the cremation money. Hadden talked of those not present. 'Gavin's twisted because he won't get a consultant post until someone dies, and the longer that takes the more people in the rush for the shoes. Alester doesn't like him but he needs him. Lochhead doesn't like him and doesn't need him but most of the time is too nice a chap to let it show. Gavin's worried. He's done most of the right things so all he's got to do now is play safe and stay out of trouble. So nothing is ever old sloping-shoulders' fault.'

'What?'

Hadden balanced a digestive biscuit on the shoulder of his white coat, sat to attention, gave himself the order, 'Slo . . . ope shoulders,' and the biscuit fell to the floor and broke. 'Consultants are paid more so they have to catch the biscuit.'

'Mrs Noble again.'

'Sort of. But she's complicated. She could have happened to anyone.'

Campbell wondered how an omniscient independent tribunal would apportion blame for Mrs Noble between the consultant Lochhead, the senior registrar Laird and Hadden himself, who had opened her up in the first place. The concept of responsibility seemed rather abstract for the surgical mind: they appeared to prefer a system with an adequate provision of natural disasters.

At half past ten Campbell was summoned to Casualty again. His patient was in the resuscitation room, which was filled with nursing and medical staff. Most of the doctors were coloured and therefore specialist registrars of one sort and another: mainstream medicine and surgical specialities at the Institute were whites only. If the number and polychromaticism of her attendants were anything to go by, the patient must have quite a lot wrong with her.

An Indian lady with a sari under her white coat politely addressed Campbell. 'Doctor, are you the general surgeon?' He nodded and she smiled. 'Dr Chotahwallah from neurosurgery. I think this is your patient. She has facial injuries and has a knock on the head but her neurological state satisfies me. I have written, call us if more neurological opinion is required.'

Campbell thanked her and she left. The crowd round his patient opened and he could see that her top half was hidden by green towels. The duty anaesthetist, masked and gowned, was finishing off an emergency tracheostomy. A tall African with a gold and white smile told Campbell, 'She was in some kind of road traffic accident. I was asked to look at de chest. It's OK. Maybe a cracked rib on the right, but nothing to worry about from our point of view.' He too walked out.

'Her facial skeletal problems can wait,' said an Arab dentist whom the system graced with the title of duty oral surgeon, 'but I took the liberty of ensuring her airway with a tracheostomy. He is almost finished. We will come and see her in the morning. It is no trouble.'

A white man with an unseasonal tan was watching the departing specialists with some amusement. Campbell recognised him as an Australian from orthopaedics. He grinned. 'You gotta problem here, doc. It's yours all right, and her face is a bit of a mess too.' He switched from his own voice to comic stage Indian. 'But in my department of de long bones there are no acute problems of a traumatic variety whatsoever at all thank you doctor.' He laughed, not unkindly, and left.

The anaesthetist was taking off the green towels. The patient's face really was a mess. He looked up and said to Campbell, 'Bloody Arabs telling me my own job. Anyway, her airway's OK now. You can have her. Pressure's a bit down. Don't know what's doing it.' He picked up his emergency bag and strolled out, leaving a nurse to pack up his surgical tray. Campbell was now the only doctor in the room. He began to examine the patient, then the Casualty SHO, who must have convened the now dispersed galaxy of surgical talent, looked into the resuscitation room. 'Hello Campbell. So she was general surgical after all. Funny. You know I thought she was.'

Campbell finished examining the patient then rang up Hadden. He at least had some positive thoughts on her management. 'Well, if the United Nations Committee on Everything Else are sure it's for us we'd better have her. Take up the white man's burden, lad, and it sounds as if she needs a drip. That's general surgical too.'

A leisurely assessment of the patient up on the ward did little to advance the diagnosis. Hadden agreed with the houseman's findings that she was critically ill with a persistent low blood pressure and an abnormally silent abdomen. There were no clues other than the history of a road traffic accident and a small area of fabric pattern imprinted on the skin of her abdomen from her girdle. Both of these pointed to blunt violence and the possibility of internal injuries, the most likely being a ruptured liver or spleen. As either should have produced more obvious clinical signs Hadden decided to have her observed in the ward. Meanwhile they would open the theatre and operate on the perforated ulcer.

At midnight, since no new cases in Casualty awaited surgical attention, Gray invoked the terms of the houseman's agreement to catch up on sleep for his day off. As he went Campbell realised that without malice aforethought or uncomradely contrivance his co-resident had had a much quieter day and looked like having a better night as well. There would be other receiving nights.

On the way into theatre he had a shower which proved refreshing, as did the appearance of the night-theatre staff, a troupe of aseptic houris in thin blue pyjamas, one of whom Hadden chaffed gently as he operated. 'I see your eye make-up is shower-proof, Nurse Affleck. You should write up your method as a short communication to the *British Journal of Cosmetic Technology*. Or is it perhaps that you have contravened part three cap one para four of the Teateroberführer's standing orders in that you did knowingly and wilfully omit to have an adequate shower before joining us for this evening's little entertainment? How do you plead?' Giggles and blushes behind facemasks helped to pass the time.

Hadden cut down into the abdomen, tying off bleeding points, until the perforation was exposed to view, a neat punched-out hole a quarter of an inch across in the front of the duodenum, still leaking greenish beads of digestive juice. The houseman was invited to put two catgut stitches across the hole and draw them tight. The perforation winked shut.

'Tie it then. Left over right. One plain one purl and shout at your assistant for cutting the ends too short. That's it. Arise, sir surgeon. May I close the wound up for you, sir?'

Through Hadden's banter Campbell glimpsed something of what made surgeons do it. There had been a hole where there should not have been a hole. It had leaked and caused a lot of pain. If you closed the hole the leak stopped and the pain went away. And you did it with your own hands. He cut Hadden's stitches on the way back to the surface and did the skin sutures himself with slippy, looping black silk.

Registrar and houseman, still in theatre kit, went into the ward to review the accident victim. Her pulse rate had increased and her blood pressure had fallen and examination of her abdomen revealed no more than it had done before. Hadden went off to call the senior registrar. In the corridor a shabby little man was sitting with his cap in his hands. A nurse asked Campbell to see him.

'Good evening.'

'Good evening, doctor. Is my wife all right?'

'Mr . . .?'

'Foulis. They said my wife had got knocked down. When I came up to the Casualty they said she'd been brought up here.'

'Oh, yes.' Campbell sat down, more from fatigue than sympathy. 'We're looking after her. She's had a knock. Have you seen her?'

'No. The nurse said I had to see you first.'

'Yes. Well. She's had a knock on the face. It looks worse now than it will in a day or two.'

'Is she all right apart from that?'

'No. I mean not quite. We're a bit worried about her abdomen.'

'What, doctor?'

'She might have internal injuries.'

He twisted his cap in his hands as though trying to tear it in half. 'I see . . . I'm not keeping so well myself. Otherwise I wouldn't have sent her out.'

Hadden came out of the phone-booth. Campbell continued. 'She might need an operation. Just to see if she's injured inside.'

'Just round the corner,' said Mr Foulis.

'Have you seen the nurse about the permission slip for the operation?'

'Just a wee carry-out. Seein' it was Saturday. Thanks doctor. Can I see her?'

'She's had a fair knock on the face.'

'I still want to see her.'

'I'm just telling you so you won't get a fright. It'll look better soon.'

'Thanks, doctor.'

'The nurse might want you to sign a permission form. It's a formality.'

'Thanks doctor.'

Hadden reported Laird's views in Laird's voice. ' "Sounds as if she needs some fresh air let inside her. Just carry on and open her up and I'll be along shortly. Right paramedian. Cut confidently." '

In theatre again Hadden was less light-hearted: he cut through the abdominal wall in a long exploratory incision then checked the organs one by one, reaching round inside as Campbell retracted the edges of the wound. Liver and spleen were normal. There was no free blood or other fluid in the peritoneal space. Stomach and duodenum were normal and the whole of the intestine checked from end to end seemed intact. They waited for Mr Laird.

'How's your end?' Hadden asked the anaesthetist.

'Still quite pink.'

'What d'you mean still?'

'Well, her pressure's kind of low, and not going up.'

'You worried?'

'Be nice to know what's going on.'

'It would.'

Eventually Laird padded into theatre masked and gowned and Hadden told him what they'd done. He re-explored the abdomen with the registrar assisting and the houseman now redundant standing to one side. There was still no answer and Laird began to dither. The anaesthetist interrupted them. 'Hang on. There's some stuff coming up here out of her trachy wound. Looks like bile. She must have a leak somewhere and it's wandering up through her chest. Are you sure her duodenum's all right.'

'Ah,' said Mr Laird, 'a posterior duodenal rupture. I thought it might be. Who's on tonight? Mr Lochhead? Stick around, you chaps. I'll just give him a tinkle.' He took off his gloves and went to the phone then came back smiling enigmatically.

'Is he coming in?'

'And so he jolly well ought to,' said Mr Laird. 'It's tiger country in there at the back of the duodenum. People get into trouble. Pancreas and all that sort of thing to worry about. Chaps like us can offer our assistance and nothing more.' They waited in silence.

Mr Lochhead came in, tall and calm, and fresh as he was in the middle of the morning. He spent three hours working deep in the abdomen, dissecting the duodenum free from the neighbouring organs with patient skill to expose its posterior wall where they found, as the anaesthetist had predicted, a little tear leaking bile. Laird as first assistant held and cut with him and Hadden manipulated a suction probe to keep the field clear of blood and bile. Campbell, with a wound retractor, fought to keep awake: cramp, thirst, hunger and an inaccessible itch between his shoulders were added to the usual miseries of aseptic immobility. At half past three the prettiest of the theatre nurses brought them glasses of squash, slipping flexible straws behind their facemasks. Images of houris bearing sherbet to exhausted warriors in a Moslem paradise beset the houseman and tedium briefly gave way to lust, which theatre pyjamas and a thin green gown did little to conceal.

After hours without apparent progress the repair was suddenly complete. Morale surged as Lochhead asked for suture material to begin closing. He left two suction drains by the reconstituted duodenum and swiftly repaired the successive layers of the abdomen with his own deft, economical technique. They came out of theatre at half past five in the morning.

To Campbell's relief the patient was too ill to go back to the ward. Instead she went for mechanical ventilation in a special unit run by anaesthetists. It was one fewer critically ill patient to look after, and meant he had a chance to get to bed before morning. Her husband, still sitting half asleep in the corridor when she was wheeled past, did not notice and the houseman told him what had happened. He looked years older.

Campbell had been in bed for ten minutes when the switchboard rang.

'Doctor to speak to you, doctor.'

'Hello, doctor, Dr MacVittie of Tansey Street here. I've just been up to see one of my patients. A young man of twenty-three with a history of abdominal pain. About twelve hours and getting worse. He's quite tender at McBurney's point.'

Go on. Surprise me.

'I'm almost certain he's got appendicitis so I'd like to send him up to you. He'll be in in about half to three-quarters of an hour. Oh, and he's not the brightest . . . Nice lad though. I think you'll like him. Good night, doctor. Thank you. Good night.'

Good fucking morning. Campbell lay seething for forty minutes until Casualty phoned.

'You expecting an appendix?'

'Yes. From MacVittie in Tansey Street. Is there a letter?'

'No letter . . . but he says he's from Dr MacVittie.' The Casualty SHO lowered his voice. 'He's thick as they come.'

Campbell dressed and went down to Casualty. His patient, whose eyebrows met in the middle and proceeded together halfway down his nose, was co-operative but unhelpful.

'Dr MacVittie says I've got a pendy sytus.'

'Any pain?'

'Yes . . . It's sore.'

'Where?' He pointed to the right lower quadrant of his abdomen.

'How long?'

'Since my tea.'

'Been sick?'

'No, mister.'

'Feel sick?'

'No.'

'You sure your doctor didn't give you a letter?'

'No.'

'What?'

'He didnae, mister. He said just to come here.' Such an omission was a breach of basic medical protocol. Campbell wondered if perhaps the GP had also omitted to examine the patient. Full clinical assessments by telephone were not unknown.

'Did you phone your doctor or go to see him or what?'

'Went to see him.'

'Where?'

'In his garden.'

'What?'

'In his garden.'

'Did he examine you?'

'What?'

'Did he look at you?'

'Yes. I told you.'

'Where?'

'In his garden like I told you. He was in his house. At his bedroom window. Upstairs.'

'I see. How did he know what was wrong with you?'

'He says, Put your hand in your trouser pocket, Bobby, your right hand. So I did. Then he says press hard, Bobby. That's my name, see? Bobby. Is that sore? he says. It was quite sore, so he says, You've got appendicitis, Bobby. Away ye go up to the Institute.'

The nurses put him on a trolley and Campbell examined him. There was a minor abnormality.

'When did you last go to the toilet?'

'Pardon, mister?'

'When did your bowels last move?'

'What?'

132

'When did you last go for a shit?'

'Oh, about ten days ago, or a week maybe.'

A suppository confirmed the diagnosis and at the same time effected a spectacular cure. Bobby left the department puzzled but grateful. Campbell went upstairs to his ward in the grey early morning daylight. As he went in Sister said good morning and asked if he had forgotten to shave when he got up.

21

At no time on Sunday did Campbell get more than an hour to himself. Lochhead came in again and conducted a ward round that was early, swift and decisive. Ravelston Orr came in later in his morning suit, after the service at the High Kirk where he was an elder. He held court over coffee for three-quarters of an hour before going into the wards, where he was rude again to the breast cancer patient. She cried once more and he decided she was depressed. Neither Hadden nor the houseman, who had seen a lot more of her than their chief had, thought she was, if only because they were usually more polite, but the chief was adamant.

'Without in any way claiming psychiatric expertise I flatter myself in being able even as a simple surgeon to spot when one of my post-operative patients is having a particularly melancholy convalescence. So I want her seen by a psychiatrist.'

'Yessir.'

'And I don't want just any old psychiatrist. I don't know what it's like at the medical school now, but in my time those who saw psychiatry as their destiny were a lazy lot. Long on ideas but short on facts. The bottom half of the class. No. I want an honest-to-goodness psychiatrist who knows a bit about medicine and surgery as well. Ah yes. Old what's his name. Jewish chap. McSomething. McIsaac. Sound on depression. Yes, get McIsaac to see her first thing on Monday morning and you can tell me on the grand round what he thinks.'

'Yessir.'

'Good.' The chief swept out pausing only to stop momentarily outside Mrs Noble's side-room and screw up his nose.

'Who the hell's McIsaac?'

'Never heard of him,' said Hadden. 'We'd better ask one of the psychs. I'll do it now.' The registrar went off to ring someone from his year in the medical school, from the bottom half of the class.

Over the afternoon Mrs Noble's drip stopped twice and her veins became harder than ever to find. Throughout visiting time relatives queued for good news, bad news and comforting half-truths. One of the girls who had been admitted as a possible appendix and observed overnight with mysterious and inconclusive symptoms, confessed she was pregnant and became hysterical when informed that she could not have an abortion that day.

By nine o'clock on Sunday evening Campbell had been to bed five times and managed to get to sleep only once, and that for twenty minutes. He went round the patients of both wards in detail, trying to anticipate every preventable cause of trouble overnight, then phoned Alison and arranged to meet her on Monday evening, and went hopefully to bed.

'Dr Campbell, night nurse speaking. Mrs Noble's readings have been going off since about half past ten. Her pressure's down and her temp's up to forty-one. Would you come up and look at her?'

'Thank you, nurse.'

Mrs Noble rose horizontally from her bed with her arms folded across her chest, hovered for a moment then floated upright and soared out of the window. She was wearing a silver bikini that showed off her miraculously reconstructed abdomen to advantage and had shaken off the drip lines and ECG leads, the symbols of her mortality. She rose over the rooftops of the Institute and circled the clock tower, paused to make a gracious gesture of forgiveness to the dark windows of the operating theatre then disappeared into the night sky.

'Dr Campbell, night nurse here again. We phoned you about ten minutes ago about Mrs Noble. Are you coming up?'

'Thank you, nurse. I'll be right up. What time is it?'

'Just gone eleven.'

'Thanks.'

Mrs Noble, flushed and bright-eyed, was plucking at the bruised purple edges of her wound. The first-year nurse who was specialling her was upset, and got more upset when Campbell asked her to tie her patient's hands to the cot sides of the bed. He checked the readings and took two samples of blood for bacteriology then tried to examine Mrs Noble's chest. The dapper clinicians whose line drawings in textbooks showed you the proper Edinburgh way of doing it had not foreseen problems like these: basically, if you rolled her over or sat her up, her insides began to fall out.

He rang Hadden, who woke slowly. 'Well, she's got a septicaemia, hasn't she? If she doesn't die of this one she'll die of the next.'

'Is that how we're playing it?'

'What's she on?'

'Ampicillin. Tons of it.'

'And she's had lots of others.'

'Most things. Except gentamicin and carbenicillin.'

'Let's hang on with those in case things get worse. Cool her down.'

'Tepid sponging?'

'Yes. Keeps Nurse busy and happy. And cools the patient. Have we got an electric fan?'

'I think so.'

'And speed up her drip. Having got her this far we can hardly let her die of thirst. Ring me in two hours and tell me how it's going.'

'Right. Thanks.'

'Oh, and ring Big John Lochhead and let him know what you're doing to his patients. Good night. And Happy Advent.'

'What?'

'Christmas is coming. . . . So beware.'

Campbell laughed and put the phone down.

The nurse rang again at half past one. 'Her temp's down to thirty-eight and she's not half so daft. We've untied her and she wants her husband.'

'What do you think?'

'Getting him in?'

'Yes.'

'Well, the night super thinks it might be a good idea.'

'So tonight's the night.'

'She thinks it might be.'

'Get him in then. Good night, gorgeous.'

'Oh . . . Dr Campbell . . .'

'What?'

'One of her drips has stopped again.'

'OK, ugly. I'll be right up.'

Putting another drip up took half an hour. When Campbell emerged Mr Noble was waiting outside. 'Is it serious, doctor?'

'I'm afraid so.'

'What's wrong with her?'

'Well, it's a form of blood-poisoning.'

'Oh, I see. The badness going through the system.'

'Sort of.'

'Doctor, man to man, is she going to make it?'

135

'We're very concerned about her. We're doing our best.'

'I'm sure you are. You know, I thought you were worried even last week.'

'We were.'

'Can I wait here after I've been in to see her?'

'By all means. They'll probably give you tea as well.'

Campbell rang Hadden. That crisis was over.

At half past three the night nurse, near panic, rang his room again. 'There's an awful lot of what looks like blood coming out in her abdominal suction.'

'Mix some plasma. Quickly. Put it up on her right-hand drip instead of the saline and run it in fast.'

'It'll need to be written up. Night sister says . . .'

'I'm coming.'

He dressed as quickly as he had ever done and ran upstairs. The night sister was there and even the night superintendent had got there before him. Perhaps she had been called earlier. Mrs Noble was pale, quiet and sweating. In the bottles by the suction pump under her bed was a pint or more of blood. The night sister was holding one unit of reconstituted plasma.

'Just sign here, doctor, and we can get it up.'

'Thanks. Go and ring Dr. Hadden. Four two nine six one six eight. Ask him to come in straight away. And get a porter to take blood down to BTS.'

'All right, Dr Campbell, no need to shout.'

He drew blood for cross-matching and ran in the plasma as fast as it would go, filled up the request form for the blood transfusion service, checked the patient's pulse and blood pressure, then went and rang Mr Lochhead. Mr Noble, sitting in the corridor, was rightly suspicious of the flurry of activity round his wife's side-room.

The consultant got to the ward before Hadden did. From the immaculate gloss on his shoes Campbell concluded that he must polish them the night before in case of emergencies such as this. He thanked the houseman for calling him in, thanked the night sister and the superintendent and indicated that the ward staff could cope, made his own assessment of the patient and then spoke to her husband.

Hadden arrived as Lochhead and Campbell were going into the duty room: he joined the little council of war. The consultant was as calm as ever.

'We'll get a couple of pints into her then take her to the theatre.' He sounded as if he were planning a social evening with an old girlfriend. 'Not happy, David? Well I'll do the operation and you can doze over a retractor. No, no. You can't let people bleed to death in a surgical ward. It's messy and it's bad for morale. Shall we say quarter to five?'

They had tea and toast and talked of other things until the patient and theatre were ready. Mrs Noble died under the anaesthetic and no attempt was made to resuscitate her. Afterwards Mr Lochhead spent half an hour with the husband. Campbell shaved, had breakfast and went on the ward again for his morning blood round.

The early duty nurses were bustling all over the ward. An impression in Campbell's mind that they had been there since Saturday morning collapsed in resentment when he realised that they had a full two nights to rest and were the seventh shift of nurses in a fifty-hour period in which he had had at most three hours sleep. Not that thinking about it helped: in his current state blood sampling was difficult enough without mental arithmetic. He finished his round too late for the regular laboratory collection and had to send his senior student down with the specimens, reminding him to hurry back for the grand round. The junior staff was gathering already.

By ten to ten it was beginning to look as if the grand round might turn out to be less grand than had originally been intended. Mr Laird phoned in to say that he had 'flu and could not make himself responsible for an outbreak among the staff of the unit. Mr Cairns, the junior consultant, also rang in to say he too had 'flu, though in the light of his previous statements on the grand round his indisposition was more likely to be diplomatic. With five minutes to go the group waiting in the duty room of the male ward consisted of Mr Lochhead, Hadden, the SHO, a research fellow of Ravelston Orr's whom Campbell had never seen before, the two housemen and the students attached to the wards. All those present could have been more usefully employed elsewhere: Mr Lochhead's theatre list had been delayed two hours for the round; Hadden could have been in theatre assisting him; both housemen had enough routine work to keep them going all day and one of the medical students pointed out that but for this ritual he would have been watching the climax of a space drama, broadcast live from the moon, on their common-room television.

As they waited Campbell consoled himself with a comforting metaphor from a tuneful, rather bloody war film he had seen a few weeks before: he was a First World War infantry officer on the western front, shell-shocked and muddied after a forty-eight-hour bombardment. On the third day at dawn they were to be called back to a safe area, where a glittering dyspeptic general, played by Alester Ravelston Orr, would come clinking up from his chateau on a charger to damn or praise the efforts of the sector, depending on the state of his digestion. Campbell was half asleep and the images flowed as freely as dreams: Hadden the cynical veteran at twenty-eight; Lochhead a fatherly and diplomatic company commander; himself a sulbaltern – doomed youth getting on with the shapeless, horrifying tasks of war. Patients, depending on how you looked at them, were either own troops, to be cared for unsparingly, or an invading horde blindly assaulting what might otherwise be a tidy and fairly habitable bit of trench.

The noise of the ward's outer doors crashing together jerked the houseman back from Flanders, and the group as a whole fell silent.

Hadden, close at hand, muttered, 'Bandmaster, "Hail to the Chief!" ' The students snorted and Lochhead chided them gently. 'Not to be snide about Chiefy. Time enough for levity when this is all over.'

When this bloody war is over, thought Campbell, half-way back to France again. The inner doors swung open and an auxiliary carrying disposable urine bottles and picking her nose with her free hand strolled past the door of the duty room.

'False alarm, chaps,' said Lochhead. They stood for ten minutes. Campbell resolved that if ever by any chance he became a chief he would be punctual on such occasions: every minute's delay was a millenium in the purgatory of unanimous resentment generated. They talked and some sat down. Campbell didn't: had he done so he would have fallen instantly asleep.

By half past ten even Lochhead, that most fatherly and diplomatic of field officers, was having trouble maintaining morale in his sector. The student who had intended to watch the space programme became more vociferous as time for the touchdown approached. Gray confessed an interest in the moon-landing which drew from Lochhead an elaborate pun about the houseman's intended career in lunacy. At twenty to eleven the grand round was officially despaired of and Lochhead, who had trained at the Institute, pointed out that if the housemen invited those present down to the Residency they could use the time allotted to the grand round for pleasure and instruction in the television lounge instead. So they adjourned.

In the Residency Lochhead became quite affable: for a consultant at the Institute, almost frolicsome. Perhaps it was the effect of returning to youthful haunts, or a by-product of finally getting Mrs Noble off the books, or simply that his views on the chief's latest whim, though never stated, coincided with everyone else's. He settled in the lounge with the remnants of the grand round and chatted happily while Gray went to the servery to organise some coffee.

A commentator with gigantic glasses explained something that was perfectly obvious from the previous direct coverage. One of the students laboured to jest of green cheese. The moon grew larger on the screen and Campbell dozed off for a few minutes. He woke to find that he had missed the touchdown and his coffee was cold. The commentator floundered in new depths of bathos and Mr Lochhead got up from his chair. A sudden clammy feeling, that they had all been playing truant, and taken a teacher along with them, descended. The TV was switched off. In the corner beside Campbell the telephone rang and he answered it. It was the sister on the male ward: a coarse and unprepossessing woman. She sounded angry.

'So that's where you are. My, you're all for it. "I demand explanations or resignations," is what he said. D'you know Mr Ravelston Orr was on the ward half an hour waiting for you lot?'

'Did you try bleeping us?'

'Do you think I'm daft, Dr Campbell? We bleeped both of you, both ordinary and cardiac arrest, at least five times. The exchange must think we've got Jack the Ripper up here.'

'Well, we've both got our bleeps. Is the chief still on the unit?'

'No, He's gone off to a nursing home to see some private patients now. He's left a telephone number. He says he's no stranger to clinical responsibility and he's to be called for any emergency whatsoever.' The idea of Ravelston Orr being called from half-way across town to a cardiac arrest was beyond ridicule. He would be twenty minutes too late to save the patient and at least as many years behind in his resuscitation technique. 'But if he is called both you housemen are to consider yourselves sacked. He's dictated a letter for you about that. I suppose the whole lot of you are down in that television lounge, watching television.'

'We're just coming up.'

'If you're lucky I'll keep the emergencies till you get here.'

Numbers dwindled as the group proceeded through the corridors and back to the wards. The students went off to their common room for more coffee, Hadden to the out-patient department to check the unit's appointments, the research man back to his cancerous white mice and even Lochhead, remembering an overdue consultation on the medical side, left them to it. The housemen ascended the last flight of stairs alone.

'It might be a blessing in disguise,' said Gray. 'There must be easier ways of getting some registrable surgical experience.'

Campbell worried about the possible effects of this incident on his career prospects, if any. Hadden had said, 'If you step out of line just once, they've got you by the testimonials.'

'Sometimes I feel sorry for him,' said Gray. There was no need to ask who he meant, but it was a very oblique, psychiatric way of looking at their predicament.

'How d'you mean?'

'He probably forgot all about it, or got the time wrong. He couldn't admit to a thing like that though.'

'Maybe.'

'That would tend to tip the diagnosis towards dementia.'

'What?'

'Senile dementia. Rather than depression. Ravelston Orr.'

'Oh, I see.'

Back in his ward Campbell tried to pick up the broken threads of the morning's work. The nursing staff looked at him with awe and pity, as though Ravelston Orr might at any moment come charging down the ward, rip his houseman's white coat from his shoulders, ceremonially re-possess his bleep and trample his stethoscope underfoot. He began to wonder if even the patients knew about his fall from grace: Mrs Munro seemed very concerned about his welfare when he went to look at her mastectomy wound.

By half past twelve it was clear that Mr Lochhead had been working quietly behind the scenes to sort out the mess: he found Campbell and Hadden in the duty room and explained what had happened. One of the aerials transmitting the signal for the bleep system had been out of action all morning, and a phone call to Ravelston Orr's secretary over in his research laboratories confirmed that he had been under the impression that the grand round was to start at ten-thirty, not ten as had been arranged. So responsibility was shared between blind fate and an old man's memory, but there lingered for the housemen the thought that they had been where they should not have been, and had done what they should not have done.

It appeared that Mr Lochhead's explanation to the chief had been fairly detailed too, for soon afterwards they heard Ravelston Orr's voice in the ward secretary's office, booming out a letter to the Board of Governors.

' "The requirements for communication between doctors are modest a comma but their reliability is essential to the care of patients full stop new sentence. In an age which has witnessed perfect and instantaneous communication between the moon and places as remote as Texas a comma it seems to me extraordinary that a hospital such as the Institute can fail to provide . . ." '

One problem only remained, and Campbell had completely forgotten about it. Mr Ravelston Orr finished his letter and came into the duty room to remind him.

'Dr Campbell, what were Dr McIsaac's views on that unfortunate depressive post-operative breast of mine . . . Mrs Whatsername . . . Or was it Miss?'

'Pardon, sir?'

'You may recall, Dr Campbell, when you have completely returned from your lunar perambulation, that I requested that you arrange a consultation. A simple matter of obtaining a psychiatric opinion. I take it you can use the telephone, or even write a letter if need be.'

Campbell was trying to speak but the chief struck up again. 'An emergency is no less an emergency for being psychiatric. Particularly a melancholia. After all the poor woman may do herself some injury.'

Campbell tried again to admit that he had forgotten all about it, but Hadden stepped in. 'I rang up the department, sir, and was told that Dr McIsaac went to Australia as a professor ten years ago . . .'

The chief was only briefly nonplussed. 'I am delighted to hear that common-sense is no bar to advancement in the specialty . . . In the Antipodes at any rate, if not nearer home, eh? eh?'

Hadden waited politely and continued. 'And eight years ago he committed suicide.'

'Good Lord! Did he? Old Rube? . . . Amazing . . .'

'Would you like some other psychiatrist to see the depressed lady, sir?'

22

Campbell had arranged to pick Alison up from her flat at half past seven. Before leaving the Institute he spent half and hour in a bath trying to convince himself it would be as beneficial as two hours' sleep. The symptoms of fatigue were now becoming a little alarming. In the early evening he had rung the exchange convinced that his bleep had gone off, to be told quite curtly that it hadn't. In the bath he wandered on the slightly delusional frontier of drowsing and waking at which the Institute's bathroom furnishings assumed a threatening aspect: a Shanks' Patent Hygeia Fountain 1898 Cistern, seven feet up on the wall, wavered menacingly and the Barrhead Sanitas Major pedestal beneath gaped with its wooden O poised like a trap for the unwary. When he concentrated things became normal again and a walk round the Institute's three car parks helped some more.

On the way down he drove carefully. Fortunately the laws which compelled proper rest for public transport and long distance lorry drivers did not apply to private motorists. Anticipating difficulty he had booked a table at a restaurant within walking distance from her address. Traffic seemed awkward and he chalked up a near-miss on a zebra crossing.

She lived in a grey Georgian crescent in the New Town: poetry must have paid around the turn of the century. He rang the bell on the biggest door he had ever encountered socially and after a delay Alison appeared, pink and furtive in a dressing gown. Campbell slid round the edge of the great grey door into a hall which receded yards and yards into the house and would have done for a burgh museum: walls and tables were covered with pictures, statuary and miscellaneous darkly

141

gleaming objects. Campbell, who regarded all antiques with ignorant reverence, was impressed. Alison noticed.

'It's a bit fearsome, isn't it? I can't think what to do with it.' Slender and barefoot and strangely incongruous in her own home she seemed to Campbell more desirable than ever before. For a tired mad moment he actually wondered if she had planned something wild before dinner, but had dismissed the thought even before she explained, 'Sorry to be like this. I was kept ages late at work. I really would have been ready otherwise.'

'Don't apologise. I'm a bit early.'

'I'll get you a drink. Come in here.'

Victorian Oil Landscapes and Edinburgh Interior *c.* 1912. The museum spread on through the house. Stags glowered mistily from mountains in paintings that looked as if they had been varnished with gravy. From the depths of a mahogany sideboard, possibly Edwardian, she produced contemporary drinks.

'What would you like? I've got most things.'

'Gin and tonic?'

'Yes.'

'Thanks.'

'Please sit down.'

She brought his drink over, leaning forward to give it to him. He reached for the glass without looking at it and she put up her hand to hold her dressing gown, then laughed and said, 'I'm just going upstairs to slip into something less comfortable. Won't be a minute.'

The sofa was a huge billowing affair covered in mushroom coloured velvety stuff. Campbell sat back with his drink and took in his surroundings. This room was less cluttered than the hall but straight away he noted in addition to the gloomy Highland scenes, some oriental brass and ivory, ebony bookends, possibly African, weapons various to be swung or thrown arranged in a quaint lethal fan on the wall, and a bookcase solid with the proceedings of learned societies. If the collection here and in the hall was of any biographical significance the poet must have led an active life.

There were very few traces of female occupancy. Very few, considering that only she lived here. One magazine in a heap on the lower deck of a bamboo occasional table gave her away. *Vogue.* Also present were *Field, Punch, Country Life* and the *Spectator.* He finished his drink, picked up the *Spectator* and lay back to read it.

Alison's voice woke him. He shook his head fiercely and said, 'Sorry. Dozed off. Let's go.' She was smiling.

He sat up and looked around. In her hands there was a tray with two cups of coffee and two glasses of orange juice. The curtains were open and grey daylight filled the room. Someone had covered him up with a dark green rug.

'Bloody hell. What time is it?'

Alison laughed. 'About twenty to eight. I didn't know when you have to be up there in the mornings, so I woke you early.'

'Gosh, I'm sorry.'

'It's all right. Quite amusing even. Now I almost believe your hard luck stories . . .'

'What did you do all evening?'

'Sat here reading for a while and went to bed early. I thought of cooking for us but you looked so happy just lying there snoring.'

'Snoring? I don't do I?'

'Not unpleasantly.'

'Gosh, I'm sorry.'

'Don't worry. It's all right. What would you like for breakfast?'

'Anything.'

'Scrambled eggs?'

'Lovely.'

They breakfasted together in a thoroughly modern kitchen. At half past eight they said goodbye behind the grey door.

'Won't your neighbours think things?'

'Oh no. They're sweet. All about ninety-five and terribly broad-minded. If they see you they'll make all sorts of wrong assumptions and probably approve.'

Campbell made a lecherous growling sound.

'Down boy,' said Alison.

'I feel as if I ought to have a bowler hat and a rolled umbrella and the *Times* under my arm.'

She pecked his cheek. 'Have a good day at the office, dear . . . You're all bristly.'

'If I'd known we were going to do this I'd have brought my shaving kit. Listen . . . I still feel awful about last night. Would you like to come out and eat somewhere on Wednesday to make up for it?'

'We could try.'

'I'll phone you.'

'Bye.'

'Bye.'

23

In one aspect of housemanship Campbell excelled: he knew far more than any of his contemporaries about the Second World War. While this conveyed no particular advantage in the day-to-day care of patients, it was of immense value in dealings with senior consultants, most of whom had served in the happy band of medical officers. To hear them talk it was as though, for the survivors at least, Hitler had offered life instead of mere existence. They had ranged over oceans, jungles and deserts, collecting medal ribbons and anecdotes, esteemed by their non-medical colleagues and running among themselves a genially masonic system of professional self-interest. They had enjoyed it and the vast majority of them still enjoyed talking about it. Scratch a miserable old consultant, Campbell often thought, and you will find the ruins of a happy young major.

He had stumbled upon this as a student and had made something of a speciality of it over the last few years, acquiring lore and jargon without any particular effort and reading with genuine interest a selection of the deluge of books on the subject. Like all specialities it showed a tendency to divide into subspecialities and at the changeover from medicine to surgery Campbell found himself inconvenienced by this. His medical job had been fought East of Suez: with Creech he had toured Burma and the Malay peninsula and even on occasions ventured as far as the fleshpots of Singapore. Slim, Wingate and Giffard had been his idols and the Forgotten Fourteenth his vicarious comrades-in-arms. A discreet display of knowledge about the triumph at Imphal had averted the revelation of his ignorance of iron-deficiency anaemia, and even Bertram, who rarely missed a trick in the business of handling his superiors, stood in envy of Campbell's grasp of these crucial inessentials of the consultant mentality.

The change to surgery and the Western Desert called for some homework: at his bedside these days lay a well-reviewed paperback history of the campaign and an obscure out-of-print hardback called *With Sword and Scalpel in the Sands* by a contemporary of Ravelston Orr's and mentioned by Lochhead as the chief's favourite reading.

Such preparation for survival in theatre with Ravelston Orr was not excessive. He was proverbially overbearing and as part of his memorable style cultivated idiosyncrasies and tantrums few could withstand. One resident in the early sixties had shown more spirit than most, asking the famous Mr Ravelston Orr, 'How would you like your stitches cut today, sir? Too long or too short?' He was now believed to be practising dermatology near Wigan.

So Campbell approached his first morning in theatre with his chief in a state of watchful preparedness. His unexpected night out had precluded a revision of the fall of Tobruk, after which Ravelston Orr had been captured, but otherwise he felt quietly confident that he could cope.

Theatre opened at nine and Campbell assisted the senior registrar in a couple of minor operations. At half past the chief's secretary rang to say that he had left his office. Yellow alert. Shortly afterwards the theatre orderly posted near the door by Sister spotted him going into the changing room. Up to red. At twenty to ten there was a sound of puffing and heavy rubber footsteps in the sterile corridor and the surgeon and scientist showed himself to his acolytes.

When the chief scrubbed the theatre sister supervised the ceremony personally as only she understood the list of twenty-one nevers and twenty-seven alwayses that had accumulated round it over the years. A student nurse who had presumed once to do it in accordance with the theatre supervisor's handbook had required to rest in the nurses' sick bay for eight hours after the experience.

This morning the chief was happy. What chance of traffic, morning mail or the breakfast menu had precipitated it no one knew, but all present basked in the benign rays of his good cheer. He reassured the patient, joked with the anaesthetist when he had put her under, bade a cheerful good morning to his senior registrar and even remembered without prompting the houseman's name.

'Ah, Campbell, so we are to operate together this morning. Pleasant to see a new face among one's little band of colleagues. Perhaps Mr Laird has told you: we like things done here in certain ways that we have found most convenient over the years.'

Rage, violence and abuse. Weeping nurses and ejected students. Thrown instruments and cut fingers. Endless correspondences with the dean and the matron.

'Yessir. I've heard. I mean I've been told.'

'Good. Well, I'm sure we'll get on splendidly. I see our anaesthetist colleague has Mrs Rintoul quite ready.'

The patient was a woman in her fifties who had begun to experience pain in her left calf when walking. X-ray examination of her arteries by radio-opaque infusion had shown a short blockage of the artery in the thigh. Mr Ravelston Orr had deliberated upon the case and deemed it suitable for surgery: the blockage could be cleared, or by-passed by a graft, and circulation to the calf improved.

As he began the chief showed signs of tetchiness over the positioning of the patient's leg. 'Just a leetle more abduction. A leetle-leetle-leetle more. Too much! Back a leetle. Stop! Well. That *might* do.' His assistants glanced round amongst themselves: was this the end of happiness? The chief whistled breathily and tunelessly as he mopped the skin on the operating field. Green towels flew around for a moment, clips snapped on and all was ready for the first cut. Blood ran and Mr Laird dabbed at it. Mr Ravelston Orr suddenly remarked, 'I enjoy thighs.'

Like the Polynesian cannibals? Or as opposed to being a tit-man,

145

Campbell wondered. The chief went on, as if someone had asked, 'And would you be so kind, Mr Ravelston Orr, as to explain this preference?'

'The anatomy is so elegant . . .' He interrupted himself as though the invisible interviewer had ventured to smile. 'I refer to the deep anatomy of course. There is a grand sweep about the musculature. . . . The tissue planes intersect with such subtlety. . . . Ah, sartorius. The tailor's friend.' The audience relaxed and the phantom interlocutor got little opportunity to speak. 'And Hunter's canal, whereby the artery sidles out of harm's way. So that we may sit on our bottoms and kneel on our knees without getting cramp in our toes. Wonderful how the blood supply avoids the extensor aspects. A principle of anatomy, eh, Campbell?'

'Yessir.' This was getting dangerous. He would be asking about the deep relations of the popliteal artery next. Campbell, whose last acquaintance in depth with the thigh was five years previously when it had been dead and drenched in formalin, had cause for anxiety.

'Oh, I do enjoy the thigh,' mused the chief. 'Always have done. Even though I was in a South African Rifleman's thigh – retract Gavin. Just a bit farther. Thank you – trying to separate the femoral artery from the shrapnel when Tobruk fell.'

Campbell felt now as he had once felt as a student, turning over an exam paper and finding a question everyone had said would come up and which he, out of negligence or nonconformism, had omitted to revise. And in this particular examination there was no room for manoeuvre. The assumed silent question was being answered already.

'June forty-two. A balls-up. An utter bloody balls-up.' Strange, people who otherwise rarely swore made an exception for their military reminiscences. The phantom questioner had speeded up. 'All Ritchie's fault. The Springboks could have held on for weeks in Tobruk. Thank you, Gavin, Cut there. Thank you. There was a perfectly good line of defence – Not that, Gavin. That – from Acroma to Bir el Gubi. Running through a little place near us . . . El something.'

All this one-sided conversation was a bit eccentric: Campbell decided to take a chance. 'El Adem, sir?'

'Yes, El Adem. But bloody Ritchie in his infinite wisdom. . . . But wait a minute. My dear boy, how pleasant to meet a houseman who's read something other than an anatomy book. D'you read much?'

'A bit, sir. An interesting . . .'

'Fascinating. But Ritchie said no go and half the brass believed him. And that was where the rot set in at Tobruk. Thank you, Gavin. Mop there. Thank you. "For if the trumpet give forth an uncertain sound . . ."' Cut, thank you. Poor Ritchie never really had a chance. Shouldn't have been left with it. It was like putting a chap who's been a bad senior registrar in charge of a unit after making him a consultant too early in the first place.' That might have been a barb directed at Gavin, or perhaps just an exceptionally thoughtless analogy. 'So for reasons unknown even to the official historians we were packed off to Sidi something on the other side of Piccadilly, as our London-obsessed betters used to call it. Thank you, Gavin.'

'Don't you mean Knightsbridge, sir?'

Ravelston Orr laid down his scalpel. Under the mask his jaw jutted forward. His eyes narrowed. Sister snatched a handful of loose instruments from the green towelling and Laird stepped back six inches rather slowly and averted his eyes.

There was a short silence in which the chief's eyes softened and a faraway look came into them. He chuckled then laughed more and more loudly all by himself amid his silent wondering audience.

'Fancy that . . .' he managed between bursts of horribly braying. 'Fancy my own houseman correcting me in my memoirs . . . You're perfectly right, dear boy. Knightsbridge it was. London-obsessed oafs. And the other place was Sidi Mufti. It all comes back.'

It did. How it did. They rumbled through dust and gunfire all the way down to quite a passable and not too bloody exposure of the femoral artery and its branches. 'Ah. There we are. Profunda in all its glory. So with half of A squadron brewed up and B pinned in a wadi and the command in pieces – Thank you, Gavin – we fell back on Bir Lefa and then . . .'

'Sir.' One of the theatre nurses interrupted with suitable deference, 'A phone call for you sir. From your secretary's office. She says it's quite urgent.'

The chief laid down his knife and with gloved hands raised up before him followed the nurse into the ante-room like a short but high-powered ecclesiastical procession. Mr Ravelston Orr's telephone nurse too had her routine worked out over the years.

He returned visibly annoyed. 'Urgent be blowed! Idiotic London-based committees. Where were we?'

'Bir Lefa,' and 'Branches of the profunda,' said Campbell and Laird simultaneously.

'London . . . Urgent . . . Ugh. I'll give 'em urgency the next time I'm down there. What's that, Campbell?' He was pointing to something that looked like the leftovers from a cheap cut of liver.

'Profunda, sir?'

'Profunda?' Millimetre by millimetre the jaw was coming forward again.

'It's the lateral circumflex artery, doctor, that's what it is.' The eyes were slitting down too. 'Would you kindly name for me the branches of the lateral circumflex artery?'

Five years ago most arteries tended to have superficial and deep branches. It seemed a safe generality to risk. Campbell coughed and

147

began with some confidence. 'Well sir, there's the superficial branch of the lateral circumflex artery . . .'

'Go on.'

'And there's the deep branch which arises from the lateral circumflex artery . . .'

The eyes were now very narrow indeed and the jaw jutted half-way across the table. Sister had cleared away all loose objects within reach.

'Rubbish! Sheer unadulterated eyewash! You say you qualified last summer? I don't know how you crept through the net of 2nd MB. D'you hear that, Gavin? D'you see what they're sending us as housemen? I despair.' His gesture of despair brought a scalpel within an inch of his senior registrar's ear. Laird retreated still farther and the chief paused to draw breath. He spoke again, not shouting but in the measured tones of a reasonable man. 'My secretary keeps a store of useful books for occasions such as this, one of which, by Dr Jamieson, contains a good account of the anatomy you have been attempting so feebly to discuss.' He paused again then bellowed, 'Get out! Get out and read it! And read it till you know it! And when I finish here you will know, draw and describe for me every branch of every artery from the navel to the knee.'

With his peroration still echoing round the theatre he dropped his voice to a near whisper and said pityingly, 'I use the lay terms advisedly, out of consideration for your present state of ignorance.'

Campbell took off his gloves and his green gown and stole out of theatre to the sound of the senior student's voice reciting in order and in commendable detail the branches of the lateral circumflex artery.

24

Lunch in the Residency was as always crowded, the food as usual was bad but Campbell went into the dining room anyway, as did most residents, because meals were sociable, and a chance to sit down away from the ward with a clear conscience. There was a place free beside Mac, who was now houseman in the thoracic surgery unit. He was happy in his work. 'It's all right I suppose. Fifteen men on a dead man's chest, yo ho ho and a bottle of whisky from the cremation money. So I can't complain. All part of the rich tapestry. And the theatre staff really are quite something. All that death makes them sex-mad.' Mac's social life altered between active phases where he went out of his way hunting round the Institute and passive ones where he just amused himself with whatever the lottery of nursing organisation happened to send along to where he was working at the time. He was in the passive phase, contentedly. 'And how's the bold Ravelston Orr?'

'He has his moments.'

'I suppose you count your fingers every time you've been into theatre with him.'

'It's not as bad as that. Not quite.'

'They say he's mellowed.'

'Everybody says that. I don't know though. He was pretty fierce this morning.'

'Hardly fair. Hitting a man when he's down.'

'What do you mean?'

'You know. Tired. Come on, don't be shy. Living it up these days, aren't you?'

'Me?'

'I did just happen to notice last night that your car wasn't in the car park. Three this morning.'

'Did you?'

'Come on. Who's the lucky girl then? Have you finally got into old bigears.'

'Who?'

'Staffs in your ward. Got big ears and short legs. I heard from somewhere that she's yours for the asking.'

'Thank you kindly. I can't say I know who you mean.'

'The only thing that stands out about her is her ears. And her boobs.'

'Well, I'll leave her to you, if she'll have you. I'm going off the big Institute scene.'

'Come on. It's part of the deal. The work's hard and the pay's lousy, so you have to take what's going. Perks of the job. Staff nurse on your own ward? She's in lieu of social disabilities incurred as a result of having to work one night in two. And if she doesn't like the idea she can always say no.'

Though Campbell wouldn't have put it so strongly, it was more or less true. Healthy young human animals of both sexes, many of them single, were thrown together at all hours of the day and night. It was hardly surprising that romances, affairs and sundry more transient liaisons resulted. Mac got going. 'They've got us cold on poverty and obedience. Thank God there's still room for a little discretion on the question of chastity. So gather ye rosebuds while ye may.'

'Well, I'm beginning to think it's bad for people.'

'Because of something that happened last night?'

'No. That was nothing to do with this place.'

'Oh. Going extra-mural are we?'

'Yes.'

Bouncing Mac, Grand Hero of the Order of the Bedspring, who

149

kissed and fucked and told and asked. How would he cope with the end of housemanship, when another generation of residents clocked in at the rosebud factory? General practice in the shires of Scotland was not yet ready for his way of life. Campbell changed the subject.

'Have you got a job for June?'

'I think the best people are going to be unemployed.'

'Two of us anyway. Have you really nothing lined up?'

'Not a nibble. I would quite like to do an obstetrics residency at the Haig Memorial Pavilion, just to stay around the scene. Twelve months at HMP would do wonders for my social life. All those Irish pupil midwives straight out of convents at the Infirmary of Our Lady of the Bleeding Sorrows County Monaghan or wherever and raring to go. Trouble is the jobs there have all been booked for months, but if one of the lucky sods who's got one drops dead from over-exertion in the first week I'll be free to step in at a moment's notice.'

Poor Mac. What would Gray make of him? A minimally socialised psychopath with features of compulsive promiscuity related to early weaning. Something like that. He was always on about tits.

'I don't know. I used to think I wanted to be a great teaching hospital physician but I'm going off the idea. It makes as much sense as a duckling wanting to be Konrad Lorenz.'

'Who?'

'Ethology chap. Hand-reared chooks follow him around. Simple psychology for medical students?'

'Oh, him. Yes. I see what you mean. In second year I wanted to be a great anatomist. Then in third year the scales dropped from my eyes and I realised that physiology was the only possible career for a thinking man. Pathology took me over in fourth, then obstetrics in fifth. Asking ladies to lie down and open their legs all day. It's funny though, I still fancy obstetrics.'

'So you were saying.'

'So maybe obstetrics in the periphery. Down in the jungle with dark proud mysterious registrars.' He beat a tom-tom rhythm on the edge of the table and John, the steward, rushed up with a plate of soup.

25

Late on Wednesday evening Campbell was lying on the mushroom-coloured sofa again. This time his head was comfortable in Alison's lap.

'You've got lovely breasts.'

'Go on. You just say that to all your women.'

'No, really. They're lovely. Haven't dozens of chaps told you?'

She tweaked his ear and made a frowning schoolmarmy face down at him, incongruous over her naked breasts.

'They're so lovely it's hard to decide which I prefer.'

'Gerroff.'

'That's better. Symmetrically erect. Orllpresentandcorrect.'

'I prefer the right one,' said Alison.

'What?'

'It started first.'

'Really?'

'About three weeks before the other one.'

'What . . .? Oh. Ages ago.'

'Well, when I was twelve. And the left one never really caught up. It's still a teeny bit smaller.'

'Come down here. From down here they both look lovely. No, maybe you're right. The right one billows out just a leetle-leetle-leetle bit more. Close haul the starboard bosom, mister bosun. Look to it smartly, I say, or ye'll be all night up there, ye blackguards.' Campbell shifted his head slightly and looked from one to the other in supine deliberation. Decisions, decisions.

'You look as if you're watching tennis.' She giggled and ruffled his hair. They were both quiet and a little arpeggio, starting as a tinkle and ending like the sound of a distant motor cycle, came from inside her. Campbell listened thoughtfully and then said, 'Normal sounds. Not obstructed. All quite physiological. I declare this abdomen MOT"d till 1st April.'

She pummelled his chest with a fist. 'You're dreadful. Did medicine make you dreadful or did you start off like that?'

'Medicine made me dreadfuller. I owe it all to the long-suffering taxpayer.'

'I pay tax.'

'Thank you.'

She sat stroking his cheek and Campbell lay thinking that if this was what the psychologists meant by infantilisation then there was a lot to be said for it in its place. Suddenly in a small distant voice she said, 'Let's go somewhere more comfortable.'

Campbell was shocked: convention dictated that such decisions were reached via a fixed succession of events, a pattern of usually wordless pressures and retreats culminating in the inevitable made explicit. It was most unusual just to blurt it out like this, over the soup, as it were.

'Mmmmm,' he said.

'I mean bed.'

That was what he had thought she meant: the use of the word like that shocked him a little more. Realising that any delay on his part would be a monstrous insult but not wishing to abandon all pretence of the customary male initiative Campbell first sat up, kissing her cheek as it passed, then knelt on the floor in front of her with his hands on her waist. She leant forward and kissed his forehead and they stood up together. A mirror over the fireplace caught them in picture. She looked even lovelier in its reflection. His own appearance, tousled and with a fair amount of shirt-tail showing, held less promise of romance for her but she did not seem to be put off by it. Hand in hand they walked out of the room. At the door she paused, looked around and then switched off the light.

Miscellaneous Antiquities, Domestic and Exotic. The hall, half-lit by a hanging thing like a sacristy lamp, was crowded and menacing. Still hand-in-hand in the manner of the Babes in the Wood they made their way through it and on to a staircase of needless grandeur. At the landing a stag's head presided.

'That's Seamus,' said Alison. 'Seamus, David.'

He had just been introduced to a stag's head by a lovely girl who was naked to the waist and with whom he was about to sleep. That sort of thing happened only to schizophrenics and exceptionally lucky sane people.

Just as the mausoleum and the drawing room downstairs captured a confident Edwardian provincialism or something, Alison's bedroom caught for another posterity the spirit of the contemporary colour supplement. It might have been designed by a trendy achondroplastic dwarf: no item of furniture reached more than about twenty-four inches from the floor and the main light, a vast coloured paper globe, was at less than chest height. There were glossy surfaces, primary colours and arty books. Campbell noted with relief that she had a very large bed.

Alison, rather matter-of-factly, was spreading out a duvet. Her stooped torso, lit from behind, seemed utterly desirable, too beautiful for life, more something from art, and that the best of highbrow Danish pornography. Was that why it had all been so easy? In a panic moment he glanced round for signs of hidden cameras, floodlights, one-way mirrors and the like, remembering a very worrying film in which an honest copper was compromised by something quite like this.

When she turned round he repented of the thought instantly. She looked at him and said, 'There's a loo two doors along on the right.' His apprehension must have been evident, if misinterpreted. It seemed a good idea. The bathroom afforded another time-machine trip, this one back to the twenties, with fittings only a little less massive than the Institute's. When he returned to the bedroom Alison was standing naked, waiting.

'Won't be a minute,' she said, passing him at the door and turning right towards the loo. There was something very odd about all this: a girl with whom he had not indulged even in what Kinsey called moderately heavy petting was acting as if they'd been married or at least living together for months.

Campbell determined to play the married game too, within the limits of politeness. He undressed and got into bed under the duvet and took a book from the shelf. By the sound of things she was having a shower. While he waited he multiplied his knowledge of da Vinci many times by flicking through the introduction of a paperback about him. Alison reappeared at the door, switched off the main light and got into bed beside him. He put an arm round her and she turned and pecked his cheek, much as she had done at the door on Tuesday morning. Campbell felt immeasurably less lustful than he could ever have imagined.

'D'you want the bed light on or off?' she asked. One lump or two, vicar?

He reached out and switched it off: the fact that she had mentioned it at all seemed to suggest that she wanted it off since the assumed norm for persons of their age, class and marital status was sex-with-the-light-on, at least initially.

In the dark a tender shoot of romantic love began to sprout again. She lay full length against him enfolded by his arms. Thoughtfully and silently they kissed and kissed again. Campbell began to feel better, i.e. randier, and confidence that expectations would be fulfilled began to grow, eventually becoming very firm indeed. In the dark touch-world under the duvet she seemed quite pleased by this development and Campbell set about catching up on the preliminaries that would in more normal circumstances have taken place on the mushroom-coloured sofa. That too seemed to please her.

Progress was satisfactory but silent. Campbell had the feeling, perhaps to do with being of a species a little lower than the angels, that they should be conversing or at least exchanging sweet nothings; but he could not think of anything to say without risk of jarring misunderstanding. Rapport between them had evaporated.

Alison broke the silence. Half turning to lie on her back she said, 'Come on.'

He did so, wondering what had happened to all the tenderness and sympathy there had once been between them. A moment he had dreamed of was about to rush past like a crowded bus on a rainy night. Despairingly, Campbell asked, 'Are you on pills or anything?'

'Don't worry. I'm very regular and this is a safe day. Two days before. Are you ready?' More in confusion than in ardour Campbell positioned himself. 'Come on then,' she said.

She tensed as he pressed towards her, and drew in a sudden sharp breath then moaned. A minor technical hitch. Do not adjust your

153

receivers. He positioned himself again and pressed. She moaned once more. 'Ooooh. It's a bit sore.'

'Sorry. Wait one.'

'Ouch. That's sore.'

Campbell paused in dispassionate assessment: superficial dyspareunia, as her complaint was known in the trade, had about a dozen possible causes. He tried to remember them. A page of half-forgotten gynae lecture notes reassembled in his mind. All passion fled. Some of the causes were unpleasant, some were downright nasty and contagious too.

'I'm sorry,' said Alison softly, with her face in the pillow. 'I haven't done very much of this sort of thing before. In fact none at all.'

Campbell burst out laughing and fell back giggling helplessly beside her then turned and embraced her. She had started to giggle too. He kissed her and to his surprise thought he tasted tears on her cheek.

'I'm, sorry,' he whispered.

'What for?'

'For hurting you. And for laughing.'

'Don't be,' she said, giggling damply. 'I suppose it's funny.'

'Yes. You were so tough and adult-movie coming upstairs.'

'I know. I wasn't going to tell you. Even afterwards. Just to pass it over.' Campbell burst out laughing again.

'You're not very soothing for my first night nerves,' she said, a little primly.

'How was I supposed to know? A grown-up secretary from the wicked world of art? Who drives a red mini.'

'Red minis have got nothing to do with it.'

'You really were piling it on a bit: "Let's go somewhere comfortable," "After you for the loo," and all that.'

She elbowed him in the ribs. 'Unfair to twenty-four year old virgins.'

'Sorry. Shall we try again. Once more with feeling?'

She snorted in the dark and said in a little girl voice, 'To screw will be an awfully big adventure.'

They tried again gently, and everything was all right.

Quite early next morning Campbell woke in a strange large comfortable bed. A blonde girl was lying beside him with her arms round him. In early light the curtains looked rather pretty. He was not at the Institute. He was with Alison and they had slept together in every sense from rampant ecstasy to probably snoring. He lay looking at her hair in the growing winter dawn. Her face against his chest was calm and beautiful in sleep.

He stirred and she began to wake up. Campbell watched as though it was the first dawn of creation. She rubbed her face against his chest, her eyes opened and then widened, and her lips parted but a little thread of saliva still linked them. She closed her eyes and pressed her cheek against him. Campbell moved to put his arms around her and kissed the top of her head. There was a muffled 'good morning' against his chest.

'Good morning.'

'Mmmmmmmmm.'

'Mmmmmmmmm.'

'My hand feels funny.'

'Sorry. I've been lying on your arm.' He lifted himself off it.

'Pins and needles in some of my fingers.'

'Pressure neuropathy. Usually ulnar nerve.'

She kissed him quiet. 'You're off duty . . .' Then she looked up at him. 'Last night was lovely.'

'My pleasure ma'am. Still sore?'

'Mmm. No. Not sore. It feels funny, but nice funny.'

'Grrrr.'

'That just feels nice.'

'Mmmmm. It does. Lovely,' said Campbell. She was moaning softly and began to move against his hand.

'Are you ready?' said Campbell. 'Here's comfortable enough.'

'Oh unfair,' she muttered into his shoulder. 'You're teasing and being awful again. Unfair.'

'To twenty-four year old ex-virgins?'

She giggled and said, 'Come on, then.'

They got up and had scrambled eggs for breakfast. Once more Campbell prepared to say goodbye at the grey door.

'Can I phone you?'

'I'll feel so awful if you don't.'

'Bye.'

'Bye.'

26

Much fortified by an uninterrupted night's sleep Campbell went on to his ward at quarter to nine. Hadden had come in early and gone round dealing with all the clinical problems so that the houseman's duties apart from routine bloodletting were mainly social. The week's appendices were all well and happy. Mrs Calder was her usual cheerful self and very pleased with her mastectomy scar. Mrs Rintoul, whose lateral circumflex artery had so confounded him, was also for the most part happy. 'My foot's that warm it's lovely. And my husband always used to say my left foot was cooler in bed, even before the pain came on. He'll be that pleased. Mind you one of my toes is a wee bit sore. That Mr Hadden had a look at it.'

'May I see it?'

'Of course, son.'

Her middle toe had a bluish tinge and was cool to touch. The rest of the foot was all right and normal pulses could be felt at the ankle.

'The circulation to the foot as a whole has improved. But this one toe might cause a bit of trouble.'

'That's more or less what Mr Hadden said.'

Campbell discussed it with Hadden, who was pessimistic. 'She'll lose the toe. There must be a clot forming and flicking off from the by-pass site, and it's blocked the digital artery. Let's hope that's all it does.'

Mr Ravelston Orr arrived later in the morning and reviewed the situation, then departed leaving instructions on various measures directed at decreasing the clotting tendency of the blood. These were so complex that any further disaster in the leg could easily be attributed to the failure of the junior staff to carry them out in detail. Not for the first time Ravelston Orr was putting his men on the spot.

That evening while he was on duty at the Institute Campbell rang Alison to arrange a meeting on Friday.

'Mmmmm. Friday's difficult.'

'Oh?'

'Yes. Something fixed up a long time ago. A lawyer chap. Business really, clearing things up after grandpa. But he's more like a family friend. . . . Sorry. Not Friday.'

'Well, how about something next week?'

'Ring me at the weekend.'

'Right.'

'Next week might be fairly busy. . . . But we'll manage something.'

'Good.'

When he rang off Campbell had doubts but was too preoccupied by his work to develop them in detail. The shade of blue round Mrs Rintoul's toe had deepened considerably and Mr Ravelston Orr's grand anti-coagulant strategy proved predictably tricky to manage.

On Friday he went to the concert hall by himself and sat in a half empty auditorium listening to a Mahler symphony that went on and on but was pleasant enough for thinking about Alison to. It also provided an opportunity to reconsider and amplify the doubts raised by the phone call: where was she now and with what sort of lawyer chap? Campbell knew nothing of lawyers but went over the phone call in detail and decided that while lawyer could mean anything, the term 'family friend', last applied to the idiot general practitioner whose arrival on Creech's unit had caused him such difficulty, was more reassuring. If she was having dinner somewhere with a Dickensian figure in steel-rimmed spectacles then all the uncertain agonies of his jealousy were misplaced.

The last movement of the Mahler turned out to be a sort of catholic nursery rhyme in German set to music and sung by a blonde soprano who, from the distance imposed by economy, looked like a bigger, heavier version of Alison. It was strange, how an excess of contemplation doth multiply likenesses, as Francis Bacon or someone like that would have said if they had thought of it. There was a girl in the third row of the stalls who looked quite like Alison from the back, as did twenty or thirty other girls with medium-length blonde hair sitting around the place.

In the bar at the interval Campbell discovered to his surprise and discomfiture that one of them, probably the one from the third row, was indeed Alison. She was talking animatedly to a middle-aged man with glasses, who was laughing a lot. It seemed unlikely that they were discussing how best to dispose of the landscapes to endow an owl sanctuary at Glenlivet though in a theoretical sort of way it was just possible. Campbell had a double gin quickly. Alison saw him and gave him a tiny cold smile then left the bar, holding on to the middle-aged man's arm.

Campbell left the concert hall at the interval and walked through the cold rain to the pub opposite the Institute. It was full and noisy and there were lots of people he knew at least by sight. Mac was there with some of the other housemen and was quick to notice Campbell coming in. 'Look who's just rejoined the human race. Jump in, the beer's lovely.' He was flushed and cheerful. It was quite possible he'd been there since five and unlikely he'd be entirely sober again before Monday morning. He was the anchor man of the hard-drinking-housemen set, who might be found on duty round a bottle of whisky in the lounge or off-duty in this handy bar. If the quickest way out of Manchester was drink, the same was probably true of being a houseman at the Institute.

Campbell bought himself a pint and filled up the glasses of one or two of the others and joined the group. Familiar faces, bright with drink, were a welcome sight. Next to Mac was a very drunk student nurse trying to recount between hiccoughs and giggles some bon mot from gynae theatre. 'An' the registrar said, "Her old man's not going to like this," and the anaesthetist – you know the funny old one who drives the white Maserati. Him – he said – Oh, I can't tell you: it's too terrible.' She spluttered and giggled and Mac slapped her back. 'He said, "Don't worry, you can send it home in a bottle for the mantelpiece.

. . . !" She choked again. 'He probably hasn't done anything more than look at it for years . . .!" Isn't that terrible? And him a doctor.' Mac held her glass and she drank some more.

Various tables of nurses and doctors and students, not all as drunk as Mac and his circle, filled the bar. In front of him were several pints of beer and a couple of whiskies. Campbell caught Mac's attention across the din of the table. 'Anything on tonight?'

Mac leaned across and screwed up his face, sniffing in a passable imitation of Billy. 'Eighty-five Thirlestane Street. Staff-nurses from Casualty. Might be advisable to go early because it'll be very busy. You know what they're like down there. Rowdy.' He flicked his wrist and took a quick Billyish gulp of beer then said in his own voice, 'I thought you were sick of it all.'

'I thought I was. But there are times . . .' Mac's remaining powers of concentration had returned to the student nurse. Someone had gone for more drinks and as closing time approached Campbell found himself about a pint and a half behind and drank steadily to catch up. The noise-level in the bar was rising and a lot of people were standing up near the counter. Groups were looser and people were talking and shouting over longer and longer distances, mostly about parties. Trade in last-minute carry-outs slowed the flow of full glasses from the bar and social contacts were much increased by people trafficking through the various groups on the way to and from the toilet.

The lights flickered on and off and raiding parties of barmaids swept through picking up empty glasses. Campbell, still more than a pint behind (where had the last one come from?), took large cold gulps. Mac was emptying the glasses in front of him with the brisk detachment of a businessman clearing his desk, and someone had organised a large carry-out and appeared to think that everyone at the table should contribute. The student nurse had gone off to the toilet. Campbell hoped it was nothing serious.

The famous Casualty staff-nurses of eighty-five Thirlestane Street lived on the top floor. Everyone with a flat seemed to. It really was inconsiderate. Hordes of drunks of both sexes with clinking paper bags were moving upstairs so slowly it was practically a queue. Campbell was still sober enough to worry about what they would be like on the way down.

Maureen the lovely dumb blonde was at the door welcoming people. She greeted Mac with unaffected warmth. Was she too nice, or too stupid, to harbour grudges? Perhaps she had forgotten. She was a long time ago. Now they were just good friends.

Campbell decided to have something to eat but found the drinks table first and with a can in each hand to save a double journey went through to a lighted talking place. Everybody seemed to be talking to everybody else already and he could not be bothered squaring up to join in so he stood in a corner and drank a can of beer. A short fat girl with big ears came up and spoke to him.

'Hello, Dr Campbell.'

'Hello.'

'Don't you remember me? You were rude to me the day before yesterday.'

Campbell looked at her and experienced no contact. He mumbled, 'I don't think we've been introduced,' and she tossed her head so far back that he could see right into her nostrils then she walked away. He remembered: Bigears from the ward. He opened the second can. Billy was working his way through the crowd in the centre of the room and getting dangerously close. It was too much trouble to avoid him.

'Hello, David. Rare party, eh?'

'Uncommonly so.'

'Oh . . . Yes . . . Haven't seen you for ages. Thought you'd signed the pledge.'

'Maybe tomorrow.'

The second can seemed smaller than the first and the third one produced strange perceptual distortions. People with noses of anything greater than standard size had grown monstrous shining schnozzles. Bigears had sprouted taxi doors. A fat girl had become practically spherical and even poor lovely Maureen, whose plumpness Campbell had not previously noticed, was now a bloated caricature of the late Monroe. She asked him if he was feeling all right. Voices were the same but quieter. He said he was.

There was a queue for the loo, mixed and sluggish, and the people in it seemed to be pretending it was not a matter of the orderly arrangement of biological necessity but some kind of random linear social grouping. The small-talk was appalling. Campbell stood in silence contemplating his internal discomfort. Two girls came out giggling and tidy and he found he had a room, albeit a small one, to himself. That and a much delayed pee relieved his misanthropy. While washing his hands he ventured an affectionate curiosity for the owners of the various odd little toilet things on the shelves and was depressed to discover the origins of Maureen's blondeness. An associated meditation on Alison's blondeness – real or chemical, but now irrelevant – and on her lawyer, or whatever he was, depressed him yet further. The front of the queue was angry when he went out and he made his way through the crowds to find another can. As there were only a few left he took two to be sure. A Casualty registrar from Belfast had done the same and they talked for a few minutes without mentioning the impending beer shortage.

Campbell found a darker room which was more restful on the eyes

159

and sat down beside a little girl who said she was a trainee in the dietetic department. He asked her if she were happy in her work and she talked for a long time without saying whether she was or not. After a while she got up and went away. Immediately her place was taken by someone taller and thinner and older, who turned to Campbell as though she had just noticed him.

'Oh. Dr Campbell.'

It was Maggie.

27

Campbell began the second surgical receiving day of his career with a very substantial hangover which several bouts of vomiting both induced and inevitable had done little to relieve. At breakfast Mac was mockingly fresh and clear-eyed as usual, and unsparing in his account of the previous night.

'You really weren't very kind to Maggie, considering all she's been through.'

'Oh?'

'But you fell asleep about half past one. Maureen put you to bed in her room to stop people walking over you. And I drove you home about three.'

'Thanks.'

'And I've cleaned out my car. I'd settle for twenty cigarettes and a pint for working under extremely unpleasant conditions.'

'Ugh. Did I?'

'More than somewhat. Mostly in the door pocket. How do you feel?'

'Hellish.'

'Serve you right.'

When he went on to the ward he learned that he was to go straight into theatre with Mr Lochhead. Overnight Mrs Rintoul had complained of more pain in her foot and Gray had noted the disappearance of the newly acquired pulses at and below her left knee. Despite Ravelston Orr's anticoagulant directive and the best efforts of the junior staff she was clotting from the by-pass down.

Mr Lochhead was calm and cheerful. 'Chiefy's flown down to London for a working lunch and an afternoon committee, so it's up to you and me, David. I'll handle the plumbing but first I thought you might like to tweak off that toe. It's obviously not going to do and she might as well lose it under the one anaesthetic.'

Campbell's inside, which had been turning over most unpleasantly before any mention of direct involvement in surgery, stopped dead and began to turn the other way, even more uncomfortably. A sweaty swimmy feeling rose to engulf him and he only just fought it off.

'I haven't done much cutting sir.'

'Good one to start with. More chiropody than surgery. I'll give you a hand.'

Mrs Rintoul was wheeled in asleep and then draped with green towels. Her toe would have looked unpleasant to a well-rested teetotaller in midafternoon: there was a focal area of black at the base of the toenail from which successive shades of purple blue and red receded. Even at its root it did not look at all healthy.

'It's quite simple,' said Lochhead. 'We just trim back until we get some nice fresh stuff that's going to heal. A deep vee-shaped incision back into the foot, a quick nibble at the bone there to get it out of the way and cobble it all up by coffee time. If you make a neat job of it when it's healed she'll never know you've done it unless she counts her toes.' Campbell wondered if this were part of a subtle campaign directed at his recent alcoholic indiscretion. He seemed to be laying on the cheerful surgical bloodthirst a bit thick. 'That's right. In there. Deep and wide. She's got big feet. Lovely. Isn't that blood an encouraging sight? If it bleeds like that it'll heal, even without my wonder operation to clear the drains above. Good. Come on, David, your hand's shaking and Hogmanay's still three weeks away. I hope we don't have to do anything like this on New Year's morning.'

He must have guessed: was it the tremor, or his greenish sweating face, or the grey-brown circles round his eyes or simply the boozy staleness of his breath that had given him away? Observant chaps, these young surgeons. And he wasn't letting up. 'Good. Just tie off that little bleeder there. Splendid. Ever used bone-nibblers before? First time for everything. Squeeze hard.' The sound of crunching metatarsal bone was horrible beyond imagination and travelled through the instrument right up his arm and into the middle of his head. 'Good so far. A bit farther. Then rasp it down with this.' Campbell swallowed a mouthful of something nasty that might have been saliva and rounded the bone stump with a shiny blacksmith's file. 'Good. Now, firm but not too tight with your stitches. Always. But especially whcre the blood supply's dodgy.'

With shaking hands Campbell closed the wound. The final result was just as Lochhead had predicted and much more plesant to look at than either the toe or the wound. The consultant seemed satisfied. 'Well done, David. If you'd like to go and ask Mr Hadden to come in and see a little coarse de-clotting you can run along and have a quiet Alka-Seltzer with your coffee. . . . Oh, and don't do it again. Chiefy wouldn't like it.'

161

28

Over the weekend Campbell brooded on what had happened on Friday night, as though interpreting it and re-interpreting it would somehow reduce its significance. His facts were few: she had said she couldn't meet him on Friday because she was meeting a lawyer, which might be true. She might have been less than frank about the nature of the meeting but that was still within the socially permitted limits of feminine dishonesty. The things that really grated were two in number: *i.* her behaviour in the bar, and *ii.* something that didn't quite fit about the role and behaviour of the alleged lawyer. Middle-aged doctors were certainly not to be found disporting at concerts with young female patients. Did the Law Society take a more liberal view on these matters than did the General Medical Council? And then there was the question of her recognition of him. On the one hand she had not ignored him and on the other hand her expression had been neutral if not downright cool. But whatever else, Campbell thought to himself at least thirty times in the course of the weekend, she had slept with him and enjoyed it, and had not slept with anyone else before and was presumably, on common-sense grounds, not sleeping around in the interim. And they had agreed that he should phone her at the weekend.

He did so on Sunday evening and she was curt and rather distant as if there was someone else in the room. They made no arrangement to meet but she promised to ring him the next day. Campbell's customary Sunday night touch of existentialism took on the black vacuity of real depression, and he listened to a broadcast requiem with a sense of personal involvement.

She rang him on Monday morning in the middle of a ward round when he was least expecting it and he had to switch suddenly from the context of work and hospital to the softer more subtle problems of trying to sort things out with someone in whose company he had been briefly and intensely happy. She sounded cheerful and affectionate – what he had come to think of as her normal self – and suggested that if he could possibly get out at lunch-time they could meet somewhere near the Institute. They decided on the second-nearest pub.

Campbell's optimism lasted about ten minutes. Standing in a bored group, senior elements of which were discussing someone's varicose veins in repetitive detail, he realised that there were two entirely different reasons for which she might want to see him as soon as possible, and on balance the less favourable was the more likely. Through the rest of the ward round – veins, hernias and a couple of cancers – he prepared himself for sudden demise.

The pub was full of engineering students gibbering about cars and girls. Campbell swigged half a pint and looked and listened. Whose was the hand that slanted back those brows? Alison arrived about five minutes late and said something about parking. She did not want to stay in the pub either so they decided to go for a short walk. Behind the pub was a large, well-kept and on the whole cheerful graveyard which seemed to Campbell as good a place as any for the impending conversation.

It was mild outside, refreshingly cool rather than cold, and winter sun had brought a scattering of students and office workers to the churchyard paths. Campbell and Alison took a short-cut across the grass and a man with a barrow sweeping leaves shouted, 'Dinnae walk on thae bodies.' Campbell smiled and waved back shouting, 'It's all right I've got nice warm feet.' The man looked puzzled and went back to his leaves. Alison laughed and Campbell experienced a brief irrelevant optimism.

They went down a mossy path over broken steps to the lowest part of the cemetery, where there were rows of family tombs: great masonry stockades any one of which could have housed the finale of an open-air Romeo and Juliet. In front of one was a greenish slab carved with a baby, a skull and the city's coat of arms. They stopped and Alison bent over it to read the inscription '*Hodie mihi cras tibi*'. Campbell translated it, ' " The bells of hell go ting-a-ling-a-ling. Me today. You tomorrow." Of course it gains a great deal in translation.'

She turned to him and said, 'Oh, David, I like you so much for silly things like that . . . and . . . oh, everything.' Campbell wondered despairingly if she had flicked through one of the swinging new etiquette guides that morning looking for the chapter on chucking people. Next would come the 'It's been so super' bit.

She took his hands and looked him straight in the face. Had she rehearsed it as well as revised it? 'It's been so . . .'

'Super?'

She started to giggle again. 'Don't you take anything seriously? It has. It really has. It's been super. To go on would . . . spoil everything. But I'll always remember you. You're so . . . different.'

Campbell winced. 'Different' had been the peak of Maggie's achievement with Mac. But that was an idiosyncratic reaction. She was doing it nicely, with a proper concern for his feelings, every bit as well tuned as her gratitude on his handling of the death of her grandfather. It was another ready-made but well-tailored response from a nice well-educated girl.

He let go her hands wondering if that too were supposed to happen as per the programme and they walked from the infant's gravestone to the churchyard gate. What she had said was sufficient and unhurtful but far short of the whole story. Campbell resolved to slog it out a bit longer.

'I was happy with you.'

'Sorry.'

'And I thought you were happier with me . . . than you actually must have been.'

'I was happy. I really was, David.'

'So what happened? Or didn't that was supposed to? Or whatever.'

'Nothing, David. Absolutely nothing. You're being analytical and I don't want you to be. Just accept it.'

'Am I allowed to be just even curious? When something looks like something and turns out to be something else again. And what's this I'm supposed to accept? Being shot at dawn first thing this afternoon and not even getting to know what for?'

She laughed sadly. 'Please don't. You're not on trial. You're fine. Too nice, if anything. Too innocent.'

'Me? Innocent? Now I really resent that. Coming from a twenty-four-year-old recent ex-virgin. It's the pot calling the kettle white.'

'I wasn't. Not then, anyway.'

'I thought you were.'

'You liked that, didn't you. Not nastily, I mean, but nicely and protectively. You being too nice again. You really were. You were marvellous.' She smiled and laughed in a way that five minutes before would have had Campbell swooning on a tombstone. Now he got a little angry.

'OK. But why did you bother?'

She laughed again. 'I just felt a bit innocent that evening. A touch of the virginals. And I thought you'd enjoy it.'

Campbell bit back an oath.

'You did, didn't you? It brought out the best in you. Like grandpa dying. Kind, coping Campbell.'

Kind, coping Campbell could very easily have lost his temper and hit her. He said nothing. She smiled at him.

'I really felt awful when you began to get so . . . involved. You see it was all a sort of mistake. Bumping into you and all that nonsense about your wallet, then the concert and dinner. It wasn't meant to happen. It only happened because it happened a little bit at a time and I got to like you a bit and you were so hopelessly keen. But it was definitely a mistake.'

Campbell shook his head wearily. This was painful enough to be the truth. 'It was a nice mistake while it lasted.'

'It was. We were curious about each other and liked each other and could pass the time together and sex was super. But we're not each other's types.'

164

'But what about . . .' She put a hand up to his mouth to silence him. He was not going to find out about last Friday's concert or the man who was with her or what exactly she meant by types.

'No, David, there's no point.'

'Point about what?'

They walked in silence to the churchyard gate and parted. Campbell walked back to the Institute and as he did so surprised himself by thinking more about lunch than about what had just happened. He crossed the consultants' car park and strode up the steps towards the main door whistling a cheerful little tune.

Just inside the door the sergeant porter was leaning on his desk: he got up and came after Campbell. 'Dr Campbell, sir, you must know about the anti-noise campaign. Whistling indeed.' Campbell remembered that NCOs at Sandhurst were said to have developed the use of the word 'sir' as a term of contempt. 'And such a tune. Really.'

'Oh?'

'The Internationale!'

'Really?' A polite and measured response was dictated by the unforseeable consequences of telling the wrinkled old retainer to bugger off.

'The Internationale indeed, sir. Now what would the Board of Governors think of that, sir? Indeed.'

29

By the third week in December, Christmas stalked the Institute like a disease. Early signs multiplied and the diagnosis loomed to certainty. Campbell stood by with frozen loathing. As a medical student he had seen it all before: student nurses dragooned into making paper-chains and painting ward windows with tableaux maudlin, religious or satiric as sisters competed with bitter cheerless ferocity and intrigue for the Matron's ward decoration prize; consultants active and retired jostling for the honours of the turkey; festive fare atomised and squeezed down the nasogastric tubes of the moribund; the wall of silent opprobrium surrounding anyone sufficiently lacking in finesse as to appear likely to die on the day; and the miserable confusion awaiting the bereaved. The skull grinned far too close beneath the smile of a hospital Christmas for Campbell's liking.

There was no escape: at three one morning Campbell was called out to clear a drip-line and found that the night nurse had been too busy with little decorations for the ward Christmas tree to notice that a bottle of intravenous fluid had been running three hours behind. He pointed this out and they said, 'But Dr Campbell, it's Christmas.'

In over-reacting he spoiled their night and his own and felt compelled to ring up at four to apologise. Throughout the day, nursing and medical staff talked of nothing but presents, visitors, cakes, turkeys, puddings, drinks, last-minute shopping, last-minute preparations and last-minute change of plan in a stifling crescendo which reduced Campbell to curses and expletives the mildest of which was 'Humbug'.

Only the increased availability of alcohol and a seasonal loosening of the Institute's conventions on its use gave consolation. In the Residency the hard-drinking set met more frequently and had expanded to include a number of former moderates. A recurrent image of the coming of Christmas was that of half a dozen bleeps lying on the lounge table amid the glasses and cans and bottles of yet another session.

On the morning of 22nd December Mac came down with what looked like a hangover. At breakfast he was subdued: his face was puffy, his eyes were hollow and he refused the steward's offer of a plate of black pudding and tomato. This invited comment which he answered in terms of unnatural self-pity. More frequent sufferers mockingly asked him how he felt and welcomed him to their circle, but Soutar was sceptical and suggested that Mac take his temperature when he went up to his ward.

Mac did not appear for lunch and word got around that he was suffering, as Soutar had suggested, from 'flu. The prospect of an epidemic working its way through the Residency over Christmas did nothing to cheer the housemen.

That afternoon Campbell spent an hour in theatre with Mr Lochhead doing a left mid-thigh amputation on Mrs Rintoul: the artery had clotted irretrievably at the level of Ravelston Orr's operation and from the knee down her leg was dead already. Lochhead sliced away at the muscles of the thigh then sawed through the femur, muttering about grand old 'tweendecks surgery. Afterwards Campbell carried the leg across to Pathology feeling sorry for Mrs Rintoul and a little sorry for himself as well: the toe operation for which he had suffered so much had been in vain.

From Pathology he went up to Mac's room. It was empty. John, the steward, had an explanation. 'The medical registrar didnae like the colour o' his watter, sir, so they put him in a ward to keep an eye on it.'

'Where is he?'

'Eight, sir.'

'Thank you, John.'

An hour later Campbell went down to Eight to see Mac. A nurse told him that he had been removed to the Isolation Unit.

'What's wrong with him?'

'He's comfortable,' said the nurse. Campbell grimaced. She smiled and said, 'You could see the doctor over there, doctor, if you want to know any more.'

Campbell hurried along to the Isolation Unit, a building on its own beyond the coke dumps and some disused tennis courts. Formerly a satellite of the Haig Memorial Pavilion reserved for the delivery of venereally infected women, it had been taken over by a special medical unit to provide intensive care and barrier nursing facilities for dangerously infectious patients. In the dark he stumbled along a path strewn with lumps of coke. Mac's transfer to the Isolation Unit made the diagnosis inevitable.

The nurse in charge needed pressing to let him in. He put on a disposable mask, overshoes, a gown, a white unfestive paper hat and a facemask. Mac was sitting up in his cubicle, smiling and faintly jaundiced.

'Welcome to the pest house. They tell me I've got the yellow peril and it'll be six months off the booze.'

'Hard luck,' said Campbell. 'We'll have to bring you black grapes instead.'

'Yes. A dry Christmas. And a dry New Year too more's the pity.' Mac was just a little too flip about it to be convincing.

'Which of the yellow perils is it?' Campbell asked. 'Plain or fancy?' There were two kinds of hepatitis, one of which killed people. Serum hepatitis did, and was less common, but was more likely to occur among hospital staff.

'They're running a test now. But from the way they're treating me I'd say they think it's the real fancy no-messing-about nasty serum stuff. They're taking no chances. You know Ivor, the SHO here? Came at me for blood dressed like a deep-sea diver: boots, gauntlets, a thing like a welder's mask on his face and funny paper hat like yours. It made me feel I wasn't nice to know.'

'They've got to be careful. Since the last time.'

'I suppose so. Ted. He did cross my mind once or twice.'

'But then again it might be the nice harmless one you get from fish in doubtful restaurants on the Costa del Sol.'

'I haven't been to any,' said Mac thoughtfully.

'No. But it's vaguely endemic in this country. People are always going down with the yellow John Ds.'

'Junior hospital doctors aren't always.' said Mac.

'A medical degree doesn't make you immune from benign infectious jaundice.'

'No. It only makes it a bit more likely it's the other, nasty kind.'

'Maybe. When will your test be through?'

'This evening.'

'Will Ivor tell you?'

'I don't know.'

At dinner the steward put down a piece of virulently yellow coloured fish in front of Campbell and said, 'I heard from one of the porters, sir, that Dr MacDonald's got the serious hepatitis.'

'Serum hepatitis?'

'Something like that, sir. A shame with Christmas coming on.'

30

A playful fate that had dogged Campbell's duty rosters ever since he had become a houseman now determined that he should be the receiving house surgeon on Christmas Day. He woke with yet another hangover and lay cherishing the hope that most people, GPs and patients alike, would want to hang on to their surgical emergencies until Boxing Day. Even before he got up a local GP, well known for his common-sense and conscientiousness, phoned in and offered him a young female appendicitis who had been observed overnight at home and sounded like the real thing. Campbell thanked him and returned his seasonal greetings quite sincerely, wishing every GP he dealt with was as good, then got up hoping that was surgery for the day.

In the dining room, holly, paper chains and a more than ordinarily crapulous steward made Christmas breakfast a little different, but the fundamental nature of the Institute reasserted itself in leathery fried eggs and cheap, fatty overdone bacon. For obscure English reasons, the only newspapers available were the Scottish ones which at any other season Campbell would have ignored. Most of their news had been in cold storage since the same time last year. 'Skiers throng Christmas Slopes,' 'Holiday Roads Threat,' and 'Yes, It's a White Christmas – For Some!' that last accompanied by a picture of a grinning Highland postman up to his insteps in snow. There was an inside-page story about Mac: 'Hepatitis returns to Institute.... One new case.... Mild. First for five months. No further cases. No cause for alarm .... Routine precautions. .... Spokesman ... sporadic cases occurred from time to time ... another large outbreak unlikely.' How did spokesmen always know?

Since it was Christmas Campbell lingered a little over coffee before bracing himself to go up to the unit. Neither of the sisters had won the Matron's ward decoration prize, and they were agreed that the winner had stolen ideas from both of them. Campbell's duty room had been decorated and many of the medical staff had brought in their families for the unit's annual informal children's fancy dress, deportment and

Christmas present competition. A dozen assorted kids, scrubbed and packaged for the occasion in smart, colourful and uncomfortable looking clothes, some dragging dolls and other toys, formed the clamorous social undergrowth of a forest of mixed adults also uncomfortably tidy-looking, which drank cheap sherry.

Campbell's desk was a bar, his paperwork had been tossed into a cupboard and his chair had been removed. He poured himself a large drink and found Hadden.

'Cheer up, lad. 'Tis but once a year.'

'I've got an appendix coming in.'

'There's another on its way up from Casualty. Gray saw her. And a possible perf. coming in from the outback.'

'Merry Christmas.'

'Cheers.'

A child tugged at Campbell's trouser leg and when he looked down sprayed a rattling sparking volley of toy machine-gun fire in his face. 'Don't tread on it,' advised Hadden. 'It's Gavin's.' He patted the child on the head. 'Save your ammo for consultants, sonny. Think of your dad's career prospects.' The child trotted off in the direction indicated. 'Are you coming into theatre?'

'It can't be too soon,' said Campbell.

'Say half an hour. Try the dark brown stuff. It's not so bad.'

In theatre Campbell performed his fifth or sixth appendicectomy. It was a routine one that had progressed far enough to make the operation quite worthwhile but not so far as to make it difficult. The offending organ was fat and pink and accessible. With Hadden assisting Campbell isolated it from its blood supply, tied off its base, cut it free and dropped it into the waiting specimen dish, then popped the stump back and fastened it into the large bowel with a purse-string suture, leaving a neat grey dimple where once abdominal catastrophe had threatened.

'A pretty scar is the least you can give her as a Christmas present,' said Hadden. 'She's definitely the bikini-wearing type.' He showed Campbell how to close the two-and-a-half-inch wound with sub-cutaneous continuous nylon which could be pulled out from one end in due course, leaving no stitch scars.

The next appendix was less straightforward: a thirty-five-year-old man who had complained of a week's abdominal pain and vomiting and now had good signs of right lower quadrant inflammation. The history was too long for appendicitis and before they went in Hadden raised the possibility of Crohn's disease. Inside the abdomen they found not appendicitis or Crohn's but an appendix almost obliterated by a pinkish crumbling cancer which had spread beyond hope of cure to the lymph glands in front of the spine.

Hadden rang Laird who had just returned home from the sherry party and came in grumbling, but turned to and resected the tumour and some of the glands, then diverted the intestine to the surface of the abdomen. 'That'll do for now. We can join him up later. Interesting case. You should think about presenting him at one of the surgical meetings. The microscopic sections should be fascinating. And we should get a PM fairly soon. Just finish sewing him up, thank you, and I'll pop along home to my seasonal paternal duties.'

Late in the morning the perforation arrived from the country. While the ward prepared him Campbell and Hadden lunched in the theatre rest room where the duty nurses had arranged drinks and turkey sandwiches. The registrar spread himself in an armchair with his mask flopping under his chin, ate sandwiches two at a time and drank beer straight from the bottle. He was in expansive form. 'God bless us all, said Tiny Tim, and God bless Alester Scrooge and old Sir Hector Marley and even Fräulein Goody Twoshoes and the Beast of Theatre Office. May all her lampshades be nice tattooed ones!' He handed a bottle to the houseman. 'Think of your fluid balance, lad. Surgery can be a very dehydrating experience.'

'Cheers.'

'Here's to Christmas Day in the Workhouse.'

As they rested between cases in the air-conditioned cocoon of the theatre suite, away from consultants, sisters and patients, Christmas seemed momentarily worthwhile. The ward could take as long as they wanted to get the perf. ready.

Campbell's bleep screeching the cardiac-arrest tone shattered their peace. Houseman and registrar leapt to their feet scattering beer and sandwiches then ran through the shower compartment and out into the unsterile corridor. Heavy but fast, Hadden took the lead and burst out of theatre skidding right into the female ward.

All the patients who could sit were lined along a central table at the head of which was a half-dismantled turkey. No one was eating and most were staring at an odd little group half-way down on the right. Sister was there and so was the chief, in a long white cook's apron and a yellow paper hat in the shape of a crown. He was still holding the carving set and bending over a woman with one leg who had fallen from her chair and lay blue and lifeless on the floor.

Campbell pushed past the chief, dropped on his knees, struck the patient on the chest and began to pound it in a regular one-per-second rhythm. Hadden joined the houseman on the floor, with the ward resuscitation tray, and lugged the patient's head round free of the chairs to put a tube in her trachea. He got it in first shot and attached a ventilation bag which he operated with one hand, relieving Campbell of the external cardiac compression with the other, so that the houseman could set up an IV line. He did so and ran in bicarbonate solution.

'She's getting pinker.'

Hadden, working like a one-man-band on circulation and respiration stopped compressing her chest and felt for a pulse in her neck.

'Feels like sinus rhythm. This could be a good one.'

Still kneeling over the patient, Campbell held the bottle of intravenous fluid up in the air.

'Take that, someone.'

As it was removed a large carving-knife clattered to the floor beside him.

'Were her pupils dilated when we started?'

'No. She should be fine. She's gagging on her tube.'

The duty anaesthetist arrived and joined Campbell and Hadden on the floor beside the patient.

'She'll be fine. We can take that out.' He removed the respiration bag and the endotracheal tube. Mrs Rintoul coughed and opened her eyes. A gurgle deep in her throat prompted Hadden to seize her bodily and turn her half over on her side. She vomited profusely over his theatre clothes.

'That's fine, Mrs Rintoul. Get it all up. That's it.'

She spluttered and spat then tried to sit up.

'No, no. Just lie where you are. You'll be more comfortable.'

She lay semi-prone, mumbling something about the linoleum then looked up and said, 'Sorry, all this trouble . . . Christmas.'

'Don't worry about that. You're fine now. Just lie quietly.'

Word of the success zipped round the table in both directions from Mrs Rintoul's neighbours. Excited chatter filled the ward. A nurse wheeled a trolley in and they lifted the patient on to it. Ravelston Orr handed the bottle of intravenous fluid to someone more junior.

As Mrs Rintoul was wheeled from the ward an old lady near the top of the table began to sing in a piercing shaky voice, 'For she's a jolly good fellow,' and the whole table joined in. There was confusion in their chorus as to its subject. Some sang, 'For she's a jolly good fellow,' some 'they' and a few stuck out for 'he'.

Mr Ravelston Orr followed the trolley up the ward and was back at the turkey as the chorus ended. He nodded diffident acknowledgement and set about his carving like a man who was only doing his job and wanted nothing more than to be left to get on with it.

Later in the afternoon Campbell caught Mr Rintoul at the beginning of visiting hour and explained in some detail what had happened and why his wife was now in the intensive care unit. He took it very calmly.

'That's fair enough, doctor. It's best she's down there. Not that she didn't like it up here, but like you said, being dead, even for a wee while, must be an awful shock to the system.'

31

The week between Christmas and New Year dragged interminably. Both wards emptied as the acutely admitted patients left and were not replaced by patients from the waiting list. Scottish patients, even after years of trouble from hernias or piles, were not willing to pay the price of missing Hogmanay as part of their treatment. So there was little work and, as Christmas faded, little festivity, as though the world were drawing breath for the older, wilder rites of the turn of the year. In the Residency there was a backlog of Christmas presents to work off, so on his duty nights and even on some nights when he could have been else-where Campbell sat gloomily drinking in the lounge. At these sessions they remembered Mac, now snatched from their midst to six months abstinence. Little bulletins about him came up from the isolation unit as housemen, singly or in groups, went down to see how he was faring. The diagnosis of serum hepatitis was confirmed by further tests and his condition remained stable. He was yellow and sometimes depressed and had lost his appetite. And he was neglecting his stack of girlie magazines in favour of flicking through the first chapters of *War and Peace* anticipating, as he said, plenty of time to get through it with an unclouded mind.

Mr Ravelston Orr, after the ceremonial of Christmas Day, announced his intention of taking two consecutive long weekends and was not expected on the unit all week. Mr Lochhead came in every day, toying from time to time in theatre with some morsel of minor surgery and generally keeping an eye on things. Campbell spent long periods sitting at his desk looking out of the window at the traffic on the crossroads through the branches of trees that had long since shed their leaves and looked to him as though they had long since given up hope of growing any more. Day by day his mood darkened. Even Hadden's cheerful banter was intrusive and irritating and he spent more and more time alone in the duty room or in his bedroom, discontent but unable to wish for anything more specific than the end of house jobs. He looked forward to that as a time of quiet and unburdening, a release from the unending stream of trivia and disaster that had been his life for almost seven months. There were five more to go. In spring would come an optimism perhaps, though that seemed far away, and on the 1st June it would all stop as suddenly as it had begun. There would be sudden total silence:

no bleeps, no night calls, no exhausted sojourns at the tail of ward rounds, no sessions in theatre making night and day indistinguishable. Campbell still had no job to go to in June but that did not seem to matter. Again Flanders offered a simile: it would be sufficient to survive till then and live afterwards. On 1st June would come the silence of armistice and he would put down the burdens of war and walk away forever from the mud and the guns.

On the Wednesday of that week, the 29th December, his depression was joined by two new symptoms: in the morning he developed low backache and in the afternoon a throbbing frontal headache. It was uncomfortable but not disabling and he carried on with such work as there was, mentioning it to Hadden at tea-time. For once the registrar was serious. 'I noticed you were less than your usual cheerful self. Might be something viral. You should take a couple of days off. The ward's quiet, Chiefy's away and Lochhead's reasonable. Gray and I can cope. We could even get the SHO in to cover your duty nights. He doesn't do much for his pittance.' Campbell found the SHO, handed him his bleep, went out of the Institute for half a dozen paperbacks and took to his bed.

By eight that evening he was so stiff and shivery that he found it difficult to turn the pages of his book. The headache was worse. Housemanlike, he decided to review the situation later and fell asleep. Vivid dreams of surrealist absurdity and violence woke him and he found the sheets moist with sweat. A new symptom, dragging abdominal pain, had joined the aches and stiffness. After further doubt and delay he rang the exchange and asked the operator to get the medical registrar to ring his number. The duty man turned out to be Stangoe, the perfectly adapted teaching hospital animal. At least the bedside manner of the forthcoming consultation would be above reproach. He was also widely read, in the limited medical sense, and had the reputation of being an astute clinician as well as the author of several learned papers on intestinal rarities. He was very much the coming man: Bertram, the registrar on Creech's unit and a rival in the promotion stakes, had described him as being a good doctor for all the wrong reasons. But would he know about 'flu?

He knocked on Campbell's door and came in: a neat lean little man with the groomed alertness of a fox-terrier in the show-ring.

'Hello, David, what's up?' Campbell, who could not see how collecting housemen's first names aided promotion, was surprised to be thus addressed.

'Headache, backache, rigors, general stiffness and upper abdominal pain. And I feel awful.' Both appreciated the value of concise, lucid history.

'Since when?'

173

'In that order. Starting this morning.'
'Vomited?'
'No. But some nausea.'
'Eyes hurt?'
'No photophobia.'
'Uhuh. Neck sore?'
'Not particularly. But stiff, like everything else.'
'Notice anything else?'
'Such as?'
'Colour of urine?'
'Nothing special. Haven't pee'd since lunch-time though.'
'Bowels?'
'Regular.'
'I meant colour.'
'Nothing special.'
'Let's have a look at you. Tongue. Good. No glands in your neck. Eyes. Look down. Across. Again. Put your tongue out again. Point it up. As though you were trying to lick the end of your nose. Fine. Lie flat. Good. No. Relax. That's better.' He pressed the edge of his hand up under Campbell's ribs on the right. 'Sore in there?'
'Like a kick in the crutch.'
'Sorry.'
'It's all right.'
'Now, just pop that under your tongue. Fine. Well, we'll need some urine and some blood, but that can wait until we've moved you.'
'Where?'
'Mind that thermometer. Isolation unit. Can't really handle the specimens properly on an open ward.'
'Christ.'
'What?'
Campbell took the thermometer out of his mouth. 'Have I got hepatitis?'
'You're jaundiced and you're a houseman. There's been a case from the Residency last week. Nothing else to say you have. But we've got to think of it. For public relations if for no other reason. Did you see the papers this morning?' Stangoe had moved over to the wash-hand basin. 'Put that thermometer back in your mouth. Well, they're getting on their high horses again. Uninformed alarmism of course. But it does mean we've got to be extra careful.' He sounded like a whole committee-ful of consultants already. And he was washing his hands very thoroughly.

Shaking and ill, Campbell packed some things he thought he might need. Stangoe accompanied him as he was pushed along the coke-strewn path in a large wheelchair. The Isolation Unit stood in the dark, gloomy and forbidding like an outlying fortress of the main defence works of the Institute. When they went inside Mac waved, cheerful and surprised, from behind the glass of his cubicle. Campbell got out of his chair and put a hand on the door handle to go in and talk to him. The nurse in charge stopped him. 'You can't go in there. You should know better than that, Dr Campbell. Going in there without proper protective clothing indeed.'

'But I've probably got the same as he has.'

'This is an isolation unit.'

She put on gown, paper hat, mask and gloves and showed him into an empty cubicle next to Mac's.

'Take off all your clothes and put them in that plastic bag. We'll put it inside another and seal it. You'll get them when you get out. No smoking. If you want to urinate use one of those disposable bottles and stand it over there. If you want to move your bowels tell us. Seeing you're a doctor here we'll be fairly generous about visiting same as we are for Dr MacDonald. But no smoking and they must wear protective clothing. Right?'

'Thank you.'

'Any questions?'

'Perhaps later.'

'See the night nurse then.'

'Thank you.'

'Now . . . Date of birth? Next of kin? Religion?'

The sheets were fresh and cold. Squash seemed to come free with every cubicle. Campbell turned off all the lights except the bed-light and lay looking round his new abode. The wall with the door was glass from waist-level up, so that the staff at the nursing station could observe all the patients at once. The other walls were pale institutional green. Opposite him hung a faded impressionist reproduction with a label on its frame giving more prominence to the donors, 'The Circle of Friends of the Institute,' than it did to the artist.

He had a bed, a chair, a standard old-type hospital locker and there was a thing in the corner that looked like a commercial spin-drier, which must be for disinfecting the various disposable cups, plates etc they had in these places. He wondered if his paperbacks would be minced and drenched in disinfectant when he had read them.

As he warmed up the shaking stopped and despite a headache, various cramps and the abdominal pain he began to feel more comfortable, and proceeded to review his situation: Stangoe's kind thoughts on how it might not be, we're just being careful, were to be reluctantly dismissed as a softener for bad news. Campbell had done the same himself for many patients and realised now that it probably did help. The most likely, the almost inevitable diagnosis was serum hepatitis, and nothing would change that. A conversation with Mac just prior to the result of his test came to mind: serum hepatitis was the one that junior hospital doctors got. Serum hepatitis. Every day they came into contact with the blood, urine and other secretions of dozens of people, any one of whom might be carrying the disease, perhaps even without ever having been jaundiced. And although blood from BTS was supposedly safe, mysterious cases still occurred among its recipients: Campbell remembered the number of times he had handled the stuff in the last few months and gave up trying to recall specific incidents.

Apart from the multiplicity of possible contacts there was the problem of the incubation period: different outbreaks put it as widely as from forty to a hundred-and-something days, though in any one outbreak it was usually fairly constant. Tomorrow Ivor would come round and ask him if he could remember any particular incident when he might have been at risk. There were so many, and the time stretched back so far that it was hardly worth asking.

At half past one the next morning Campbell was wakened by the sound of tapping on the glass of his door. It was Mac in his dressing gown, beckoning him out. Campbell sat up: his headache had gone and the abdominal pain was less severe. He switched on his bed-light and noticed for the first time that his skin was faintly yellow against the sheets. Mac beckoned again then came into his cubicle.

'The staff nurse is off to tea. Come on through. The auxiliary's making some coffee, but she'll do cocoa or anything you want.'

'Oh, thanks. Cocoa would be nice. Good to see you.'

'Got to drop in and make the new neighbours feel at home. Decent thing to do. How d'you feel?'

'Not nearly as bad as I did last night.'

'That's the viraemic phase. The beasties wandering round looking for your liver. They'll have found it now and be setting up shop. The worst bit's over.'

'Good. . . . Fine. I'll just get my dressing gown.'

'I'll be in Daffodil Cottage next door. We've got about forty minutes.'

They compared their degrees of jaundice, putting their forearms together like typists on a package tour.

'Yes. Mine is just a little richer. That golden blush that makes all the difference. Still, you're coming on. I shouldn't be surprised if you see the New Year in a better colour than me. Mine might have started to go by then.'

'I don't know if I want to. But we can wait and see.'

'What do you think of the pest house?'

'Strange. A sort of sci-fi jail. With a touch of the sensory deprivation.'

'Yes. That's what's getting me down. It's nice to have company. Had all four cells to myself most of the week. A crumble died and never called me neighbour.' He paused and switched to stage doric. 'Wull ye have a wee drink, doctor? A braw wee whisky?' He produced a medicine bottle from his locker.

'How d'you get that in here?'

'Friends in high places. The man who checks the oxygen.' He poured some into two paper cups.

'I don't know if I should but I will. A wee one,' said Campbell. 'It's the sort of thing we're always telling patients not to do. I don't know if they pay any attention.'

'I don't think they do. I've cut it down though.'

'How do you get rid of the bottles?'

'My man takes the empties away. Like milk.'

They sipped their whiskies and the auxiliary came in with coffee and cocoa.

'There ye are. Ye're awfy laddies, the pair o' ye.'

Mac thanked her.

'What are the nurses like here?'

'Not bad. Most of them. Old Annie Auschwitz, the one who admitted you last night, is the worst. The rest are all right. Night-staff's the nicest. Oh, and an old friend of yours is coming here when Annie moves on at the beginning of January.'

'Who's that?'

'Joan somebody.'

'Masson?'

'The one who got appendicitis.'

'Really?'

'So Annie says.'

Campbell looked at his whisky. He had not thought of Joan for weeks and had seen her only once or twice around the hospital since their muddled, unplanned parting. The prospect of being nursed by her in the near future was to say the least thought-provoking. In Annie's choice phrase, he would have to tell her every time he wanted to move his bowels. It would not be the most romantic of encounters, he decided, but it would be better than nothing and she couldn't just turn on her heel, however people did that, and say she never wanted to see him again, because of the bowel thing, and having his temperature taken and his pillows fluffed up and all the sundry little services that would make a prolonged frozen withdrawal on her part difficult or impossible. They might even screw in his cubicle on her nights on.

'That was meant to cheer you up,' said Mac, 'so forget it.'

177

'No, it's not like that. I wouldn't mind seeing her again. Even here.'

'Nice girl. Never got round to her.'

'Well don't start in here.'

Mac grinned. 'Ooooh the heavy husband.'

'Piss off . . . . What doctors are here?'

'Well, there's Ivor the brave SHO who dices with death at every venepuncture. He's all right. It's quite amusing being admitted by him.'

'Yes. I was going to ask about that. Does he want to know every time you pricked your finger or did a messy blood thing in the last four months?'

'More or less. But they're not very hopeful of tracking anything down. They think we're sporadic. At least I am.'

'One's a case and two's a series,' said Campbell, narrowing his eyes and slugging the last of his whisky, cowboy-style. 'Together the two of us could make a great little epidemic for ourselves in this town.'

'Maybe so.'

'Have you read about yourself in the papers? Stangoe said something about it just before I came in here.'

'Yes. Today's. 'Is the Institute telling the whole truth?' They think they're trying to cover something up. And they dangled Ted Main's bones a bit too. Half-way down page three. It's funny. You read that stuff but you don't feel it's you. I'm a twenty-five-year-old surgeon in a go-ahead chest unit. My SHO'll be jealous. And a mild case.'

'That's nice.'

'But I'm getting a bit of a thing about this Institute spokesman chap. Who the hell's he?'

'Dunno. Whoever's in the office when the phone rings, I suppose. But I've heard they pay porters for information too.'

'It's probably better.'

The unthinkable had happened and so far it wasn't too bad: a vague ill feeling and nagging abdominal pain no worse than might accompany 'flu, together with a yellowish skin discoloration to remind you it was a bit more serious than that. Campbell felt well enough to wonder almost guiltily about the ward. Sitting down here swilling cocoa and chatting with Mac verged on being a pleasant alternative to duty. The drawback was that sometimes people died of serum hepatitis and that made the cocoa taste a little different. It was necessary to talk of other things.

'Anything new on the job front?'

Mac hesitated. 'Well there is a sort of something in the wind. Nothing very definite yet.'

'Obstetrics somewhere? Out in the woods?'

'No. Nearer.'

'At the Haig?'

'No. Not obstetrics.'

'Is it top secret or something?'

'Well, it's a bit . . . vague still. But medical.'

'Medical? What about your vocation for asking ladies to lie down?'

'That's funny. I've got a theory since this job came up that the most miserable people in this whole miserable place are the ones who are offered jobs that aren't what they wanted and take them because they're a bit flattering. Know what I mean?'

'I think so.'

'Well, I've practically accepted one.'

'Really? Where?'

'Well, I was asked to keep it sort of quiet for now. . . . It was odd. Old Temple, my medical chief, must have liked the way I ate my egg sandwiches or something, because he recommended me to someone in Creech's unit.'

'Someone in Creech's? Who?'

'Rosamund Fyvie. I didn't know much about her.'

'Rosamund? She's a raging monomaniac, a research plagiarist and a bit of a coprophiliac on the side too.' Gray's diagnostic habits were catching.

'So you didn't get on with her?'

'Oh, she's pleasant enough socially and she can be very nice if she wants you to do something she can't order you to do.'

'She was nice to me. She wants me to do some of her coprophiliac research.'

'God, not that faecal vitamin thing.'

'How did you know about it? She said it was very hush-hush. Because she had some great ideas that only needed a few experiments.'

'Elder had the great ideas.'

'Oh. Why doesn't he do the experiments then?'

'Because he's gone now. They had a hell of a row. About a month ago. Rosamund submitted Elder's ideas as her own, to get cash out of some research foundation.'

'First I've heard of it.'

'Elder's out in practice now.'

'Christ. Rosamund made it sound really great. Teaching, research and a bit of clinical experience. She even made the coprophiliac research bit sound great too. "You'll be the link man of the faecal vitamin research pilot study," she said, "then as it develops you'll be in there with a specialty of your own." '

'Have you said you will?'

'Almost . . . I suppose I could still get out of it.'

'You'll be lucky. She's a persuasive old bitch.'

179

'Well, I've got time in here to think about it. And there's always the chance she won't want me after this.'

'After the yellow peril? Don't bank on it. If she wants you she'll have you. Any colour.'

'What about you?'

'Still nothing. It's as if I can't really believe that house jobs are going to end until they have. I don't even read the ads.'

'Time's getting on. At least as far as the big scene goes.'

'Every time I hear of somebody getting a shitty awful job like yours – sorry – I think that's another one I'm spared the bother of thinking about.'

'Come on. It's not as bad as that. It's a job, and it means I'll be staying around. I have to think about the continuity of my social life.'

'We'll be lucky if anyone so much as speaks to either of us after this.'

'Oh, I don't think it's as bad as that. There are quite a few survivors floating around. They just don't talk about it as a rule. Some surprising people. Did you know Maggie's had it?'

'Maggie? You're kidding.'

'No.'

'When?'

'About a year ago. She was quite lucky. It was mild at the time. But her liver function tests still aren't quite right.'

'She never told me.'

'Why should she?'

'She just kept saying she wasn't supposed to be drinking.'

'That's right. She's still off the booze.'

Campbell sat silent, with a ghastly sensation of falling and accelerating and knowing that the worst feeling was still to come. When it did it was a horrible realisation.

'Christ! It's bloody Maggie!'

'What is?' said Mac gently.

'Maggie. Spreading it. Giving us bloody hepatitis.'

'How do you mean?'

'When was that Residency party. When you chucked her.'

'Oh. That one. Maureen. . . . Towards the end of medical jobs. . . . about middle or late September.'

'Three months. About ninety days. No. More. Maybe a hundred.'

'Jesus. I see what you mean. But it's a long shot.'

'Maybe not. You went out with her for about a week. Starting on a . . .'

'Billiard table?'

'Ha bloody ha. On a Friday on a billiard table. Because it all came to light on Saturday at lunch-time.'

'Oh, yes. The green baize conservation society.'

'And I felt sorry for her about a week later. A Residency party. A Saturday night.'

'And you came in here a week after me.'

'Christ yes. It all fits.'

'Is that in the books?'

'Getting serum hepatitis that way?'

'Yes.'

'There've been a couple of things in the journals. Lots of positives in certain groups.'

'What sort of groups?' said Mac.

'VD out-patients.'

'Ugh.'

'Unpleasant but relevant.'

'I suppose so . . . Jesus.'

'Listen,' said Campbell. 'This is nasty and I'm sorry but it's important. When you were stopping by with old Maggie, did you use . . . what you might call an obstructive method of contraception?'

'Nope,' said Mac. 'Bareback.'

'Charming. Me too.'

The housemen sat silent, looking into their cups. Campbell spoke again.

'I didn't because she said something about just finishing a period.'

'That's not true. Not that week anyway. But she's got something far wrong with her cycle. Always dripping.'

'Charming. It *was* . . . just a little messy. Blood. Serum. Hepatitis.'

'Jesus.'

'Right,' said Campbell. 'It all hangs together. Horribly well.'

'So what happens now?'

'Well, do we tell Ivor?'

'Or Maggie?'

'What's she been up to since then?'

'Nothing much, I think. Not since that fiasco with you when she got a bit obvious.'

'I hope not. Mind you it would be bloody funny if, say, Creech, Ravelston Orr, old Temple, the Medical Superintendent and both Chaplains were wheeled in here bright yellow on successive days next week.'

'It's highly unlikely.'

'Agreed. But seriously. Do we tell Ivor?'

'We don't have to decide now. And visiting time is almost over for tonight. If I'd a Pavlov-type ward-sister's bell I'd be ringing it. Staff'll be back any minute.'

'OK. Well, good night . . . Christ, it's rather awful, isn't it?'

'Yes, but knowing that hardly affects us now.'

'No.'

'See you about the same time tomorrow night then?'

'Fine. Thanks for the booze.'

'It's all the life-bringing oxygen man really.'

'Well, thank him from me. Good night.'

'Good night.'

'Hang on a minute. About Maggie. If she had it way back, where did she get it from?'

'She was in the dialysis unit during the big outbreak. She was one of the last to get it.'

'Poor old Maggie. Always missing the bus.'

'She didn't quite.'

'I wish now she had,' said Campbell. Another sickening wave of suspicion welled within. 'Christ!'

'What?'

'Maggie was at Ted's funeral.'

'Oh hell. Yes. I'd forgotten about that. Sheeyit.'

'So maybe he was number one on an interesting list. Had he been knocking around with old Maggie?'

'Ted? Yes. Brief and torrid. A treasure hunt. Bloody hell.'

'A what?'

'One of those silly car things where you drive around then meet and get drunk. Organised by nine and ten theatre. I was on the ward as a senior. Ted was working there and Maggie was muscling into everything social at the time.'

'You mean they went out together?'

'Not regularly. They sort of got lost. On the treasure hunt.'

'She was in it with Ted?'

'Well, he won her in a sort of raffle they had for crews. You know, grimmies and people without cars.'

'Some raffle.'

'They took a long time coming back from one of the task things. You know, going places to find things. A list you had to get. Some of it was a bit corny. Article of female apparel. That sort of thing.'

'So Ted won her in a raffle and literally shagged the knickers off her for some silly bloody game.'

'Maybe so.'

'It's jumping to conclusions a bit. *De mortuis* and all that.'

'Oh, I don't know. He won.'

'And now he's dead.'

'Perhaps he didn't screw her. Maybe he got it in the line of duty. Like the last outbreak.'

'Hard to find out now.'

182

Cocoa, coffee and whisky were finished. Time was running out.

'Look. You'd better push off or they'll stop our fruit squash and withdraw visiting privileges. Staff should've been back five minutes ago. Good night.'

'Good night.'

'Tomorrow night?'

'Tomorrow night.'

32

Next morning the SHO came in to question and examine Campbell, who found himself anticipating things and giving answers too pat or too oblique and continually putting himself in the SHO's shoes because he was more used to asking the questions himself. The Maggie thing was a major complication and made him feel like a crooked detective being put on the spot by a former colleague. At least Mac, his accomplice in this disingenuous exercise in discretion, could be relied upon not to give anything away until they had discussed it further. If they decided to 'remember', one of them could do it and Ivor could be clever and come and ask the other, and put it all together for himself. He was the sort of chap who would enjoy doing that. Campbell wondered if he would write it up for the journals. Probably yes. Every scribble helped.

The SHO went out and came back further protected by boots, a long plastic apron, goggles and a perspex visor. Ivor the diver. He drew off twenty mils of blood, which was more uncomfortable than a familiarity with the other end of the procedure had led Campbell to believe.

After coffee time sensory deprivation began to take its toll: reading became a bore and eventually a wandering fly proved fascinating. It seemed to like the Impressionist flowers best, then the squash bottle, then the counterpane. Campbell dipped his fingers in squash and lay in wait for it with a newspaper in the other hand, but the fly was too wary to be caught. Some visitors arrived. A couple of housemen came and said much the same to Campbell as he had said in similar circumstances to Mac. Mac's parents came to visit next door: his father turned out to be a tall, rather saintly looking Church of Scotland minister, and his mother a short cuddly person with a queen-mother coat. In the afternoon Ivor went in to see Mac again, spent some time with him and then went away and came back with the consultant, who was with him for half an hour, and looked in to see Campbell on the way out.

Mac did not visit him that night. During the staff nurse's meal-break the cocoa lady explained that he wasn't well, was an awful colour and had started talking daft. Mac's parents arrived again very early the next morning, and the consultant came in both in the morning and the afternoon. Once or twice Campbell heard Mac's voice, shouting incoherently.

The following day, the last of the old year, there was tremendous activity in the next cubicle. An extra nurse appeared and spent all her time with Mac. Porters carrying the large purple boxes from the Blood Transfusion Service came and went all morning. When Campbell asked Staff Nurse Auschwitz how Mac was, she snapped that he was critical but comfortable and would not discuss the matter further. In the late afternoon when Campbell was waiting for tea to arrive there was a further increase in activity: Ivor was dashing around, the consultant swept in and shortly afterwards two porters, puffing and cursing, manoeuvred a portable electrocardiographic monitor into Mac's cubicle. Then the duty-anaesthetist rushed past with his white coat flapping like frantic white wings.

Mac must have arrested. Thumps, scuffling and frantic muffled voices came through the partition for fully twenty minutes then the activity tailed away and all the doctors came out and trooped slowly past Campbell's cubicle towards the door. Ivor, at the end of the line, threw a worried look at Campbell. So that was it.

Campbell's first reaction was one of furious disbelief. It couldn't have been Mac: it must have been someone else. Mac was elsewhere and all right. It wasn't Mac's voice that he had heard in delirious raving. Someone else had been admitted to his cubicle and died and Mac was in another cubicle or back in the wards because he didn't have serum hepatitis at all. Somehow Mac was not lying yellow and inert with dull staring eyes and white lips waiting to be taken away like offal. Campbell's denial mounted to panicky absurdity then collapsed.

It was Mac all right and he was dead. The pathetic inevitable details – the bruised ribs, the electrode jelly everywhere, the ECG leads, and the yards and yards of untidy hopeless trace – all unseen next door, made Campbell shudder, then weep. There would even be a puncture mark over his heart from the last despairing shot of adrenalin. Mac the life-force, the tippling rollicking wenching blithe animal spirit, was cooling inexorably next door at the rate of one and a half Fahrenheit degrees per hour.

Nothing in Campbell's life had prepared him for the death of a friend in the next room. Even Ted's death had come as information, not experience. And death as he met it professionally just wasn't relevant. On the wards it was a seemly, notice-giving, almost apologetic visitor whose calls if not always expected were at least familiar. Here it was brazen and fierce and had just snatched someone with whom he had a conversation to finish: it was an obscene and extravagant assertion of death as the ancients had known it – random, sudden and implacable, the seizer of all men, guided by blind fate.

Then Campbell got scared: Mac's death was not, as far as he was concerned, a random event: Campbell had got the same disease from the same source. For just over three months Campbell had been following Mac at a distance of seven days and now Mac's journey had ended. He lay hugging a childish resolution not to die that day or the next day or the day after that and to carry on like that taking the days one by one and then one day it would be more than seven days and the spell would have been broken. Ten minutes later a professional detachment put him at the other end of the bed and he saw himself as just another case of liver disease. That broke the superstitious ties with Ted and Mac. Two out of three was bad, but it didn't make three out of three inevitable. It was not a nightmare or a divine thunderbolt but a disease with known pathology and variable outcome. Some died quickly and some got better. There was acute fulminating hepatitis that killed you straight off and yet the milder cases made a complete recovery. The small print categorised the in-between states: chronic relapsing hepatitis, the subacute progressive one and so on. It was nasty but it was not new or unknown.

That lasted until another disturbance occurred outside his cubicle. With much grunting and wheezing porters manoeuvred something else into the unit. Campbell looked round and saw that someone had drawn the screens across in front of his door and glass wall. The long zinc coffin on wheels, tastefully disguised with sheets, pillows and a cheerful pink blanket, must have come for Mac. The doom-buggy that housemen joked about had claimed one of their number.

There was more scuffling in the next room and on the other side of the screens the porters wheeled Mac away. Soon someone was going to find the medicine bottle in his locker. Campbell remembered that he owed Mac twenty cigarettes and a pint of beer.

33

The next twenty-four hours passed without form or incident: Campbell lay passive, eating little, reading nothing and resenting the regular visitations of gowned masked gloved figures who talked at him, took his temperature, prodded his abdomen, looked into his eyes and once more with great ceremony sampled his blood. He was ill and angry and sad and slept fitfully through the day and lay awake at night, resentful and sometimes fearful, thinking of medicine, and Mac who was dead and Maggie who was outside somewhere and must have heard what was going on.

On Sunday morning Campbell woke from a doze to find a man in a dark suit, with a flower in his buttonhole, sitting beside his bed like a visitor from another world. It was Creech. And it was the first time since the early morning session with Mac that he had seen anyone close to without a gown and facemask. Creech's nose and mouth and yellowish irregular teeth seemed things of extraordinary subtlety and interest. He offered an ungloved hand which Campbell shook with real pleasure. It was warm and dry and not rubbery.

'It's perhaps an odd thing to wish you a Happy New Year. In the circumstances. If you see what I mean. But I do.'

'Thank you, sir. And a Happy New Year to you. It was very good of you to come in.'

'Oh, not at all. I just popped in on my way from church up to the unit . . . I hope you'll excuse my informal dress.'

'Of course, sir. It's really nice to see someone not all dressed up in that stuff.'

'The girl on duty out there didn't think so. At first. But I told her. And I explained. You see I'm not afraid of what you've got. I've had it myself. A long time ago, in Burma in '43.'

'With the Fourteenth?'

'That's right. It's nice when someone remembers the Forgotten Fourteenth. It was about this time of year too, because I had a dry Hogmanay.'

'I didn't mind that,' said Campbell.

'Neither did I, although I pretended to. Everyone seemed to expect it of a Scottish doctor . . . I was about the same colour as you. I got it from a dirty syringe. A dozen of us did. I felt really . . . hellish at the time. For about a month. But I've been right as rain ever since. It was just before Imphal.'

They had a pleasant chat ending with the liberation of Singapore. Creech got up. 'Well, I musn't keep them waiting on the ward. They'll be asking after you. I expect some of them will be down. Dr Fyvie seemed quite interested in your progress.'

'Really?'

'And Sister sends her regards.'

Campbell was grateful, and thought more highly of his medical chief now than he had ever done when he was working for him.

The following day Campbell decided to tell Ivor about the Maggie thing. It could not now affect Mac because he was dead and it would not reach his parents because it was medical-in-confidence. The only person other than himself who might be concerned was Maggie. Her position would be difficult, but even so it ought to be discussed and defined, by blood tests if necessary. He made up his mind to present the idea to Ivor as a remote possibility he had just thought of, suitably laced with ignorant reservations along the lines of 'can you as a clever doctor tell me if people can possibly get it that way?'

Ivor came in in the morning to bleed him. While the needle was in his arm Campbell said. 'I've been thinking about this disease. You know, where I might have got it. . . . I went out for a while with a girl who'd had it herself, a long time before.' Ivor, intent on his death-defying manipulation of Campbell's perhaps lethal blood, showed no signs of acknowledgement, but peered through his mask at the needle. He finished and went out and came back moments later with a newspaper folded to display a story on the bottom half of the front page. Campbell read the headline: 'Nurse found dead in Home.'

'We knew,' said Ivor.

Campbell read on. 'Sister Margaret Birss, 29, . . . found dead yesterday in her room in the Sisters' Wing of the Argyll Robertson Home at the R.C.I. . . . Empty sedative bottles. . . . Foul play not suspected. . . .'

'Christ,' said Campbell. 'Is that how you know?'

'No. She phoned in on Friday. This' – he pointed to the newspaper – 'is a bit of a surprise. Maybe we should have thought of it.'

In the late morning the duty staff-nurse put her head round Campbell's door. 'Dr Fyvie to see you, Dr Campbell.'

Rosamund, in full kit, was taking no chances. She wished her former houseman a Happy New Year and seemed most concerned about his welfare. She talked first generally and then about what Campbell was going to do in June. Campbell listened with growing revulsion as she circled in towards her offer.

'You could do research and still not get behind with clinical experience. And there's the teaching. You enjoyed that when you were our houseman.'

Campbell said he wasn't sure, but thought probably not.

'Well,' said Rosamund, 'you should think about it anyway. It's worth serious consideration. You'll have opportunities on both the clinical and research sides and you'll be the link man of what might turn out to be an entirely new specialty.'

Campbell said it sounded good, but he wasn't sure.

'And it's not just anyone I'm looking for. The research money's just come through and you're the first person I've approached. You made a good impression as a houseman and that's why I'm offering it to you. Think about it. Give yourself a few days.'

When she had gone Campbell lay in bed, a delicate shade of yellow against the sheets, turning over in his mind the possibilities of a career in hospital medicine. There was the day-to-day care of patients, teaching and research, the continuity of a sort of social life and eventual promotion, depending on original publications, a certain political agility and the continuing availability of dead men's shoes.

187